MW01688661

Black Tide

A Matt Rowley Novel

By

Patrick Freivald

JournalStone
San Francisco

JOURNALSTONE
YOUR LINK TO ARTISTIC TALENT

Copyright © 2015 by Patrick Freivald

All rights reserved. No part of this book may be used or reproduced by any means, graphic, electronic, or mechanical, including photocopying, recording, taping or by any information storage retrieval system without the written permission of the publisher except in the case of brief quotations embodied in critical articles and reviews.

This is a work of fiction. All of the characters, names, incidents, organizations, and dialogue in this novel are either the products of the author's imagination or are used fictitiously.

JournalStone books may be ordered through booksellers or by contacting:

JournalStone
www.journalstone.com

The views expressed in this work are solely those of the authors and do not necessarily reflect the views of the publisher, and the publisher hereby disclaims any responsibility for them.

ISBN: 978-1-942712-00-8 (sc)
ISBN: 978-1-942712-01-5 (ebook)

Library of Congress Control Number: 2015932366

Printed in the United States of America
JournalStone rev. date: April 17, 2015

Cover Design: Rob Grom
Cover Photograph © Shutterstock.com

Edited by: Vincenzo Bilof and Amy Lynne Eye

Black Tide

Chapter 1

Matt Rowley tightened the turban across his face and hoped his light brown eyes wouldn't blow his cover. The dark contacts he'd worn had crusted with grit during the sandstorm, so he'd torn them out. The pre-dawn gloom had shielded him this far. He took a deep breath and stepped into the tent.

Beneath cloying sage lay the acrid stink of human sweat and a lingering tang of gunpowder. Through the haze he identified four targets: three obvious guards held AK-47s in casual grips, and a fourth lurked behind the muslin curtain. The infrared signature of the last man spiked white at its core, even through the cloth—far too hot to be human. His eyes widened at the TV in the corner. The fifty-plus-inch flat-panel clashed with the austere, faux-Bedouin pile of rugs and tapestries that made up the rest of the decor.

On the muted TV, Ramiel stood in front of a crowd in Cairo, black hair slicked back, fine suit bulging to contain his enormous musculature as he used his fist like a gavel to punctuate each point. The podium cracked under the last blow. The caption on top said "LIVE," and in the bottom corner 3:36 p.m. *Four minutes.* Matt wondered how many there were, and if destroying this Ramiel would destroy them all.

"As-salaamu ʿalaykum," the front guard said in a Syrian accent, running a hand across his stubbled chin. "Place your hands on your

head." Matt suffered through the frisk as the wind howled outside, drowning the sound of automatic weapons chattering in the besieged town a kilometer away. The ground shuddered, and moments later the explosion reached his ears.

He lowered his hands and tried his own Arabic. "I'm here to see Ramiel." Their eyes narrowed. His eidetic memory enabled him to learn languages much faster than most, but though he had an ear for accents, he had no tongue. Although not a betting man, he'd still wager that Tennessee-tinted Arabic didn't get much play this side of Damascus. That, and he'd used the egregoroi's name, and none of their intel could nail down whether or not that constituted blasphemy in this cult.

"You are American?" the guard continued in Arabic. A helicopter roared overhead.

He nodded without taking his eyes from the mujahidin. The other two tightened their holds on the AKs but didn't raise them.

"And yet you submit yourself to Allah, Mohammed His prophet, and Ramiel His emissary?"

"I don't. I'm just here to see him."

The weapons came up as the front guard stepped back. All pretense of calm or compassion had disappeared from his voice. "Kneel."

"No. I'm here to talk to Ramiel, not let you shoot me in the head."

"Kneel!" The guard's knuckles turned white, his finger eased toward the trigger.

"I'd rather not kill your guards," Matt said to the figure behind the curtain. "But if they don't put down those weapons, I'm going to have to." Of the abilities he had lost when Gerstner stepped off of the table, he missed precognition the most—though not the psychotic whispers that came with it. Even without, his augmented reflexes and strength made dealing with three normals a trivial exercise, especially at point-blank range.

"You seem . . . confident." Ramiel spoke perfect Oxford English with a slight brogue, his voice a deep baritone. The guards froze at the sound, their watery eyes darting in the hazy smoke. "I'd like to see this." He barked out an order in Arabic. "Kill him."

Matt stepped forward and drove his forehead into the bridge of the front guard's nose. The man's cranium imploded, and Matt wrested the AK from his grip as he fell. The left guard's weapon barked, shredding the air Matt had just occupied. In a single movement Matt drove his fingers into the shooting man's throat and snap-kicked the other in the leg.

A sickening crack accompanied the second man to the floor, and he screamed and writhed, hands gripping his shattered knee. The gunfire stopped as the shooter reached up to his ruined throat, eyes wide in shock and incomprehension. Matt jerked his hand back in a spray of arterial blood, brought up the AK and pointed it at the squirming, screaming man on the ground.

Next to him, the choking guard fell. Bright crimson bubbles gurgled from his obliterated pharynx as he gasped for breath. Matt fired two tight bursts, one at each target, and the room fell silent. Then the dead men's bowels let go, completing the smell of death Matt found all too familiar: blood, gunpowder, and shit.

The curtain parted and Ramiel stepped through, heat pouring off him in waves. Matt trained the AK-47 on the shirtless man, a wall of rippling muscle in draw-string khaki pants and bare feet. The fallen angel smiled at the gun and then at Matt. "So much changed during my eternity in the Pit. Such disrespect for your betters."

"You've enslaved thousands of people." He caught the TV in his peripheral vision. 3:39. *One minute.* "Most of us don't go for that these days, respect-wise."

"Do they wear chains? Is worship slavery?"

A memory shuddered through Matt, a ram-headed angel with wings of silver feathers, a surrender of everything in three impossible words. *I am yours.*

He snarled his answer. "Yes. It is."

Ramiel shrugged. "This new ideology is much as the old: convert or die. Your illusion of choice is alien to me, your sacrificed Jew a fairy tale invented by the young." The room grew dark, the wind howled. Sulfur mingled with the sage and blood and shit, and black worms writhed beneath Ramiel's skin. Despair and hopelessness stabbed Matt's mind, and he gritted his teeth at the psychic barbs. "You can't hurt me, Mister Rowley, not with fists or feet or that sad little instrument. So kneel, and face your true purpose."

A soft white glow enveloped the attack, worming into and through the tendrils of black thought, and Ramiel's grin faltered.

"There's something in you." The disjointed shards of millions of Jade addicts, dull impressions of the living and bright incoherent sparks of the dead, swirled unseen in the space between space, a spiritual white noise that had grown along with his returning abilities. He sometimes recognized splintered remnants of personalities, Janet LaLonde; his wife, Monica; their son, Adam. Most of the time it blended into an indecipherable blur. Now it tensed, squeezed, and shattered Ramiel's probing attack.

The angel stumbled back a step, then regained his composure.

"I've got a lot of company these days." Matt tapped his temple.

Ramiel put a finger to the side of his nose, a pensive gesture at odds with the situation. "Yes, them, anybody can see them. Hard to see anything else through the beehive you've got around you. But under them, under you . . ." His face brightened in wonder and joy. "She's there. Our daughter is alive."

The TV clicked to 3:40, and a metal hook cut through the canvas. Matt grabbed the wobbling steel and clamped it on a post. The tent tore away from the ground. Ramiel looked up at the helicopter buzzing past, tow cable lashing back and forth in the buffeting wind. Matt squinted against the sand in his eyes and pulled the trigger.

A spray of bullets shredded the meat of Ramiel's face, exposing black bone and red-hot embers. The angel stumbled backward as Matt emptied the magazine. It clicked dry and Matt grabbed the barrel, skin smoking and hissing where it touched the metal, and swung.

Ramiel blocked the blow with his arm, and the weapon bent. Gritting his teeth against the skin sloughing off of his fingers, Matt swung again, and this time the angel caught it. A fist crushed into Matt's sternum and he fell back, coughing blood, his chest a red fire. He dropped to one knee and groped for another assault rifle, sand clumping on his bloody fingers.

His watch beeped. He dove to the side, and on cue a streak of fire impacted the angel center-of-mass.

Ramiel disappeared in a fireball that blasted Matt to the ground. Ears throbbing, Matt scrambled sideways, his chest screaming agony with each movement. Another AGM-176 missile followed, and another, and another. Payload spent, the drone banked skyward, and Matt struggled to his feet.

Matt and the egregoroi—a Watcher freed from Tartarus by Frau Gerstner, the last of the Nephilim—had an audience now. Dozens of men milled about in confused panic, cowered from the skies. Some readied surface-to-air missiles, and gaped in astonishment at the remains of the man they believed to be Allah's emissary.

Ramiel knelt in a pool of molten sand, the glowing red silicon no brighter than the coals that smoldered beneath his exposed bones. Every scrap of flesh had burned away. The shreds not destroyed by the missiles had been consumed by the furnace raging in his chest. Withered, skeletal wings unfolded behind the abomination, and it roared through rows of serrated black teeth.

Matt braced for the psychic shockwave that poured out of Ramiel and closed his eyes against the hot, gritty wind. Ramiel's rage burned through him, scoured his bones, wracked his soul. A vast nothing opened in his mind, a dark wind of insatiable need and want and bloodlust, an unquenchable thirst devoid of human pity. White filament wrapped his arms and legs, held him above the eye of the storm and the gaping pit below. He lifted from the ground, higher and higher, until he opened his eyes.

The tent city lay before him, lashed with the dying gasps of the sandstorm. A hundred-odd men stared wide-eyed at the creature screaming in the glowing pit of molten sand. A man cried, "Efrit!" Another joined him, and another. The crowd stumbled forward, shrieking their reproach as the winch hauled Matt up to the helicopter. They cried "Efrit!" again and again, and with each utterance the egregoroi withered.

Matt flipped upright, his chest a tight knot of pain as he grabbed Tsuji "Blossom" Sakura's offered hand. With the help of a uniformed man beside her, she hauled him onboard. He landed in the seat amidst the deafening roar and Sakura gave him a thumbs-up.

He leaned back, wiped sand and blood from his lips, and put on a pair of headphones with an integrated microphone. "How'd we do?"

Sakura slammed the door shut. "Good. Cameras caught all of it." She pointed to the bank of monitors linked to the video feed from the C-130 far above. "Uplink is live. The world knows."

On the monitors, a half-dozen Ramiels stumbled to their knees and smoldered. CNN, Al Jazeera, FOX, BBC, they all zoomed in as the charismatic leader who'd enraptured thousands faltered in his live speech at six different locations. Split-screen, the hacked signal broadcast the growing, shouting crowd around the blackened, demonic skeleton.

It looked up, crouched, and leapt.

The pilot jinked right, and the black form streaked past them, missing the rotors by centimeters. Skeletal wings spread, it roared and dove. Claws four inches long punched right through the door. The soldier scrambled in mad panic, a useless gesture in his flight harness. Matt helped himself to the man's service pistol and shot the claws, point-blank.

Shards of boiling-hot keratin ricocheted through the cabin, and Sakura cried out. Matt fired again anyway as the bolts holding the door shuddered and bent.

"Matt!"

He turned as Sakura tossed him his AA-12 combat shotgun. Behind him, metal sheared and air rushed in, loud even through the headphones.

Hovering twenty feet away, Ramiel spun and threw the door.

The pilot jerked up and it dinged off the landing skids with a shudder.

Matt took two steps and leapt into open space, pulling the trigger as he slammed into the demonic form. His standard-issue fin-guided fragmentation rounds had been blessed by a bishop, a dubious but cooperative rabbi, and an Imam, just in case—he had no idea if any of it did any good. They entered the joint where Ramiel's wings met his back and exploded.

Chunks of smoldering flesh spattered Matt with a sizzle, and as they fell his robe caught fire. He grabbed the damaged wing one-handed and put his feet on Ramiel's back, then twisted his body. His muscles bulged. He gritted his teeth against the strain. The bone shifted in its socket, and then the tendons tore free with a dry crackle. He let go and a gust buffeted the skeletal wing upward and away.

Wind drew the fire up his robe, and burning cotton mingled with the stench of smoldering hair. Feet on Ramiel's back, he pointed the shotgun down and pulled the trigger, full-auto. Round after round plunged into the falling angel, rupturing flesh and blowing apart bone, but it healed almost as fast as he destroyed it.

Matt braced for impact. A year ago, a thirty-foot fall wouldn't have even fazed him. This wasn't a year ago. Neither his reflexes nor his regeneration worked like they used to.

He bent his knees and used Ramiel's body as a cushion, then tucked to roll as they hit. A sickening crunch, and white-hot flame seared through his right leg. His head hit the ground and he saw stars. Writhing, he rolled to put out the flame, to get away from the burning rage underneath him.

He tried to crawl with his arms and left leg, his right one hanging useless behind him. Over the howling wind the demon shrieked, and over that the crowd chanted, "Efrit! Efrit!" Someone covered him with a blanket and beat out the flames, each impact an explosion of pain from his leg. He turned his head to the side, cheek against hot sand.

Ramiel stood, a withered wing clawing its way into reality where the severed one had been, the stench of brimstone smoking off of the malformed limb. At full height Ramiel stood four meters, a titan of charred bones glowing red from internal heat. It screamed at the crowd in a language Matt didn't know, something akin to but not Hebrew. Its voice drowned in the crowd's chant of rebuke.

It withered further, tendrils of smoke where blazing shimmers of flame had been. Wisps of ash fell from his crumbling skeleton as the crowd pressed forward into the sulfurous cloud of stench, burnt matches and charred bone. Matt panted on the ground, trying not to pass out as the pain in his leg faded to a numb burning sensation. The wind screamed, joining the demon and the crowd in its fury.

A vortex formed around the demon, an opaque, howling tornado of grit and sand, shot through with gouts of flame. The crowd dropped to its knees and with a single voice praised Allah for their deliverance.

Sakura's voice cut through the noise, and Matt realized he still wore his headphones. "Matt, you alive?"

"Yeah." He gritted his teeth against the pain and the whirling sand that seared tiny holes in his exposed skin. "Can't walk, though. Extraction requested."

"Be right there."

An eternity passed, then the world shuddered. As the helicopter landed, a streak of ashy mist shot skyward from the maelstrom. The wind died, the crowd stopped, and sand rained from above, revealing the morning sun under a pale blue sky. Matt hissed as someone lifted him by the shoulders, and as they dragged him to the helicopter he looked at where Ramiel had stood.

A sand-crusted pillar, still red-hot, stood like an obelisk in a pool of hardening glass.

"Is it dead?" Sakura asked through the headphones. Automatic weapons chattered in the distance. Something exploded in the distant city, the fireball rising into the sky.

Matt shook his head. "I don't think you can kill these things, not permanently. But it won't be enslaving anyone's mind for a while. I hope."

Back on the chopper, he watched the monitors as Sakura cut off his pants and splinted his leg. Ramiel, all of them, had melted, burst into flame, or crumbled to ash the moment the wind had stopped. Sakura didn't comment on Matt's frayed, light blue boxers with red hearts, a gift from Monica too many years ago.

"How's my leg?"

"Give it a couple days. You'll be fine."

He healed a thousand times slower than he used to. From a compound fracture to Olympic sprints might take as long as a week.

"How did you know?" the soldier asked them, his accent a thick Scottish brogue.

"Know what?" Sakura asked.

"That it'd work?"

Matt shrugged. "We didn't. Ramiel went out of his way for publicity, and the more popular he got the more power he demonstrated, so we thought maybe his growing power depended upon his worshippers. Expose him for what he is, and down he goes."

"Shit. What would've happened if you were wrong?"

Matt shrugged again. "I'd be dead, and the Earth would drown in a religious firestorm."

"Jesus, Mary, and Joseph."

Matt leaned back and closed his eyes, letting the chopper's percussion sing him to sleep.

Chapter 2

Monica Rowley looked up as the deck stairs creaked. She set down her tea, rushed to the door, put her finger to her lips, and opened it.

Matt grinned, his smile as dazzling as the day he'd first sat next to her in the middle school cafeteria, his face now more rugged, more handsome than she deserved. Muscles rippling under a tight T-shirt, black with the White Spruce Volunteer Fire Department shield on the breast, he flashed his eyebrows at her and tiptoed to the door. He slipped inside and slid the door closed, turning the lock after it shut.

"He just went down." Monica kept her whisper just above silence. Their son had taken his first tentative steps the week before, and the days since ricocheted between chaos and silence with no predictable pattern.

He kissed her, and she folded into his arms. They held the embrace in the doorway, and she breathed him in, Old Spice and gun oil, rugged masculinity.

"You didn't tell me it'd be on TV."

He tightened, as she knew he would. "I couldn't. Operational secrecy."

She tried to understand, tried to let it go. His job as a police officer had barely paid the bills, and validated him as the hero only on some small scale. He'd needed more, and signed up for augmentation. She understood. Monica just wished it wasn't so damned dangerous. She ran a hand through her hair, dislodging a chestnut curl.

He swept her off her feet and kissed her nose. "Nobody can do what I do, babe. Anyone else they sent in wouldn't have come out."

"I know. But I saw you on the ground—I mean, I couldn't see your face or anything, but I knew it was you on the TV, with your leg all broke up like that, and I couldn't take it."

He set her down. She stepped back and chided herself. They'd had this conversation before, a dozen times, and it all came down to the same thing. She'd support him, and he'd try to be safe, and she'd complain about it anyway because she couldn't help but worry. Not that they had much of a choice. As the last augmented human on the planet, the tattered remains of ICAP still owned Matt for another eight years. Minimum.

He shifted from leg to leg and bounced, an almost comical slow-motion dance, one eyebrow lifted in a "See?"

She sighed. A crippling injury for anyone else, an inconvenience for her superhero husband. She turned and walked inside. He followed her into the kitchen, the nook more used than their dining room.

"Coffee? Tea?"

He shook his head. "I'm good. Where's Ted?"

"Out back, sleeping in the sun. Been there an hour, easy. I'm not sure he can handle the strain of such an intense life." Lazy and lovable, their Basset Hound liked to bark at everything and nothing, and loved Adam with both his brain cells.

"Best not wake him, then."

She looked at the clock on the wall, a mail-order internet thing that chimed bird calls on the hour. "Amy's coming in twenty minutes. I should be back around four."

He appraised her sweat pants, tank top, and sports bra. "Kung fu?"

"Sifu's got another batch of prospectives, wants me to put

them in their places." Nineteen adults from eighteen to eighty, each out to prove they're too good for the "Beginners" class, waiting their turn to get manhandled by a hundred-and-thirty-pound ass-kicking machine. If past experience held any indication, two or three of them might be right. "Not my fault their egos outmatch their ability."

Matt picked up the phone; spotty service in the Appalachian wilderness made a landline necessary, even in this day and age, even with a priority government job.

"Who are you calling?" Monica asked.

"Amy. No need to have her come this way if I'm home."

Monica chuckled, plucked the phone from his hand and hung up, invading his personal space so that her lips lay inches from his. "Don't be silly. You cancel on her too much and she'll stop saying 'yes' when we really need her." She set the phone on the counter and wrapped her arms around his neck.

"This is why I leave the important thinking to you, babe." He kissed her, a smooch, then something more. His hands wandered to her ass and she spun away.

"No time for that."

He glanced at the clock.

She followed his gaze, then grinned. "Can you be quiet and fast?"

"Fast I can do. Can you be quiet?" He picked her up and carried her to the bedroom without the slightest sign of effort.

"Let's find out."

* * *

Fifteen minutes later the doorbell rang. Matt winced and glanced at the nursery, but Adam didn't stir. Very little upset that boy, but he woke like his daddy, groggy and ungrateful. Monica answered the door, her hair a touch messier than when he'd walked up the deck stairs. Amy rounded the corner into the living room, a bottle-blonde knockout at sixteen, too young and too cute.

Your daddy's got to get a shotgun, and quick.

"Hi, Mr. Rowley!" She'd figured out how to beam with

enthusiasm and whisper at the same time, something Matt had yet to master.

"Hi, Amy. How's school?"

"Good!" She prattled on about trigonometry and US history with far too many mentions of a boy named "Frank," then excused herself to peek in on Adam.

Monica leaned in from behind and pecked him on the cheek, her breath hot in his ear. "Bye. Back in a few."

She bit his earlobe a little too hard.

"Bye, babe. Drive safe, and watch for deer."

He watched her go, and part of him lamented the moral downfall of western civilization while the rest admired her ass in the too-tight sweat pants with JUICY scrawled in block letters across them. She caught him looking, blew him a kiss and slapped her right cheek, then disappeared out the door.

"Love to, baby," he muttered.

Amy came back in and sat on the loveseat, laptop in hand. He smiled inwardly at the lack of ear-buds—wearing them a strict no-no while babysitting—and watched her shuffle a stack of textbooks, an e-reader, and her computer into the optimum working arrangement.

She smiled, almost shy. "Are you going to be here long?"

He didn't have anywhere to go, but felt awkward staying home with the babysitter. "I've got a few errands to get to, so I'll be in and out."

* * *

His phone rang halfway to the grocery store, a number he didn't know with a Washington, D.C. area code. He pulled over, killed the truck's engine, and hit "Talk."

"Rowley. Go ahead."

"Sergeant Rowley, this is Lieutenant-Commander Roger Smith, SACLANT's office, authorization eight-two-seven-one-five-five-one. Got a minute?"

The daily code checked out, and Matt had all kinds of minutes, but he didn't much want to talk to NATO's Supreme

Allied Commander Atlantic's office a half-hour after he'd gotten home from six weeks abroad. He had no idea how formal Smith might be, but Matt hadn't been a sergeant for more years than he had been, and the tired formality rubbed him wrong. "What's up, Roger?"

A pregnant pause told him everything he needed to know: Roger wasn't too keen on being "Roger" rather than "Lieutenant-Commander Smith." With ICAP's disintegration, Matt found himself without rank, command, or superiors. His reassignment to the Department of Homeland Security's newly created Special Threats Bureau came with no mission and no directives, but a shiny new ID badge that might get him out of speeding tickets. As the only Aug left in the world, the UN, NATO, and the United States never ran out of things "only he" could do.

"Mister Rowley, we have some disturbing news coming from an oil rig off-coast. I need you to report to NSA Mid-South for immediate deployment to the Gulf of Mexico. Your chopper leaves at eighteen-hundred, so get driving."

How quickly "sergeant" had become "mister." Even with lights and sirens, White Spruce to Millington, Tennessee would be a three hour drive, maybe more.

Screw this.

Matt rolled down the window to let in the late October air. "Monday work for you?"

Another pause, then, "Excuse me?"

"I just got home, and haven't seen much of my wife or boy these past weeks, so I'm thinking I'll take the weekend and go ahead show up in Millington say, eight a.m. Monday?"

"That's unacceptable."

"Tuesday, then." Matt listened to Smith about gag on his phone a moment, then continued. "Last I checked, UMS Operations Division didn't take orders from SACLANT, and my former division is in shambles. With no one on top of ICAP that ain't dead or behind bars, even with the STB designation I'm pretty sure we didn't just become a division of the Navy, or the Coast Guard. So while you figure out if you've got the authority to give me orders, send on over the files and I'll read up on whatever's got you so bent out of shape."

A pregnant pause, then, "Monday, Mr. Rowley. Eight hundred hours."

He hung up and pulled out onto the road, a content whistle on his lips.

His phone blipped eight minutes later, just as he loaded a jumbo package of diapers into his shopping cart, next to five pounds of crab meat, and a pork loin bigger than his arm. He committed the operation's credentials to memory and deleted the message, then headed for the checkout.

* * *

Monica pushed her way inside past Ted, who didn't quite get out of the way. Matt sat at the computer, brow furrowed in concentration, scrolling the mouse with his middle finger. Amy read on the loveseat, Adam in a dark blue onesie at her feet. He dropped his toy and grinned wide, just like his daddy.

"Hey there, little man."

He reached up as she approached, and she scooped him into her arms. "He good?"

Amy shrugged. "Sure. No problems at all, Mrs. Rowley."

She nodded toward her husband. "How about him? Any big diaper changes necessary?"

"Nah." Amy shook her head. "He ran out to the store for a bit, came back and got right on the computer. Ain't moved since. I'm pretty sure I could have had a string of cute boys over and he'd never have noticed."

Monica frowned. The only things that occupied that much space in her husband's mind were house repairs and mission parameters, the former coming in a distant second.

She handed Matt their son, whom he took without looking up, peeled a pair of twenties out of her purse, and handed them over. "Thanks, Amy. Same time next Saturday?"

"I'll have to check. I have cheerleading but it might be later in the afternoon . . . ."

Monica tuned her out and showed her to the door, distracted

by Matt's distraction.

She turned and watched him, Ted now asleep at his feet, Adam drooling on his shoulder, eyes closed. In the months since she'd given birth, Matt had spent three months in the hospital, and a miraculous six in physical therapy before they'd called him back to work to destroy a fallen angel named Arakiel. Two months later his scars had disappeared, he'd doubled his muscle mass, and while he couldn't bench press a car anymore, he'd still obliterate your average NFL player in a fight. Your average ninja NFL player. And his NFL ninja friends.

During his recovery he'd done little things here and there, nothing too serious until Ramiel. With three defeated egregoroi under his belt, Matt had become the worldwide expert on dealing with weird shit crawling out of the woodwork—even though he didn't know much more than anyone else. Add to that his augmentations, and left to the government's whim he'd be out of the country every week until it killed him and left her a widow.

He worked, oblivious to her presence, and she let him. Instead she plucked Adam from his shoulder, set him back on the floor, and turned on the TV. *Downton Abbey*. Perfect.

* * *

Blossom Sakura waited at her sleeping daughter's side and tried to ignore the chemicals pumping death into Kazuko's frail body. Other drugs waited nearby, plus a bag of blood to fight the marrow-killing effects of the chemotherapy. Only nine years old, and the Mayo Clinic used poison and radiation to combat her illness.

Kazuko had been fine. Her daughter dying at six, Sakura had given her second-generation regenerates with ICAP approval. At seven, Kazuko had shown full remission, and an utter fearlessness borne from being her mother's daughter and from the power of near-instantaneous healing from anything that wouldn't kill her outright. Then Matt Rowley had destroyed Gerstner, and within weeks Sakura's daughter had become an eight-year-old girl doomed to die in pain and misery instead of up and playing with the other children, working at her studies, drawing and painting and—

She glared at her ringing phone and answered it.

"Sakura Tsuji."

"Miss Sakura?" The pleasant male voice recited the day's verification codes, then prattled too long before getting to the point, a new mission for the Special Threats Bureau.

"Yes. I will meet him Monday at eight a.m. Thank you. Goodbye."

Kazuko murmured, and Blossom ran a hand gently over the hairless dome of her head. Kazuko's eyes fluttered open, a dark brown mirror of her own. "Are we done soon?"

"Yes, my Kazuko. Soon."

* * *

After a fantastic dinner—pork chops, baked risotto cakes, and a huge salad—they made love in the bedroom and then Matt let Monica nap on the couch. Once sure she'd fallen asleep for good, he pulled up the video that had come with the mission files and popped on his headphones.

Black waves glinted under a cloudy night sky. Salt crusted the ship's railing, painted some dark color Matt couldn't make out.

Men babbled in the background.

"I don't hear nothing," a man said, his accent Texas coast.

More waves, more silence.

"D'you hear that?" Another man, more frantic.

Someone cried out in the distance, high-pitched and desperate.

"There it is! There it is!"

"I heard it that time," the first man said. He raised his voice. "Are you okay?"

"Starboard, Ricky. Fuck!"

The camera swung and focused on a pale dot amidst the choppy waves, black water topped with white froth. "I got it!"

The image rocked in time with the boat, losing and regaining the object in the water, haphazardly spotlit from off to the left. They approached at low speed, and a girl's piercing voice rang out.

"HELP ME!"

"We're here!" one of the men hollered. "Just hold on!"

The camera dropped to the deck but kept recording.

"Josh, rope."

"Knot it?"

"Yes, put a fucking knot in it! Honda, with a stopper."

The girl yelled again. "HELP!"

"Ricky, man the fucking camera."

The camera swung back up. The shape resolved itself into a chunk of yellow raft, half-shredded foam sticking out from shredded rubber. A Caucasian girl, maybe ten years old, clung to it, her dark hair plastered across her face.

Someone threw the rope past her, then dragged it back with a casual expertise so that it fell right into her hands. She clutched it with white knuckles, muscles straining in near panic.

"Now climb in the loop and grab that ball."

She did as told, sputtering desperately as she lost her grip on the remains of the raft, but they pulled it taut as she put it around her thighs like a swing. She grabbed the stopper knot with both hands. They hauled her fifteen feet up, over the rail and onto the deck.

"Are . . . are you okay?"

She squirmed out of the rope to her hands and knees, coughing. Her white dress hung in wet curtains from her body. A man in overalls kneeled next to her and put a hand on her back. She coughed again and again.

"Ricky, get her a glass of— "

Vomit erupted from her mouth in a bright red river that splattered the deck and the man's legs. He scrambled back with a cry and she vomited in a continuous stream, far too much bloody fluid for a little girl. Too much for an adult. She looked up into the light, revealing black eyes, not just the pupils and irises, but everything.

"Holy shit!" The cameraman—Ricky—stepped back.

She grinned and opened her mouth and more blood dribbled out, leaking down her chin and soaking her dress. Her lips moved and words formed, every language and none, a thousand voices making an incomprehensible one. She spread her arms in defiant confrontation, black eyes blazing with un-light, and she rose from the deck, first one foot, then the other, hovering inches from the wooden boards.

"Join us." Her child's voice reverberated with a thousand more.

A metal object slammed into her head, and she tumbled to the deck.

The camera zoomed in to the crumpled form, a little girl covered in bright arterial blood, a huge bruise already forming on her temple.

"Holy shit, guys. Holy SHIT."

"Turn that off, Ricky."

She twitched, and more blood leaked from her mouth, eyes, nose, and ears.

"I SAID TURN THAT FUCKING THING OFF."

The screen went blank.

"What was that?"

Matt whirled around, the movement tearing the headphones from the computer. He stared wide-eyed at his wife, who stood behind his desk in one of his VFD T-shirts, her face raw with worry.

"We don't know. Yet. I've got to head out Monday for an eight a.m. briefing."

"Oh." She took a step back, hand to her mouth. "That's not . . . not a movie?"

He blinked, at a loss for words, and shook his head. "No, Mon. It's real."

"My God, Matt. You have to help that girl."

He cleared his throat. "I know."

* * *

Matt kissed his wife and son goodbye, scratched Ted on the bridge of his nose, and stepped out into chilly darkness. At four a.m. in mid-October the Appalachian Plateau frosted his breath and sent goose bumps up his naked arms. He almost turned back for a jacket but had already faced one worried goodbye too many. As far as deployment timelines went, "I don't know" sucked more than any other.

He fired up the sedan—he'd leave the truck for Monica in case the weather went south—and pulled out onto the winding country road. Fresh gravel pinged off the wheel wells, and the frozen air didn't quite smother the petrochemical stench of oil and tar. He turned on the radio, dialed in KIX 106, and cranked the country music as loud as the speakers could handle.

He analyzed the mission while his tires ate up the road. Eighteen men had quit their jobs and moved to a mobile home park in Cuevas, Mississippi within six months of each other. Upon arrival, every one had been hired to work on the same drillship. Twelve had abandoned their families without so much as a note. The other six had no families to speak of. The mechanics and plumbers made some level of sense, but the IT guy, the accountant, the two waiters, and the three in retail had no skills related to the job. Thirteen white, three Hispanic, two black, none with criminal records. The intel weenies hadn't uncovered anything they had in common.

Cypriana, a Greek energy company, owned the drillship and a dozen just like it scattered across the world in search of oil and natural gas. They kept their nose clean—as clean as any multinational corporation—and their paperwork in order. This ship, the *Imperator*, boasted state-of-the-art technology, a thirty-thousand-foot drilling depth, and a habitat suite complete with hydroponic gardens. Though flagged out of Vanuatu, the crew of 125 came for the most part from Turkey, Cyprus, and Greece.

Since the American men had joined the crew, nine young girls from the Cuevas area had "run away," all of them while the men were home on leave. Sara Vallimont had turned up two hundred miles off the coast, clinging to a shredded piece of a life raft, speaking in tongues and vomiting enough blood for three people.

And hovering.

Matt threw a light on top of his car and blew through the stoplights headed into Nashville. He pulled into the Estes Kefauver Federal Building and Courthouse Annex lot just before five a.m., parked across from the church and killed the motor.

Images of Sara Vallimont flashed in his mind, superimposed with his son. He'd seen terrible things while deployed in Iraq, and the charnel house in Conor Flynn's basement still haunted his dreams. Possession or madness or garden-variety fanaticism, it came back again and again to the same place.

He looked in the mirror at the pale brick church, the stained glass black under the sallow security lights. "Don't make me kill any kids. A possessed kid, forget it. Find someone else to do your dirty work."

He got out, unsure whether God heard him, or cared.

A swiped badge, a wave to the guard, and an elevator ride took him to his office, the door still emblazoned with the eye-and-thunderbolt of the International Council on Augmented Phenomena. Almost everyone in ICAP management had died the moment Gerstner had stepped off the machine, and the Augs had lost their abilities, but in the spirit of government bureaucracies everywhere, ICAP just refused to go gently into that good night.

Matt frowned at the door. His abilities had returned, and his alone. Hundreds of Augs labored in hospitals, bodies pushed beyond their limits now that supernatural muscles had faded to mortal mass, hooked to machines that pumped blood and oxygen in a parody of Gerstner's living death. Their bodies lay shattered because of him, and the righteousness of saving their souls—at least from Frau Gerstner—faded against the stark realities of their existence.

He shook off the dark thoughts and entered his office. A withered cactus slumped in a pot on the windowsill, the faint sweet tang of fermentation rising from it. He dropped the plant into the garbage, pot and all, and sat.

A sparse desk and two guest chairs that hadn't seen use in months, and aside from the electronic paperwork generator the room contained only one thing of use. He unlocked the center drawer, jerked it open, and pulled out his secondary credentials. He sighed at the smiling face that stared back at him.

"Once more into the breach."

He relocked everything and trotted up the stairs two at a time.

On the roof the AH-64 Apache sat idle, lights out and pilot absent. Matt wandered over to the edge of the building and looked south, toward White Spruce and a wife and child and bed he'd rather not have left, but saw only Nashville. A sea of streetlights over a sleeping town, only the occasional car broke the silence—retail workers and security guards working early shifts, or C-shifters heading home to an early-morning dinner and a visit with the kids before school. The air held a sharp tang of cold with an undertone of exhaust and smoked meat.

The roof access door banged behind him, but he didn't bother to turn around.

Someone cleared his throat. "Excuse me, Mr. Rowley?"

Matt smiled at the tentative greeting. An aggressive and battle-hardened pilot, Ben Marks couldn't be described as anything other than timid on the ground.

"Are we good to go?" Matt said.

"Yes, sir, Mr. Rowley. Sorry, I had to take a—use the bath—the restroom."

Matt turned and extended his hand. "Good morning."

Ben reached out, pulled his damp hand back and wiped it on his pilot's jumpsuit, then put it back out and gave Matt a limp, dead-fish shake. "Morning."

Matt flashed his secondary credentials, an unnecessary formality made necessary by bureaucracy. Since ICAP's disintegration, the attack helicopters had reverted back to Army use, except when they didn't. They walked to the chopper. Ben fired it up and got the rotors spinning while Matt strapped himself in. Matt put on the headset and closed his eyes.

"We should land in Mid-South early. You'll have time to kill."

Matt gave an "aye-aye" and fell asleep to the muted sound of thrumming rotors.

* * *

Matt stepped off the helicopter, ducked under the whirling blades, squinted against the whirlwind and the rising sun, and smiled at Sakura. She didn't smile back, and he didn't expect her to.

"How's Kazuko?"

"Resting."

Sakura had a knack for processing information quickly, and ICAP had taken advantage of her talents to make her the fastest human being ever. Since Gerstner's death—or defeat, if Ramiel spoke the truth—Blossom had slowed to human-fast, instead of supernaturally-fast. Her low levels of musculoskeletal augmentation had been replaced with a punishing workout regimen that left her in the top tenth of a percent for human physicality and a sluggish shadow of her former self.

A hardened Yakuza-hunter with the Tokyo Metropolitan Police, she'd served undercover as a teen and handled massive task forces through her twenties and thirties. As an ICAP agent she'd helped him bring down a global conspiracy and destroy the greatest threats to mankind since the split atom. She'd also poisoned his pregnant wife to save her daughter's soul, something he'd forgiven but couldn't forget.

Intensely private, she'd never ask for or expect forgiveness, nor offer any for any slight perceived or real. She lived without compromise or qualm, and either didn't know or didn't care that others didn't share her stoicism.

He walked with her down the stairs into one of the Naval Support Activity Mid-South's massive buildings. A small base on the Mississippi, it served as the center for recruitment and personnel for the US Navy. Matt presumed that SACLANT had a reason for sending him here instead of directly to the Gulf, but couldn't fathom what that might be.

"What can you tell me?" he asked her.

"Sara Vallimont has undergone surgery to drain blood from her brain, a massive hematoma caused by the wrench you saw in the video. Examination reveals physical and sexual abuse, dehydration, malnutrition. Her eyes are still black, they induced coma for the next eight days. I ordered quarantine of sailors and medical personnel, and have confiscated cell phones, tablets, and laptops."

Matt raised an eyebrow. "Why are we here?"

"You're to infiltrate the *Imperator*. I'm to provide operational support."

"But why are we still in Tennessee? Shouldn't we be on the coast?"

She shrugged. "UN Allied Naval Command decided to use

the naval base as start-off point, knew you prefer to work local."

"But if I have to get to the ship . . ." He sighed.

"It's your military. You make sense of it."

"Fat chance of that."

"I don't understand."

"Never mind."

* * *

Janet LaLonde sat at her desk at home, flipping through the grimoire she'd acquired for far too much of someone else's money. The skin had half-rotted, and mold obscured too many of the markings from an ancient stylus.

Amazing that such an artifact could survive this long. She wiped each page with a bleach-soaked cloth, committing the Uruk proto-cuneiform to memory. Blood leaked from her eyes, the dark knowledge she'd consumed stealing tears she had long refused to shed in pain or grief.

A malevolent presence pulsed behind her eyes, but she abjured it with word and ritual older than the Christ's magic by three thousand years. It shrieked and wailed as she bound it and thrust it back into the Pit. Her brother's voice pleaded, her mother's, the girl she'd kissed at a party in eleventh grade, her college lover Paul. All of them and none, she bound them and buried them under the swirling winds of death and hate and all-consuming hunger.

Dammit, brother. Where are you?

She reached back and unclasped the gold chain from around her neck, and drew out the perfect blue orb, the lapis lazuli stone writhing under the surface. The white mist inside swirled and battered at its cage, its mewling, unheard whine a dagger to her brain.

She stroked the stone with one finger, and blew on it. "Yes, I will free you, I will."

It cooed and shuddered in a hope too long buried.

"But first you must do something for me."

She sliced her palm with a fingernail and let her blood dribble onto the stone, where it disappeared inside. She chanted, and a web formed in her mind, a tangled, shifting skein of consciousness, a billion interconnected points, twisting through time, through life, into death.

"You will find my brother. By our mother's blood, follow where you must, to the edges of oblivion, but find Dawkins and bring him to me."

* * *

Jason Rees gasped awake, bright blue motes fading from his vision. He sat up, blurry-eyed, and fumbled for a bottle of Maker's Mark he'd poured down the drain days before. Head pounding, he shivered despite the heat of the rectory and lay back, pulling up the simple brown comforter that enveloped his twin bed.

He stared at the crucifix on the wall, a garish thing of mahogany and brass, polished to an unreasonable shine by diligent church ladies for most of a century. The Christ stared down at him, face twisted in suffering offered up for all men.

Or something like that.

His thoughts swirled with the events of last year, Matt Rowley and Dawkins and Gerstner, and above all Monica, smiling down at him with eyes bluer than they should be. In his mind she blinked, frowned, and flitted away, her departure a taut string in his mind that snapped under too much scrutiny.

He sighed and looked at the clock, red letters stabbing 4:24 into his brain. *Close enough.*

He stood, stumbled to the bathroom, and ignored the bloodshot, haggard eyes that stared back at him from the mirror. St. Martin's Early Bird Weekday Mass started at six a.m., and he needed to look presentable.

Chapter 3

Matt looked up at the decrepit fishing boat, wrinkling his nose at the fetid, stomach-churning aroma of rotting fish and stagnant diesel fuel. He rolled his eyes to Lieutenant-Commander Roger Smith, who stood at ease next to a black sedan with government plates and leather seats. Smith's impeccable uniform could have been more out of place on the riverside wharf, but Matt couldn't quite imagine how.

"Really, Roger?"

The small, immaculate man winced. "That is your transportation. It will take three days to reach the rig, at which point you will insinuate yourself amongst the workers, determine the nature of the threat, and if possible eliminate it."

"I don't know the slightest thing about working on an oil rig."

Roger stiffened. "Your skill set is in your dossier. I was informed that you utilized infiltration techniques to access Ramiel in Syria."

"Sure, of a sort. I know my jihadis well enough to walk by, but I don't know oil, and undercover work has never been my specialty. I mean, I'm an Appalachian country boy, so I might be able to pull off some good fishing—"

"Your flippancy has been noted, Mr. Rowley. This vessel

contains two CIA men already hired as fill-in crew for the *Imperator*. They will guide you in your infiltration and cover for your ignorance. You're under orders. I have the authority to place you under arrest if you disobey."

Matt snorted without taking his eyes from the boat. "The authority, but not the ability."

"Mister Rowley—"

"Shut up, Roger."

Roger continued, but Matt refused to listen. Instead he approached Roger and bumped up against his chest, looking down from a good nine inches above. "Rog, I'm not a violent man by nature, but I don't shy from it. And let's be honest, if it comes to consequences only one of us isn't replaceable. So when I said 'shut up,' it wasn't a suggestion."

Roger's jaw clacked shut.

It didn't seem fair to take his frustration out on LC Smith, but on some small level it felt good to cut the officious little prick's legs out from under him. As much as Monica needed it—as much as he needed it—he shouldn't have taken the weekend. Sara Vallimont had a family, too, and someone needed to decipher this mess. His power, his burden.

He picked up his duffel bag—clothing packed courtesy of the CIA—and walked up the boarding plank.

Two men greeted him at the top, both overweight, both bald, both in jeans and flannel, one clean-shaven and the other sporting a giant red beard.

"Greg Faherty," red-beard said, hand outstretched. He hauled Matt aboard and nodded to his companion. "Jim Chambers. We're here to help with your infiltration under whatever parameters might fit. Let's talk."

They shook hands, and the spooks led him to their cabin. The dark, cramped room boasted four bunks, each no larger than a cot. And it stank. The combination of sweat, salt, and stale cigarettes scoured his enhanced senses of anything pleasant.

He wrinkled his nose, set his bag on the one made bed, and turned to his companions.

"Who's our fourth?"

Jim shrugged. "Mark Talmer. Canadian, hell of a cough, keeps to himself."

The implication rang out: Talmer wasn't part of the op.

"Fair enough." Matt sat on springs too soft and too squeaky, a cheap mattress that should have been replaced many years prior. He ran his hands over the clean but threadbare sheets, pilled and abrasive. "So what now?"

Greg raised his hands to encompass the cabin. "Relax. We've all been hired to work on the *Imperator* until hurricane season picks back up. A few days transit, and boom."

"Boom?"

"If it works for you, your cover is Matt Cotton, apprentice pipe-fitter from Memphis. You work for us, mostly grunt work so far, which explains your lack of training. Your old lady Monica left you while you served in Baghdad and Fallujah, taking your son Adam with her back home to her parents in Tennessee." He grinned.

Jim didn't. "Trust me, whatever you think you're good at, you suck at this. We like to keep things slipup-proof even for experienced operatives. You say the wrong name, mention your wife or son, it sounds like a legitimate slip. Let me see your hands."

Matt held them out, and Jim grabbed them, twisting them back and forth to examine his fingers.

He sighed and looked at Greg. "A baby's ass." He looked back at Matt. "You need some calluses."

Matt raised an eyebrow. "I can't get calluses."

"What do you mean?" Greg stepped forward to look at his hands.

Matt pulled them back and held them up. "My skin's pretty tough, and any damage I sustain heals pretty fast. No scars, no calluses. No dandruff."

Greg gasped, and whispered, "You're an Aug? I mean, still an Aug?"

"Yup. The last one, far as I know."

"But . . . how? They're all gone!"

"Nobody knows." Matt hid his unease behind a shrug. *Ramiel might know.*

Jim's doubtful look poisoned the room.

Matt sighed. "Do you need proof?"

Jim spread his hands in a defensive posture. "Hey, man, your thing is your thing. Our job is to get you there and help you maintain cover. They haven't even told us why, and chances are we don't need to know."

Matt considered the value of theatrics and decided against it. "In that case, what do we do about calluses?"

Greg grimaced. "Try not to shake hands?"

"Shit," Jim said. "That's not going to work at all. You have to hope no one notices."

"I'll try a firm grip," Matt said.

* * *

Monica cranked the faucet on the wash sink, and a bare trickle came out. "Shit."

Matt hadn't been gone half a week, and already she just wanted him home. She checked the basement shelves for water filters and couldn't find any, so she bundled Adam into a red jumper and hauled the car seat out to the truck. The massive diesel motor turned over on the second crank. She put it in gear, drove to the end of the driveway, and turned right.

A charcoal-grey Chevy Cobalt eased down the road behind her, and picked up speed as she did.

That's odd. Only the Franklins lived farther down Turkey Vulture Lane, and from there the road split into dead-end dirt roads that wound through the mountain forests to various fields and hunting retreats.

She tried to put it out of her mind except as a traffic concern as she headed into White Spruce. It fell back as she sped up to sixty-two in a fifty-five, then gained ground when she hit the speed zone and slowed to thirty-five. The town unfolded before her, a main street without a stoplight that boasted a grocery store, bait shop, Wilcox Lumber and Hardware, and Big Bear Automotive Repair. A dozen houses completed the picture of smaller-than-small-town America.

She pulled in to Wilcox, hefted Adam out of the baby seat, and headed into the store.

Chris waved from behind the counter, a three-hundred-pound sack of bald townie in a green polo, with wandering eyes and an inability to take "eew" for an answer. "Mrs. Rowley, how's it hanging?"

She flipped him the bird and put Adam in a cart she otherwise didn't need. "Lower than yours."

Chris's twin brother Cory cackled and slapped the counter. "Ya gotta stop chasing that, bro."

"Nothing ventured."

"Her husband will tear your balls off, man."

Monica couldn't hear Chris's mumbled reply, and didn't care. He'd been "chasing that" since high school, with similar results. She grabbed filters, a couple of packs of light bulbs, and a solar sidewalk light to replace the one Matt had crushed with the lawn mower back in September. It felt good to buy what they needed without worrying about the cost.

She paid Cory, ignored Chris's sidelong leer, and wheeled the cart out the door. The Cobalt sat under the flag pole at the post office, empty. Monica tossed the supplies into the cab between the stick shift and the car seat, hoisted Adam onto her shoulder, and crossed the street to the post office.

She walked in past the rows of lock boxes and pushed through the door into the customer service foyer.

Sandy greeted her with a huge grin, her curly, gray hair tumbling over the shoulders of her official USPS uniform. "Hey, darling. No packages today."

Monica shrugged, peering back into the PO Box room—empty—before leaning on the counter. Sandy reached out and lifted Adam away, and for his part he smiled and grabbed a fistful of gray curls. Sandy kissed his cheek and returned his grin ten-fold.

Monica kept her voice low, even though they appeared to be the only people in the building. "Y'all have any idea who owns that Chevy under the flagpole?"

Sandy craned her neck to better see out the window. "No clue. Why? They ding ya?"

Monica shrugged. "No big reason, I guess. He was parked just past the driveway, followed me into town."

"Well that's weird. Ain't nobody lives out that way owns a Chevy."

A brown-haired man, just scruffy enough to be sexy, walked up to the car from the direction of the grocery store, smiling. In a tan turtleneck and jeans a hair too tight, he cut a handsome figure more Hollywood than Tennessee.

"Know him?" Sandy asked as he unlocked the door.

"Nope. Sure is cute, though."

He got in, checked his rear-view mirror, and lingered a little too long on Monica's truck across the street.

A nervous tingle crawled up her spine, turning to an electric jolt when he locked eyes with her through the window. His smile didn't seem so handsome right then. It reminded her more of Chris's leer, only a flatter, more dangerous sort of hunger. A small nod, a turn of the key, and he backed out and drove away.

Sandy clucked her tongue, a rapid-fire clicking, and handed Adam back to her. "You packing, honey?"

She took the weight and hugged him. He squealed and squirmed, reaching out for Sandy. "Packing?"

"Pistol, Mon. You got a gun?"

"I do, but not with the baby. Don't got anywhere to put it."

Sandy "tsked" and pointed down at her bag. "I carried every day when I had the boys. Diaper bag's got room for more than diapers."

Monica ran her tongue over her front teeth. "Yeah. Diaper bag. I'll have to consider that."

* * *

The *Imperator's* specs didn't do it justice. Two hundred and thirty meters as an abstract concept meant nothing. It smothered the horizon, the biggest boat Matt had ever seen, short of an aircraft carrier. Somehow, approaching it from the water made it seem larger even than those.

"Good God. How do we get up there?" Matt asked.

Mark Talmer rolled his eyes and used his cigarette to point at a door in the hull, thirty feet above the water line. "We don't, dumbass." The motion exposed a tattoo on his forearm, a cybernetic cat's head, half orange and half black.

"Ah," Matt said. Playing dumb didn't seem so hard when he had no idea what to do.

In their three days together, Mark's interactions with Matt had been limited to grunts, insults, and sarcasm. Mark hadn't joined their poker games, electing instead to wander the deck alone, and ate lunch by himself. Given Mark's three-pack-a-day habit and conspicuous lack of a toothbrush, Matt couldn't feel bad about it, but something about his behavior went beyond taciturn.

They pulled up alongside the enormous drillship, massive airbags inflating to keep the hulls from scraping. Men threw down huge ropes from the deck of the larger ship. Once tied together, the door on the *Imperator* opened. A small man with black hair stepped out of the way to allow them through. His choice of jeans and nothing else revealed an endless string of swirling tattoos, covering every inch of his chest, arms, even his bare, dirty feet.

Matt hesitated, expecting some form of ceremony asking and granting permission to come aboard.

"Come on," the black-haired man said. "I ain't holding the door all fucking day."

Jim stepped through, followed by Greg, Mark, and finally Matt. The sharp smell of bleach and ocean salt overpowered a faint hint of body odor.

"Welcome to the *Imperator*. You hungry? We got a shipment of blue crabs straight from Maine, fresher than you'll ever see in the stores."

They all shook their heads.

He led them through a warren of narrow tunnels, and down two flights of stairs to a massive common room filled with cots bolted to the walls and trunks bolted to the floor. "Stow your gear and get comfortable. We ain't even pumping right now, so you're likely getting paid to sit ass and play cards. Hope you brought cards."

He walked out.

The casual and abrupt departure surprised Matt. His experience on ships all entailed meeting the captain as one of the first orders of business, just to get sized up if for no other reason. Here, they didn't even get their guide's name before being left to their own devices. Investigation might prove easier than he thought.

He claimed a bunk and lay down, hands behind his head. You didn't make it through military service without learning how to wait. Or sleep.

* * *

Monica gave the chain wrench one final tug, then opened the tank valve. Water trickled into the filter housings, clean and clear. Once full, she opened the filter valve the rest of the way. She stood, wiped greasy slate from her hands on an old washrag, and turned on the valve to the hot water heater.

Hard water sucked, but it beat sulfur ten ways to Sunday. She washed her hands in the mud room sink, wiped them on her jeans, and walked into the living room. Adam beamed at her from his gated pen, the floor a chaotic mess of typing paper and crayons. "Hey, little man!"

She plopped down on the couch, turned off *The Wiggles*, and clicked through the channel guide until she found an *Outlander* marathon. She sat back to enjoy the show, then noticed a rock outside on the deck, something white just visible underneath it. Bassets were supposed to bark at everything, but Ted snored under the coffee table, oblivious to his very existence.

She peeked outside. Nothing moved but the wind in the pines, and no strange shapes appeared in the shadows beneath the boughs. She opened the door, tossed the rock into the woods, and snatched the note from the ground.

Once inside she unfolded the square of typing paper. Her throat closed at the scribble of green crayon, like the one Adam held in his fist, and she stumbled back into the counter. She couldn't read it through a sudden stream of tears, couldn't think through the tightness in her chest. Instead she went to the diaper bag, pulled out the .357, and sat on the loveseat facing the glass doors.

And shook. Madness submerged her under a wave of craving, a desperate need for escape that crushed her bones and jellied her organs, something, anything to take the edge off. Her mind raced for something in the house; they didn't even have any vanilla extract, much less a cigarette or joint or hit of meth or coke or heroin. Matt's fault, and it made her so angry and helpless and hopeless, and so terribly grateful.

Something brushed her leg, and the craving fell to a ruthless gnawing in the pit of her stomach, present but not all-consuming. She looked down at her son, who'd stretched through the gate to clutch at her jeans. He looked up, his gaze sharp and clear, devoid of the wide-eyed curiosity or worry of a near-toddler.

She wiped the tears from her cheeks and smiled. "Hey, little man."

He laughed, bursting her heart with sheer joy. She tried to return his smile but couldn't. Instead, her gaze traveled to the right, to the green scrawl on white paper.

EXODUS 22:18

The living room shelf held three Bibles: a leather-bound gift from Matt's father on their wedding day, a child's bible not even a year old—a gift from Pastor Joe—and a tattered, dog-eared paperback, the last memory she had of her grandmother. She'd never opened any of them.

She pulled the leather-bound book off the shelf and flipped to Exodus.

Thou shalt not suffer a witch to live.

She read it again, and the passages before and after, a list of old-time laws and rules from when the Jews had fled Egypt across the Red Sea. What the note meant wasn't clear, but she knew a threat when she saw it. She put her hand on the gun, then on the phone. She dialed Matt with no hope of reaching him in the field. His voicemail kicked on, and she almost cried again at the sound of his voice.

"You've reached Matt Rowley, Office of Special Threats. Leave a message."

It beeped.

"Baby, you got to call me right away." She hit "End" and stared at the phone. After a long moment she dialed another number.

The volunteer receptionist at St. Martin's church in Franklin, Kentucky, took her name and number with a promise to relay them to Father Rees. Adam scribbled, curls and loops and lines from one piece of paper to the next, content enough with the paper that little crayon marred the hardwood floor.

The phone rang five minutes later. She clicked "Talk."

"Jason?"

His cold reply contrasted with the desperate plea in her voice. "I'm not supposed to be talking to you."

Fuck you. You owe me. "I have a problem."

"He told me he'd kill me and leave me to rot in a ditch. I believe him."

"He don't bluff, but he's out of the country."

"Even more reason not to talk to you."

Monica looked at the ceiling and tried not to scream. "You called me back, so shut the fuck up a minute, huh?"

Silence. A big improvement.

She licked her lips. "What can you tell me about Exodus 22:18?"

"Uh . . . Exodus 22 is a bunch of rules to live by." Pages rustled in the background. "Yeah, eighteen . . . . 'Thou shalt not suffer a witch to live.' Yeah, that one gets a lot of play these days, especially from people attacking the Church for intolerance. Lots of other stuff about marriage and hairstyles and mixed-fiber clothing. What is this about?"

"Someone came into my house and left a note with that on it. While Adam was home." She looked down at Adam, scattering papers across the floor on his hands and knees.

"That's weird. What's witchcraft have to do with you?"

"I don't know."

"Hmmm. Humans for Humanity equated Gerstner Augmentation with witchcraft. They took credit for destroying all the witches last year through the power of prayer. Big parties, lots of enthusiastic press conferences, massive funding drives."

"I saw it on the news. But why would they be here?"

Jason didn't say anything. He often didn't, let her feel out where her thoughts were headed without interrupting.

"Do you think they're after Matt? You didn't say anything, did you? How would they even know he's still Augged?"

"He's still Augged?" The shock in Jason's voice carried through the connection.

"Maybe you're not supposed to know that . . . but maybe somebody does, and they don't like it so much."

She glanced down and gasped. Adam stared at her from the jumble of papers, where the squiggles and lines made an unmistakable image.

A fallen crucifix lay on the ground, Jason lay nailed atop it, mouth open in a wordless scream, limbs twisted to unnatural angles.

"Holy shit." She reached out her arms. "Adam, baby, stay there."

"What's wrong?" Jason asked, the edge of concern in his voice.

She wiggled her cell phone out of her pocket. Adam moved, the papers shifted, and the image disappeared. "No, wait, DAMMIT."

"Are you all right?"

"No. Yeah. Shit, I don't know."

"What happened?"

She didn't doubt for a second what she'd seen, but knew she didn't want to tell him the truth. "Nothing. Thought I saw something outside."

"Call the police. Right now. I'm hanging up."

The phone clicked dead.

She set it down and looked at her child. Chubby cheeks, big grin, not a sign of anything amiss.

"Did you do that, kid? Or did something else?"

She called 9-1-1, then spent ten minutes trying to piece

together even part of the image. When Jason called back she told him the cops were on their way. An hour later, after the cops had left, a charcoal gray Chevy Cobalt rolled past the driveway, toward town. She left the gun on the counter in easy reach.

* * *

"No, you goddamned idiot, over there!" Jim Chambers played his cover almost too well. Matt grinned his dumbest grin and carried the steel pipe in the direction Jim pointed, toward the moonpool, a massive opening in the center of the ship that provided access to the water. The water shone black under the midday sun, the blue of the sky smothered by the *Imperator's* bulk.

A giant crankshaft rotated under a gantry, or whatever they called it, spinning all the way around once every few seconds. The other end of it lay eight thousand feet under the water, just starting a test shaft to probe for oil under the ocean crust. Matt didn't know the terminology of boats or oil and without trying had solidified his reputation as the dumbest meathead aboard during his first twelve-hour shift.

Still, he couldn't shake the feeling that the attention the other crewmen paid him went beyond wariness of a newbie onboard. Untrained personnel could be dangerous and as such provoked a certain hostility, but the reactions of the established crew went beyond exasperation or even worry. Not one offered help or guidance, not one spared him a kind word after terse introductions, not one even shook his hand. The black mood pervaded every inch of the ship, even the cafeteria and the game room, where sullen men played pool, darts, and cards without banter or laughter. For blue-collar men earning six figures with overtime plus hazard pay, the malaise didn't fit.

He set the pipe down and went for another. In truth he could carry a half-dozen at a time without breaking a sweat, but didn't want to draw any more attention than he already had. His true goal had nothing to do with getting work done, and working a few days without trying anything suspicious couldn't hurt his chances of breaking away unseen.

The stop work bell rang at seven p.m. sharp. All work ceased—drilling, welding, even ship maintenance, everything but the kitchen staff, who kicked into overtime to feed the famished crew. Matt stood in line with his tray, took three scoops of pulled pork with extra bread and a carton of orange juice. The spooks sat with four other pipe layers, chowing down without much conversation, so Matt chose an unoccupied table.

The small room filled, absent the chatter one would expect in a cafeteria. The hair stood on the back of his neck as every table filled but his. Four men stood against the wall, eating off trays held in their hands rather than sitting at his table. He ignored them all, concentrating on his sandwich, muscles primed and ready to spring into action at the slightest hint of hostility.

A shadow darkened his tray. He looked up. The black-haired man who'd let them on board scowled down at him.

"What are you doing on my ship?"

Matt chewed a few more times than necessary, then swallowed. He set down his sandwich before looking up. "Trying to make a living. You Captain Galatas, then? You don't sound Greek."

"Galatas fell ill. I'm Krick, and I asked you a question."

Matt shifted his shoulders, almost a shrug. "I answered you, Captain. Not sure what else you want." Faherty and Chambers tensed in his peripheral vision.

Krick snaked out and grabbed his wrist. Matt let him, and turned his palms up, revealing a half-dozen Band-Aids he'd added to his disguise. Krick reached out to grab a bandage, and Matt jerked his hand free.

"Who hired you?"

Matt nodded toward Jim and Greg. Krick would know that from his paperwork anyway.

"Gloves or not, you've worked three days without a blister and without slowing down. What are you doing on my ship?"

He couldn't say that Jim hadn't warned him about his hands.

"Tell you what, Captain, why don't we finish this conversation somewhere private? I don't want to start any trouble."

"Too late for that, I think."

Matt held up his hands in what he hoped Krick would take as a placating gesture. "You sure?"

Krick's eyes turned jet black. Creeping black lines wormed beneath his skin.

Silver flashed to Matt's right and Greg Faherty fell away from the table, a fork buried in his neck, the oil-worker next to him grinning like a maniac with eyes as black as the captain's.

Matt dove left, away from a swipe from Krick's claws. Around him, the rest of the crew attacked, several launching themselves at Greg and Jim, the rest joining Krick.

Claws? Definitely claws, black and cruel, an extra inch at the end of each finger.

Matt sprang up and waded through the crowd toward Greg and Jim, crushing knees and cracking skulls with blunt, clinical fury. Bodies fell in his wake. Claws raked his arms and chest, ragged tears that burned well beyond physical injury, but for each one he returned a killing blow.

A moan erupted, a deep resonance that reverberated through the room from every crewman. Matt shattered a skull with a knife-hand strike, pulled back, and took a Taser to the stomach. He stumbled, gritting his teeth against the jolting paralysis, and Mark Talmer pressed his advantage. Eyes jet black, grinning like a maniac, he pulled away the Taser and grabbed Matt's neck with an iron grip.

Free from the electric shock, Matt leaned back, grabbed Talmer's wrist left-handed, then brought his right hand up into the elbow. Talmer didn't scream, didn't even react, as the joint hyperextended. Matt twisted it behind his back, forcing him to his knees, and Talmer gnashed his teeth in fury, still moaning with the crowd.

Matt brought his weight down on his elbow, driving it into the base of Talmer's neck. His body crumpled as vertebrae shattered, and Matt wasted no time. He swept the legs out from under another assailant, flipped to his feet, and struck another in the jugular. His rigid fingers pulled free in a spray of sticky fluid as black as old motor oil. A vinegar tang stung his nostrils, and his fingers burned.

Greg lay on the ground, eyes wide, throat a massive blue bruise, fork still protruding from his windpipe. Matt couldn't see Jim in the press of bodies. His flesh burned white-hot where he'd been scratched, and a hint of fatigue flooded his muscles, a sensation he hadn't felt since he left his crutches on the hospital floor.

Uh, oh.

The mob switched tactics, turning as one and grabbing for him instead of clawing. Only in the movies did one man face ten and make it out alive. At least forty still stood. Matt backpedaled to gain some space, snapping limbs and crushing bones as he went, but he impacted a wall of flesh, and a tattooed arm wrapped around his neck. Matt dropped low, and his assailant dropped with him to retain his grip, just as Matt expected him to.

Matt extended his legs, his backward leap carrying the man into the bolted-down table with a crunch he both felt and heard. He flipped back and landed feet-first on the table. Across the room, Krick stood with his arms raised, black fluid leaking from his eyes.

Jim Chambers leapt out from under the table, driving a chef's knife toward Krick's abdomen. The captain swept his hand downward and Jim caught it against his own, drawing a deep gash in Krick's forearm with the cleaver in his other hand. As one the crowd bled, black ichor leaking from their wrists.

With a wince Krick ripped his left hand up through Chambers's neck, and his blood painted the captain in crimson.

Matt leapt from table to table, lashing out to pulverize organs and snap limbs of anyone who got too close. Exhaustion pulled at him as the poison worked through his muscles, slowing his reflexes to near-human levels. He surged upward, punching his hands through drop-ceiling panels, and grabbed the thin metal supports that held up the panels. Muscles straining, he heaved himself up and through the small hole.

The darkness slithered with cables, power and internet in galvanized steel, pale yellow PEX carrying water to and from the ship's bowels. He scrambled forward on all fours, careful not to put his weight on any tiles, an insane game of "break mama's back" that carried him thirty feet to Krick's position.

Tucking into a ball, he fell through the tile and landed with a crash on the ground behind the acting captain.

Krick whirled and swiped, his claw tearing through Matt's cheek and cutting his bottom lip in half. Matt choked down the blood gushing over his tongue and grabbed the man by the shirt, pulling him to eye level. Krick's legs dangled as Matt snatched a steak knife from the table and held it to a black eye.

"Call them off." The burning itch intensified, and concentration became harder through the gray-green fuzz filling his brain. Blood dribbled from his mouth, and he spoke through it. "BACK OFF!"

Krick laughed, a haggard, wet sound over the droning voices, and closed his clawed hands around Matt's wrists. "Why bother? You're already dead."

"You first." Matt pulled back with his left hand and punched forward with his right, jamming the knife through Krick's right eye, up to the hilt. Krick twitched once.

The moaning stopped.

Bodies fell to the deck in a single mass. Matt turned, still holding the captain up. Every crew member had collapsed, eyes wide, leaking—bleeding—a viscous black substance from the right socket. Muscles twitched, bodies jerked. Matt wrapped his arm around Krick's head and wrenched, tearing it from the body.

Black fluid sprayed the floor and spattered his face, hot and too sticky, reeking of soured vinegar. The crewmen stopped moving, their necks erupting in sprays of black ichor as their heads tumbled to the floor. The room spun.

Matt stumbled and held himself up with the table. His eyelids drooped, vision blurred.

Monica. He heaved himself up onto a table, above the growing black pool of pestilent rot. *Adam.*

He dropped to his hands and knees, and the world faded.

Chapter 4

Eight girls stood around him in a circle, holding hands, their sing-song chant an unintelligible nursery rhyme. The world stank of blood and shit and death, a putrid miasma that set his stomach churning, but Matt couldn't move to cover his nose. They stared at him with eyes the void between stars, their white dresses streaked with black and red. His head rang in tune with their babble.

Their gibbering almost-words slithered between his thoughts, coaxing him to—his head rang again.

"Wake up, dammit," Sakura said.

He opened his eyes. The girls disappeared, replaced by Sakura's dour, mannish face. The smell remained, and the memory of their chant danced in his ears.

Sakura rubbed her hand on her hip. "You have hard bones. Get up."

She stood, offered a hand, and hauled him to his feet.

Corruption surrounded them. Black, liquid goo covered the floor. Clothing lay in disorganized lumps throughout the cafeteria amidst scattered trays of food, bolted-down furniture, and the dismembered bodies of Greg and Jim. Aside from the Shop guys, not a single bone or tooth lay anywhere. A pair of soldiers stood in the doorway, wide-eyed and green-faced, their wan complexions a perfect fit to Matt's state of mind.

"Forensics are on the way," Sakura said. "You shower, then we breach the closed-off section."

"There's a closed-off section?" He walked and talked, his shoes leaving sticky black tracks down the cramped hallway.

"You've been on-board three days and you didn't know?"

He shrugged. "Not a lot of unobserved time. For the most part I've been carrying pipe."

Sakura muttered something in Japanese, and ignored his pointed look as if she'd never spoken.

They wound their way to the crew quarters. Sakura found a black plastic garbage bag and opened it. "Clothes. Boots, too."

He stripped, peeling each disgusting layer from his skin and letting it fall into the open bag. He got to his boxers and hesitated.

"Hurry up." Sakura's mouth twitched, an expression that, in some alternate universe where Blossom Sakura smirked, may have been the beginnings of a smirk.

He dropped his drawers, eyes locked with Sakura. He held up the filthy, ichor-soaked underwear with a thumb and forefinger, and dropped them into the bag. Her expression never changed, even when she dropped her eyes to his groin and brought them back up.

"Acceptable, if unremarkable. Shower. Hurry up."

Sakura tied the bag as he walked into the bathroom.

He cranked the water as hot as it went and scrubbed hard, washing multiple times, scrubbing everything to eliminate any trace of the viscous black fluid. He leaned against the wall and let the clean water cascade over him, until it got too hot to breathe comfortably.

He got out reeking of lye and lavender, toweled off, and stepped into the common room. Sakura stood with her back to the room, arms crossed. A pair of used work boots in his size sat on the foot of his bed. He threw on deodorant, dressed, and approached, careful to avoid his own sticky footprints.

She half-turned at his footsteps, then took the lead. "Let's go."

Men and women in white environmental suits lumbered across their path, lugging test kits and electronics to the cafeteria-turned-abattoir. The techs had already stripped the captain's quarters, and strike teams had cleared the moonpool and bridge. That left only the rear hold, which they'd left for Matt and Sakura. Whether out of fear or respect, he couldn't tell.

A massive, rusted padlock secured the crossbars in the steel door, hinges hidden behind welded steel plates. A corpsman in full assault gear, one of six, handed him an Auto-Assault 12 combat shotgun. "Loaded for bear, sir."

He checked the drum magazine anyway and, satisfied, eyed the lock. "I don't suppose anyone has bolt cutters?"

Sakura held up a hand, and like magic a key appeared between her fingers. "In the captain's pocket."

It slid into the keyhole, and she popped the clasp with a smooth twist. She pulled out the lock, grabbed the crossbar, and looked at him, one eyebrow raised.

He half-turned. "What's on the far side?"

A marine stepped up with a tablet raised, displaying blueprints. "Engine room, sir, but there's no through access. Hull to port and starboard, one escape hatch in the aft ceiling we've got covered from above, awaiting orders."

"I'm in first with Sakura. We might have hostages inside, so check your fire and clear fast. If it freaks you out, kill it, but watch those 203's in confined quarters. Any questions?" The marines said nothing. Sakura dropped her night-vision goggles, and the marines followed suit. He raised the weapon and nodded.

Sakura pulled open the door, and he followed the shotgun through the dark entrance, scanning left and right, checking corners in full spectrum, his augmented eyes rendering goggles unnecessary. Sakura appeared at his side, NATO-issue REC-7 assault rifle up and ready. The marines piled in behind them, efficient and smooth and almost silent.

Infrared picked up a vague red heat toward the back, and the dulled, purple ultraviolet showed him too many hiding places—crates stacked to twenty-foot ceilings or under oiled canvas lashed to metal knobs on the floor, neat rows stretching back a third the length of the ship. Machinery clanked louder here, the constant shudder of the engines vibrating through the floor and walls. It smelled of machine grease and dust.

He held up a fist, turned and grabbed the switch on the wall. The marines—and Sakura—removed their goggles and he turned on the lights. Rows of fluorescent bulbs flickered to life, bathing the room in their stark, artificial glow. Aside from the added hum, no sounds greeted their arrival. He dropped his fist.

The marines fanned out to take the side aisles and they swept forward as one, shouting "Clear!" at each new row of crates. Matt slowed as he reached an open area, veering left as Sakura split right.

They stopped.

A huge chalk pentagram, thirty feet across, dominated the back of the hold. Brown-red symbols smeared across the plain steel floor, circling across riveted seams in a mad visual collage that hurt his brain to look at. Gray goose feathers lay scattered throughout the pentagram, random yet somehow part of the pattern. He glanced toward but not at Sakura, and fought down memories he'd rather not re-experience—emaciated men, thorned demons, and Akash Rastogi screaming as they tore him apart, Sakura cutting deep lines in her wrists to free the beast confined within the eldritch cage.

Gritting his teeth against the expected onslaught, he reached forward. Nothing happened as his fingers crossed the line. He stepped forward. Nothing again.

Sakura joined him, phone out, recording the symbols. "These are different."

"They are." Curved, swirling, these glyphs held nothing in common with the sharp, angular runes they'd encountered in the abandoned warehouse in Washington, D.C. Dark circles sat at every chalk intersection, crimson puddles blackened and solidified to a hard, dull mass.

He slung his AA-12 over his shoulder and dropped to a pushup to disturb as little as possible. Putting his nose millimeters from a stain, he inhaled. A sweet smell, like vanilla and old churches, it carried him to summer days on his uncle's farm. He looked up at Sakura. "Beeswax."

"Noted."

Matt pushed to his feet.

A marine yelled. "Rowley, you got to see this!"

Sakura kept filming, her jittery but somehow coordinated camera work the product of modern technology—catch it all, analyze it in slow motion or stills later. He trotted to the very back of the room.

The wall hummed, the mechanical throbbing of the drillship's engines pulsing right through it. All six marines stood, weapons down, staring at a leathery object hanging from a hook on the wall. Thick black thread stitched together pale scraps. Matt didn't have to search for recognizable pieces: ears, noses, hair tufts, eye sockets.

He swallowed and lifted it from the hook, trying not to recoil from the lustrous, well-oiled, almost slippery surface. Spread out it revealed a cloak for a large man, complete with a hood, made of sections of human faces joined with rawhide sutures. Behind him, someone threw up.

"We find our girls?" a marine asked.

Matt shook his head. "Most of these are male. From the looks I'd say adults, and some of this leather is pretty old, five or ten years, easy."

The marine straightened, his face pale. "That's pretty gross, sir."

He put the cloak back on the wall and turned around. "What's your name, Marine?"

"Hatfield, sir."

"All right, Hatfield, get that vomit cleaned up and search these crates. I expect an inventory before forensics finishes up with the cafeteria, but under no circumstances step into or interfere with that pentagram. Clear?"

Hatfield glanced over his shoulder toward the rest of the hold. "You think it's magic or something, sir?"

The doubt in his voice rankled Matt, but a year ago he'd have felt the same way. He'd seen weirder crap that he'd ever imagined, and still didn't know what to believe about any of it. No explanation would stop Hatfield's nightmares.

"Just follow your orders."

"Aye, sir."

* * *

The crates matched the cargo manifest: engine parts, cam shafts, and spare bits. In three days of searching they found nothing else of interest, so the Navy turned the sanitized ship over to Cypriana crewmen flown in from Greece.

From the deck of a US destroyer, Matt watched the *Imperator* churn water toward the Mediterranean at full steam.

* * *

Janet LaLonde walked into Matt's sparse office chomping on pale green gum and smelling of wintergreen. He couldn't help but look.

A leggy brunette prone to scandalous dresses and high heels, she hid a stunning intellect behind a white trash exterior calculated to keep people off-guard. And it worked. Her presence in the Estes Kefauver Federal Building drew too much attention, but all of it the harmless kind. Matt admired the shrewd, analytical reasoning behind her brazen disregard for dress code, even as he chided himself for falling for it and admiring the view. She pulled it off far too well.

She tossed a manila envelope on Matt's desk, blasting him with vanilla perfume tinted with pine. "So your swervy-curvies are a riff on paleo-Semitic languages, but nothing we've seen before. The grammatical structures are more modern, and it can't be paleo-anything anyway."

"Why's that?"

She opened the folder with a plastic, bright green fingernail and shuffled through the papers, still shots taken from Sakura's video interspersed between pages of linguistic analysis and translation, until she found the one she wanted and jabbed it with a finger. "That. The forty days of St. Martin."

Matt skimmed the information. The Quadragesima Sancti Martini became "Advent" in much later years. St. Martin of Tours lived from 316 AD to 397 AD, a Roman soldier-turned-priest who spent much of his youth razing pagan temples in the name of Christianity. A late pacifist symbolized by a goose, he'd hidden in a goose pen in a failed attempt to avoid appointment as a bishop, and at one time had clothed a freezing beggar with half his centurion's cloak, which he'd cut off with his gladius. After his death, his cloak became a relic, and the priest who wore it became the cloak bearer, or chaplain.

"So these whackjobs are invoking the patron saint of soldiers to do weird black-eyed stuff with little girls?"

Janet smacked her gum. "Looks that way."

"Do we know to what end?"

She sat down and leaned her chin on her folded hands. "Thought you'd never ask. Based on the incantations in that pentagram and the placement of the candles, seems those guys were binding demons into those little girls, and using the saint's body to do it."

"Why would they bind demons in little girls?"

Janet sat back, frowning. "How'd you know I was going to say that?"

Matt furrowed his brow. "You just—"

But she hadn't explained anything. He'd heard it before she'd said it.

"That's . . . interesting." Janet crossed her legs. "When did precog come back?"

"Uh . . . right now. And just that so far."

Her eyes drilled through him. "Whispers?"

"No." *Not yet.*

She uncrossed her legs and leaned forward, hands splayed flat on his desk. "Don't shit me, Rowley. I need to know who I'm working with."

"No." He held her gaze. "No whispers, not since Italy."

"If they come back—and based on the rest of this stuff I think they're going to come back—you tell me. Maybe we can figure something out."

"Why would they come back? Gerstner's dead."

She stared at him for a long, uncomfortable moment. "You weren't precognitive a minute ago, now you are. How dead do you really think she is? Dead doesn't mean what it used to."

Her eyes flicked to the desk, then the wall, then out the window, anywhere but at him.

He leaned forward, drawing her eyes back to his. "What does that mean?"

She didn't flinch, didn't lean away, just chomped on her gum. "A minute ago I tell you—well, I sort of tell you—that some whacked-up cult is possessing little girls with demons, and you don't so much as blink an eye. Your augmentations came back, just yours out of everyone in the world, and she was the source. What do you think it means?"

Her pupils dilated just a hair, and her facial temperature increased under her makeup. He didn't have anything close to Sakura's talent for identifying lies, but under her tutelage he'd learned how to make use of his augmented eyes for more than just night vision. Maybe not an outright lie, but not the full truth.

"You think she's still alive."

"I think she might still be alive, or whatever passes for alive for a Nephilim. Not the same thing. But if she is, she's got her talons so deep in you . . . ." She leaned back and booped his nose with a green fingernail. When he didn't respond, she stopped chewing and leveled him with her best all-business look. "I don't want to have to put you down."

* * *

Janet ignored the leers and glares on the way to her office, slipped inside, closed the door, and locked it. The server towers crowding her desk put off too much heat, and to compensate, the air conditioner cranked full blast. With the lights off, multicolored chaos from four screen savers blanketed the room in ethereal clown makeup.

She grabbed a roll of paper towels from the cupboard behind her desk, and set them on the floor. She opened a black plastic trash bag and set it on the floor, then kneeled in front of it.

A deep breath steadied her, then another, and another, slowing her pulse to as low as she could get it. Then she extracted a small knife from her pocket and a sprig of rosemary from her cleavage, pulled open the blade, and drew it across her index finger. The sharp blade caused almost no pain. Blood welled. She squeezed until the surface tension broke and the huge drop dribbled down her finger and across her palm.

Rosemary crushed between her palms mingled with the blood, and an acid tang assaulted her nose. The cross tattoo that spanned her back erupted in pinpricks of freezing cold fire.

"It hurts," Dawkins said. Her brother's voice came from everywhere and nowhere, clawing through her thoughts with no right to be there. Her soul shrieked at the invasion, but she snuffed it to silence through force of will. "I want . . . need . . . Oh, God. Why am I here?"

"I know, D. I'm working on it. I found you as fast as I could."

"It's been so long. How long? Can I stay?"

She wiped her nose with the back of her hand. It came away bloody. "Gerstner's fighting her way back. I think she's winning."

His despair wracked through her, an unholy, eternal madness that human thought couldn't contain. Terror snuffed his desperate thirst. "I can't stop her."

She dropped to her knees and leaned forward. Hot blood leaked from her nose and eyes, dribbling down into an expanding pool, black under the flickering server LEDs, yet neatly contained by the plastic bag. "Don't stop her. Ride her coattails, brother. Come back to me on her wings."

"I can't. I just need . . . something . . . something to take the edge off."

She hid her disgust at his hopeless timidity, so in contrast to his living spirit. "You will come back. Here. With me. I'll show you what I've learned."

Glyphs swirled through the pool of blood, curving parodies of ancient Hebrew. The ancient tongue mingled with modern thought which she stabbed like a dagger into his being. He clutched at it, and grasped for more.

She pried his icy claws from her mind and let him go, sobbing through blood as he fell.

Five minutes later she opened a tampon, smeared it through the blood, and bagged it along with the stained tissues she'd used to clean her face. She dropped the bag in the bathroom receptacle on her way out of the office.

* * *

Monica turned off the lights, plunging the dojo into the gloom of orange streetlights through giant, department-store windows.

"G'night!" Chris Malec yelled from the parking lot as she armed the security system.

"Night, Sifu." She threw a distracted wave his way and hefted the shoulder bag containing her "ass-kicking gear," as Matt called it, and all the accoutrements she needed to take care of Adam. The car seat shifted in her other hand so she set it down, the crack in the handle pinching her palm.

She jerked back and sucked at the blood blister, swearing under her breath.

Chris got in his car, a blue 1998 Dodge Avenger that looked showroom new, and it purred like a kitten. Like the few other possessions in his ascetic life, Chris cared for it with the respect one would show any priceless artifact. He beeped once on his way out of the parking lot as Monica closed the door. Thank God one of the Chrises in her life wasn't a complete asshole.

She lifted up on the car seat, and the cracked handle split the rest of the way and came off in her hand. "Screw me sideways." Her sneer faltered with a guilty glance to her dozing son. Adam's head lolled to the side with the blissful oblivion only a toddler can manage, his mouth half-open. She licked her palm—no blood, yet—ran ten feet to the truck, tossed the bag on the floor of the cab, and left the door open.

She turned around and froze.

Two men stood over Adam, identical in blue jeans, black turtle necks, gloves, and ski masks. They held pistols, orange light glistening off the black metal. Her heart thudded in her chest. The pain and soreness from the brutal workout faded as adrenaline flooded her system.

The shorter of the two men spoke, his voice a pleasant baritone with a generic Hollywood accent. "Ma'am, get your purse from the truck and set it on the ground, and nothing will happen to your boy."

Adam opened his sleep-filled eyes, groggy and disoriented, and yawned.

She reached back, grabbed the bag, and pulled it to her stomach. Slipping a hand inside, she grabbed the SP101 .357 revolver her daddy had given her when she'd turned twenty-five. The grip felt cool and comforting against her sweaty palm. An image flashed through her mind, the ICAP commando she'd blown away in their bedroom not two years prior, the look of shock and horror in his eyes as the shotgun removed a solid chunk of his chest right through his bullet-proof vest.

"Set it down and step away. No reason to get hurt." His voice snapped her back to the present. Choking down the hopeless sadness, she took a deep breath and assessed the threat as best she could. The men stood with weapons at their sides, neither pointing at her nor at Adam.

She dropped the bag and choked up the weapon, pulling the trigger twice as Matt had taught her. Nothing happened but a dull click.

She looked down, eyes wide. Her lanyard dangled from the gun, pinned under the hammer. The taller man raised his weapon, and Monica froze. She had nowhere to run, nothing to hide behind, and they had her child.

"Oh, you bitch."

His finger tightened on the trigger, and the shorter man knocked his hand to the side. He shouldered his partner out of the way, where he stumbled to his hands and knees and raised the gun again. Adam's finger brushed his pant leg, and he glanced down. His mouth opened in a soft "O."

"Come on, man," the short one said from the ground, his voice high pitched and panicked. "I didn't sign up for this."

The tall man laughed, a heartless, soulless noise more jackal than human. Then his weapon clattered to the pavement and his head lolled to the side.

Adam chortled and squealed and clapped his hands.

As the fallen man stood Monica rushed him, clearing the distance in three steps. He looked up too late, and her open-palm strike caught him on the bridge of the nose with a wet crunch. He stumbled back and she spun. The side of her foot contacted his fingers around the grip of his weapon, and it went flying.

She delivered two punishing blows to the tall man's solar plexus, kicked him in the side of the head, and stomped on his hand as he caught himself on the ground. She brought her knee up into his face with a wet thud, and stopped. Peace blossomed in her, a pure white gentleness that overwhelmed and infused her, an unknowable compassion.

Adam let go of her ankle, and she shook off the feeling, tried to think straight.

Her assailants stumbled away, and she let them go. They vanished down the alley past the grocery store.

Tears streaming down her face, she lifted her son from his seat.

"Ma. Da." He grabbed her hair and giggled, tugging at the curls with wild abandon, his daddy's brown eyes clear and free of worry.

"What was that, little man?"

"Da. Ma."

"Yeah." She kissed him, squeezed him, and frowned. *Who are you, little man?* She brought him to the truck, broken car seat in her other hand, and snatched up the gun, but it felt wrong in her hands. She put it on the dash, got him situated, and only then called the police.

A county deputy told her to go somewhere public, which at this time of night meant Tony's BBQ Bar and Grill, a honkytonk not too far from their house. She stayed in the truck, not trusting herself in a bar, even though Tony loved her too much to serve her. Deputy

Broadbent arrived eight minutes later, took her statement as Adam slept—she didn't have much to go on, but mentioned the gray Chevy Cobalt just in case they were related—then he told her to go home.

She moved Adam's crib to the bedroom and lay down.

Her alarm went off nine hours later and she opened her eyes, having slept no more than five continuous minutes. In the other room Ted whined and scratched at the door, so she forced herself to her feet and stumbled out into reality.

Chapter 5

Matt stepped into the confessional, and Father Rees hurried out, stumbling down the low step and slamming into the pews. He stalked across the church toward the rectory, and Matt followed.

The priest whirled and pointed a finger at him in a gesture that Matt took for menacing. "You get out of my church before I call the cops."

Matt held up his hands. "I'm not here to hurt you, Jason."

St. Martin's church on a Tuesday afternoon smelled warm like cheap cinnamon potpourri, but overlaid with the metallic tang of burned-out vacuum cleaner motor. The tan walls, tan carpet, and U-shaped pews inspired not the slightest reverence, and the cherry-stained mahogany cross over the altar needed a once-over with a Swiffer wand.

"I haven't spoken to her. Not once." Jason wasn't quite as tan as the last time they'd seen each other. His black hair still sported the boot camp buzz cut, and dark bags ringed his intense gray eyes, just a bit bloodshot to go with his just-too-red nose. He backed up as Matt approached, shuddering in panicked fear.

Matt stopped and folded his hands in front of him. "Father, calm down. If I wanted to hurt you, you'd be in pain already. Can we go somewhere and talk?"

Rees's eyes flicked toward the exit next to the altar. "About what?"

"St. Martin."

"What do you mean?"

"You're the priest at St. Martin's parish. I'm sure you've heard of the guy. I've got questions you seem ideally equipped to answer."

Rees leveled him with an exasperated stare, reminiscent of their time as high school friends. "Really, dude?"

"I'm here for some help. Isn't that what you do?" Matt tried to strangle his temper and only half succeeded. "You're a priest, dammit."

Rees's neck stiffened and he started to lecture. "Last time you were here you assaulted—"

"—and you tried to get me killed—"

"—trying to protect Monica—"

"—almost killed her—"

"—I thought was best—"

"You FUCKED my WIFE!" Matt's voice reverberated in the empty church. He kept his clenched fists at his side so he wouldn't use them, and almost failed.

Jason swallowed, then collapsed into a pew. "I did. A long time ago. She came to me in a moment of weakness, and I was drunk and heartsick, and I've paid for it every day of my life."

Matt let his knees buckle, sitting in the pew a few feet away. He looked at the floor, at his hands, his feet, the cross behind the altar. "That's not even why I'm here. I came to ask you about the saint."

The main door creaked open, and an old woman shuffled inside. She didn't appear to notice them as she lit a candle and knelt to pray.

"What do you want to know about St. Martin?"

"I researched him on Wikipedia and whatever, the connection to advent and chaplains and chapels. Roman soldier, monastic life, goose pen and so forth. Is there anything you can tell me that's not easy to find? Anything about little girls or demons?"

Jason shook his head. "No. Nothing like that. There's nothing in the records about him exorcising little girls."

Matt sat back.

"Why?" Jason asked. "Why come here to ask me something you could learn on the phone? Why this sudden obsession with St. Martin?"

A long, slow exhale bought him a moment. "Look, I don't know. I just got back from some weird shi—stuff, and lately I haven't been much one for coincidences."

"What kind of weird stuff?"

Matt pulled out his phone and loaded the video of the girl on the ship. "This is national security stuff. It goes nowhere, understand?"

Jason nodded.

"Like, trials and prison and rendition to black sites?"

He nodded again.

"For both of us?"

Jason rolled his eyes. "You're going to show me, so show me."

They watched it together, and when the screen went black Jason's eyes filled with tears. Matt described his time on the drillship, the missing girls, the skin cloak, his unnatural attackers. Even now, Janet LaLonde poured over the dossiers of the men involved, looking for a connection she had yet to find.

Jason turned his wet eyes to Matt. "I need to come with you."

"Pardon?"

"With you. I've been waiting for years for something more, something greater than . . ." He gestured around him. ". . . this. And that's it. I have to help you help those girls. I have to."

Matt looked up at the cross with an ironic smirk. "Will your boss allow that?"

"I've never been more sure of anything in my entire life." If Jason had caught the irony, he wasn't symptomatic.

* * *

Matt pulled into the dying strip mall, his government-owned, rusted-out '93 coupe classing up the place by at least fifteen years. Despite the time of year, the thermometers in Sparta, Georgia, flirted with a hundred degrees, and the substandard air conditioner kept the car almost but not quite pleasant. His black T-shirt clung to his enormous frame, dripping wet the moment he stepped out of the car, though the dark gray skies brought no rain.

The tiny town boasted some fantastic architecture, a majestic brick courthouse, a quaint little main street, one beautiful Victorian home, and a collection of mid-century ranches in various states of decay. Once past the half-dozen blocks that consisted of "downtown," rural life took over full force, and even the populated blocks boasted more trees than some parks. A mile out it could have been White Spruce, but hotter. And muggier.

A lady pushing a stroller looked up as the car door slammed, and waved. He returned her gesture, smiled, hopped up onto the sidewalk, and pulled open the glass-front door of J & M Recruiting. Three of the oil workers had come through this service, whose proprietor, Caren Widner, could suffocate under her rap sheet. From extortion to wire fraud to falsifying records to felony possession of a firearm to assault with a deadly weapon, the mother of five had spent as much time on trial as she had being pregnant.

The pixie-cut bottle blonde behind the desk favored him with a brilliant smile that didn't touch her green eyes. "Well, ain't you a big one?"

"Ma'am." He tipped a nonexistent hat.

"What can I help you with, Mr . . . ?"

"Dexter. Marty Dexter." He shook her proffered hand and sat down. "I was wondering if you could help me find these three gentlemen."

He put photos of the oil workers on the desk and slid them across to her.

Her smile vanished. She didn't even look at the pictures. "Get out."

"Ma'am, I—"

"GET OUT!" Her hand dropped under the desk.

Matt sat back and let a slow, lazy smile spread across his face. "A thousand dollars, you help me find them."

"I don't talk to bacon, pig, I fry it."

"I'm not a policeman." True, as far as it went. "My client hired me to track them down—"

"I don't help bounty hunters, either, or private detectives. Get the hell out of my office."

He snorted. "Or you'll shoot an unarmed man? You think life in prison will improve things around here?"

Once it left his mouth, Matt realized it would improve things. For everyone but Widner, including and perhaps especially her children. So he kept talking.

"I just need to know who hired them."

She let out a giant, exasperated, exaggerated sigh, and put her hands on the desk. "Mr. Dexter, y'all ain't from around here, so let me try this again. I. Am. Not. Going. To. Help. You. And I don't go back on my word, so you're wasting your time."

Matt chuckled. "With a rap sheet like yours, I don't think I'd be pleading integrity. Two thousand."

She scowled. "You calling me a liar?"

He looked up at the water damage on the ceiling tiles. "Well, yeah. A liar and a cheat and a fraud and a hustler, a two-bit thug too dumb to quit and not smart enough keep herself out of jail. Twenty-five hundred, final offer."

"What part of 'Get the fuck out of my office before I blow your goddamned head off' wasn't clear? I ain't afraid of jail."

Matt pulled a piece of paper from his pocket, unfolded it, and pushed it across the desk with a finger. "This part."

She flushed bright red as she scanned the federal warrant, then murdered him with her eyes. "You said you ain't no cop."

"I said I'm not a policeman, and that's true." He shrugged. "But I am a federal agent. So I need the information on those gentlemen, and I need it right now, or I'm going to take a peek under that table and see what kind of weapons charges we're talking here."

Shoulders hunched, she lowered her eyes and bowed her head. "Give me a second."

Widner stepped through the door behind her. Matt gave her three seconds, then followed—he couldn't allow her the chance to destroy whatever information she had.

The gun loomed large in his vision, the shot deafened him. The impact sent him stumbling backward as he opened the door, a raw burst of pain and shock that went right through his thickened, solid-fused ribs—so when he opened the door, he rolled right and chopped downward on Widner's wrist, pulling the blow short of snapping bone. The .45 caliber pistol fell to the floor, and she clutched her wrists to her chest and stumbled out of the back room into the office.

Matt grabbed at her shirt, letting his fingers brush her collar before she leapt over the desk and bolted for the door. He ran, human speed, and slammed his knee into the desk, knocking it askew. She reached her beat-up Camaro by the time he got to the front door, and he almost reached her trunk before she peeled away, tires shrieking as the car drifted just out of reach. He ran a dozen futile steps, then stopped and put his hands on his knees.

The moment her car disappeared from view he whirled and walked toward his car, fishing his ear bud from his pocket as he did so. He put it in.

"That went better than expected."

"Okay," Sakura said in his ear. "Headed north on . . . just turned on Route 16. Signal is strong."

"Keep on her, and call in the techs. She's got a dozen filing cabinets in that back room, and by the looks of things her file clerk is a methed-up ferret."

He got in the car, started it, and pulled out onto Jones Street in no particular hurry. It didn't matter how fast Widner drove, she couldn't outrun the magnetic tracker Sakura had slipped into her wheel well, and he had a helicopter on standby just in case.

* * *

The skies darkened as they approached Atlanta. The radio crackled bursts of static amidst country music and commercials, the first indication of unseen lightning. Their black government SUV came complete with a dark-suited government chauffer, so that they could gather operational data en route.

Matt sat in the very back, leaning over the seat to look at the computer on Sakura's lap. Jason Rees sat on her left, his black suit with a white priests' collar more in line with government dress code than Matt and Sakura's jeans and T-shirts.

Caren Widner had sped all the way to Atlanta, and the bug Sakura had placed under her dashboard picked up her side of a conversation.

* * *

"Fuck, Jimmy, I thought you'd never pick up. Some 'roided-out asshole came poking around, looking for Mark, Jeff, and Shawn. Yeah. Yup. No, he didn't get shit. Tell the *cappellani* I'm on my way, yeah. Well if he shows then we kill the motherfucker. Three more? Good. Maybe we can get another through the breach, add a panel to the new cloak. 'Kay. See you then."

* * *

"Do I even want to know?" Jason asked.

Matt exchanged looks with Sakura. She'd made it clear that she didn't welcome his presence and didn't appreciate Matt's gut feeling overriding her logical arguments.

"*Cappellani,*" Sakura said. "What does this mean?"

Matt shrugged, so Jason answered.

"Cloak bearers. It's Latin, the root of 'chapel' and 'chaplain.'" He turned to Matt and banged his fist on his knee. "Looks like your St. Martin hunch might not have been far off."

Sakura switched tabs to a real-time video, visible spectrum overlaid with infrared, depicting a downtown scene in fading twilight under black, raining skies.

Matt squinted at the screen, though it didn't make the drone's feed any clearer. "Are they touring the Coke Museum?"

"Close," a disembodied female voice said in his ear. "Widner parked by Centennial Olympic Park, and headed on foot to Georgia State University. Go Panthers. Over."

"Got it." Matt's two visits to Atlanta, both as a tourist, left far too much to be desired in the geography department. "Move tactical support into position, but keep them on standby. We have no idea how many perps we've got, or how well armed they are."

"Roger."

"Do we have eyes on?" Sakura asked.

"Yes, ma'am. She's entered an academic building and joined a good dozen people on the third floor. Can't tell what they're doing, but it's one big heat blob, so they're well-condensed. There's some janitorial staff on the first floor, a campus security kiosk out front. Over."

"Weapons?"

"Not that we've seen, ma'am. Campus security isn't exactly the airport, though. This is downtown Atlanta. I wouldn't bet on anyone being unarmed. Over."

"Thank you."

"So what's the plan?" Jason asked.

Matt looked at Sakura, then at the driver through the rear-view mirror. "Sakura and I go in stealthy, with snipers on rooftops and a couple squads behind us. You stay in the car and try not to get killed."

"Then why am I—"

Sakura put her finger square between his eyes and pressed. "You're here because Matt thought you might have something to add, which so far is a word we could look up online. You have no combat training, no tactics, no skills. So you stay in the car, in radio contact, and if you think like some action movie hero to sneak out and do something heroic, Mr. Paulson will knock you unconscious and put you in the trunk."

The chauffer gave a curt nod without shifting his eyes from the road. Sakura removed her finger.

"Sounds right," Matt said. "We'll give you a tactical helmet so you don't feel left—so you can talk to Sakura and I if something important comes up."

He let Jason's "Dude, seriously?" look roll off of him.

* * *

Matt put on his helmet and took in the heads-up display as

water sheeted off the hydrophobic visor. He disabled the Friend-or-Foe and Biometrics data; Atlanta SWAT weren't implanted, and the campus teemed with civilians, at least indoors. He pulled up the drone feed from an hour past, shaky and blurred in the driving winds and pouring rain.

A dozen people milled around the roof in disorganized clumps, two painting a giant pentagram onto the gravel, bright green in the night vision. Huge candles a foot in diameter, unlit, squatted at each corner. A wooden chest the size of a couch sat off to the side between air-conditioning units and a small water reservoir. The drone lurched, buffeted by the rising winds, and veered off toward safety.

He kept his voice neutral, letting the microphone do the work.

"Sakura and I access the roof up the south fire escape, no breach, nice and quiet. Daniels brings Alpha squad in behind us, Leftkowitz—"

"Lefty, sir."

"—Lefty brings Bravo in through the front door and sweeps upward to our position. Atlanta PD's got perimeter, plainclothes and uniforms, plus tactical support on the rooftops. Intel reports that all hostiles are on the roof, no weapons in evidence. All goes well, we hit them fast and take them in before anyone has a chance to resist. Any questions?"

A woman in Bravo Squad raised her left hand. Matt appreciated how she kept her right hand ready, near but not on the REC-7 assault rifle that hung from her shoulder.

"Go ahead," Matt said.

"Branzen, sir. This seems like a shitload of hardware for a dozen unarmed civilians."

"Acknowledged," Matt said as Sakura's sigh carried through the ear bud. "Last time I toyed with these guys they killed two CIA agents, just tore them apart with their bare hands. Best case scenario, none of you are necessary, and I get reprimanded for imprudent use of government resources. Worst case, we didn't bring enough ordnance, and you coordinate the retreat. Other questions?"

The wind raged.

* * *

Knuckles white, Matt gripped the fire escape railing and tried not to pitch to the ground three stories below. The wind lifted him again, then slammed him down, the clatter almost inaudible over the oceanic roar. He gritted his teeth and shouldered the AA-12 assault shotgun, useless under these conditions except at point-blank range.

He steadied himself, then took one last step, just enough to put his eyes over the roof's edge.

Candles flickered at each corner of the pentagram, their flames tall and true in complete defiance of the swirling rain, illuminating the rooftop in a lackluster, yellow-orange glow. Three young girls knelt in the center, their white dresses soaked gray, clinging to their shivering, huddled bodies. Nylon rope bound their hands and feet. Fifteen people stood at regular intervals around them, lips moving in unison to a chant Matt couldn't hear. Their drenched street clothes, casual and American, stood in stark contrast to their actions.

"What in God's name is that?" Jason asked in his ear.

A man raised his hands. Caren Widner followed suit, along with the woman next to her. The move cascaded around the circle, an ominous, slow-motion wave. As it reached crescendo, the candle flames stretched upward and bent, intertwining over the girls' heads, whirling higher, a twisted spear thrusting into the clouds above.

"Oh, shit," Matt said. He hated the word "magic," and hated even more any instance where it fit the bill.

The clouds spun faster and stretched down from the heavens as the fire collapsed inward on the girls. They shrieked, their voices one with the wind, a primal howl drowned and drowning in piteous agony.

Matt bolted forward as the girls caught fire. The wind threw him sideways, feet skittering through the gravel in a desperate bid for purchase. A man screamed in his ear bud, a terrified wail cut short. Matt's shotgun strap slipped from his shoulder, the weapon carried away by the unrelenting force.

He dropped to his hands and knees and scrambled as much sideways as forward. Rocks pinged off his helmet, thrown by the swirling vortex. His foot caught on a pipe protruding from the roof, and he launched himself into stillness.

Rain fell, flames crackled, yet inside the wall of swirling wind the Latin chanting overpowered a gentle breeze. He got his bearings and turned.

A tornado raged across the rooftop, scattering gravel and SWAT with indiscriminate ferocity. Daniels flew from the building, thrown like a ragdoll to tumble out of sight. Sakura huddled, arms wrapped around the fire escape railing, and her grunts of exertion carried though the headset amidst the panicked screams of Alpha squad.

The chanting stopped. He turned.

The girls hovered ten feet from the ground, unburnt limbs slack, hair limned with fire and lighting, eyes jet black, the ropes that bound their limbs reduced to smoking cinders in the gravel beneath them. The cultists faced the girls, blood streaming from wide eyes, noses, and from between their lips. Stringy runnels of mucus-thick, red fluid lifted from them to snake up under the dresses, and spread like red cancer through the white cloth. Matt stepped forward. The girls turned as one.

And screamed. Their mouths opened wide, wider than possible. Thick red tongues writhed between countless rows of needle-like teeth. The sound crackled through his mind, strangled and suffocated his thoughts. Darkness found him, smothered life and light and joy and love.

Jason babbled in his ear, a golden thread of sanity weaving through shrieking madness. Matt's numb lips murmured the Latin words, his dead tongue spoke them, again and again, stronger with each repetition. The world flashed white and faded into reality.

He screamed, a primal human sound in defiance of the noise that sought to pulp his mind.

The girls—banshees—tore at him, black claws and needle

teeth shredding his flesh right through his body armor. He grabbed one by the hair and wrested her mouth from his left shoulder. She came away with a wet tearing sound, chewing raw red meat through her demonic grin, lacerating her tongue with every shift of her jaw.

He slammed her head down onto the girl at his thigh, tried to ignore the ropy pain slithering through his quadriceps. He clutched at her to pull her away with his left arm, but the muscles wouldn't respond. Hot red blood gushed from his wounds, and his heart thudded in his ear at a steady sixty beats per second.

He whipped the first girl around by her hair, slamming her once, twice, three times into the gravel before spinning, using his momentum to throw her into the maelstrom. She disappeared in the debris-filled wind. He punched the banshee chewing on his thigh, cracking bone. He punched again and her skull caved, and still she chewed, a savage rending of skin and muscle. The third time, his fist exploded through her skull. He closed his fingers around a ropy, sinuous something and yanked.

Her tongue tore out as her body fell away, and the sinuous mass in his thigh slithered deeper toward bone. The whispers chattered their nameless hate, old, unwelcome companions giving him a glimpse of a future drenched in sorrow and despair.

He dove as teeth closed where his neck had been, and kicked. The third banshee spun out of reach, slashing his boot with her black claws. He grunted. The thick leather fell away in tatters, several toes with it.

He stumbled back as the worming pain in his leg turned to fire. His opponent leapt forward and a black blur intercepted it, a whirling mass of body armor and steel. Sakura diced the creature to pieces faster than Matt could see, her combat knives carving air and flesh with equal ease. She whirled to find the next one, and at her feet the pieces of her first opponent coalesced.

Jason yelled in his ear. "Matt, he's in the box! Open the chest!"

He limped toward the large box as weapons chatter erupted around him. Bravo Squad had reached the roof access door and spread out, indiscriminate in their fire between cultists and banshees. Cultists twitched and fell, bodies shattered by the onslaught.

Matt stumbled forward, and the third banshee shrieked, a hideous wail of despondent nihilism. Bravo Squad turned their weapons on each other and crumbled to the rooftop in sprays of bright red. Matt repeated the chant that Jason screamed in his ear, that golden thread insulating him from the worst of the inhuman scream.

Sakura continued her slaughter, hacking away at her dismembered opponent, but she'd started to slow, and it hadn't. Larger pieces formed, misshapen, almost-human chunks of pale child's flesh twitching and straining to take her life.

The last banshee fell from the sky in front of Matt, arms outstretched, hovering a foot from the ground. Its shriek wouldn't end, couldn't end, a never-ending canticle to the death of the soul, pulsing in time with every pump of his heart, every dribble of blood that fell from his wounds. The mass in his leg pulsed along with it. Matt lurched forward as Jason's golden thread frayed, his voice a panicked rasp in Matt's ear.

Matt stumbled toward the box, and the creature leapt onto him. Claws pierced his back, razor-hot knives that stabbed through his armor into his abdomen. Still he stumbled, hot red blood streaming down his legs, his thigh a squirming agony beneath the skin. Two steps, three, more, until he dropped to his knees in front of the large wooden box. With a last breath of strength he pushed on the lid, and it fell open.

A puff of wind hit him, and the banshee tore off his back with a sudden gasp. In the deafening silence, he looked down.

A mummy cowered within, shriveled and pathetic, wrapped in chains stitched with eldritch runes. It shivered, with only shreds of faded crimson wool embroidered with goose feathers to cover its nakedness. The banshee circled them, staring daggers at Matt and the mummy but without approaching. She moaned as the thing in the box spoke without a tongue.

Requiem da, Jesu Domine.

"What?" Blood dribbled from Matt's mouth. His shoulder itched, his back itched, but not enough. He leaned against the box as the world hazed out and back in.

"He's asking the Lord Jesus for rest," Jason said.

Vestementi. Pallium. Amiculum.

"Clothe him. A cloak! Give him your jacket!"

Matt groaned as he sloughed out of his shredded jacket, the slick nylon windbreaker drenched in blood. Two banshees screamed, but their piteous wails held none of their previous power. Sakura stumbled back, exhausted, pulling her knives out of the third creature, now whole. It rose from the ground to join its sisters in circling the box like starving, terrified predators wary of their prey.

Matt tried to lift the jacket and couldn't. His strength had abandoned him.

The banshees circled closer.

Sakura appeared beside him, drenched in rain and sweat, her helmet missing, a bloody gash across her cheek. She took the bloody, tattered jacket from him and laid it over the mummy.

The keening wail vanished with the wind, and the skeletal body crumbled, chains and all.

Matt closed his eyes.

Chapter 6

Monica gave the eggs one last whip and upended the bowl into the pan. She hollered into the living room so Matt could hear her over the morning news. "You want bacon or sausage, baby?"

Some talking head droned on about the upcoming election, upset at everyone for not violating the laws of nature and economics.

"Baby?" She stepped back and cast a glance over her shoulder.

Matt lay on the loveseat, legs draped over the side. Ted lay on his chest, head resting on Matt's thigh, both of them fast asleep. Monica frowned. It wasn't like him to sleep in, and since augmentation he never took naps anymore.

"Baby!"

Matt's eyes popped open and he recoiled from Ted's rear end. The dog slid off Matt, wedging between her husband's body and the back of the loveseat.

"Hey, baby. Yeah, just resting my eyes."

"Really?" She stepped back to the stove and stirred the eggs, just starting to cook under medium-low heat.

"Yeah," he said from the other room. "Oof. Just a little sore. I'll be good in a minute."

"Don't pull that macho crap on me. You don't get hurt, not for long, and you're never, ever sore, so if something's wrong you need to go to the doctor."

His arms folded around her, enveloping her in his warmth and scent, gun oil and cheap coconut shampoo and a hint of yesterday's Old Spice. "I'll be all right."

She leaned her head back against his chest. "You'd better be. You die on me, Momma will kill you."

They ate breakfast and chatted about house repairs and Christmas plans. Matt ate six eggs and four buttered biscuits, so his appetite hadn't changed, and despite his complaints he moved with the same fluid grace she'd come to expect.

She opened her mouth and he cut her off.

"Yeah, no problem."

She froze and waited.

He looked up from his plate. "What?"

"I didn't ask yet."

He looked from her to the plate and back to her. "Huh. Yeah, that's been happening more often lately."

She leaned in to look in his eyes. "Is that okay? Is it safe?"

"Yeah, of course." He answered too fast. "Just another Aug resurging, like the others. Janet knows. I'm in good hands."

"What about 'No safe levels?' Gerstner?"

He frowned. "I'm in this either way, but right now it looks like Gerstner's influence is totally gone. I shouldn't—You don't have anything to worry about."

She smiled and put her hand over his. "You know I'm going to."

He squeezed. "I know, babe. But you shouldn't have to."

She kissed his nose. "It's my job."

* * *

Matt flipped stations on his way to the store, the scan transitioning every few seconds between country music, rock and roll, and drumbeat hysteria about the looming blizzard. A familiar voice took him back to a cramped shop in St. Augustine, before they knew the truth about Jade, ICAP, and fallen angels. The discordant blend of Florida-Georgia hick and high-falutin' diction belonged to the proprietor of the tiny store Rastogi had taken them to, tall and gaunt with rotting teeth and something dark slithering behind his eyes, hostile to Augs and stingy with information. He'd found an audience on NPR.

"—aren't the cuddly cherubs of Valentine's Day cards. When God destroyed Sodom and Gomorrah, he sent his angels to do so. When the plague took the firstborn of Egypt, he sent his angel to do the reaping. They're not living creatures the way we think of them; they're embodied shards of divine will."

"And you think they're among us?" The host kept his voice too soft in the habit of public radio personalities.

"How could I doubt? God saw the hubris of augmentation and smote the wicked to the ground. Arakiel's cult slaughtered thousands before he disappeared. And let's not forget Ramiel in many places at once, until that man revealed his true form as an Ifrit, a monstrous creature of fire and sand. These names are not coincidence, they are known to us. They are the egregoroi, the Watchers, who came down from heaven to lie with human women and for their crimes were cast into the pit of Tartarus."

Matt pulled the truck into the crowded parking lot and killed the engine but not the radio. The man spoke at length, prodded by the host, about angels and devils and the occult, a mish-mash of religions and legends informing his opinions. He got the nature of Gerstner Augmentation dead wrong, but his hypotheses about Arakiel's "vanishing" hit a little too close to home. As far as Matt knew, that egregoroi—or the glass pillar he'd become—collected dust in a cold iron cage at a black site in Mumbai.

"Well," the host closed, "you're listening to Religion Today on National Public Radio. We've been talking angels with Nigel Rush of St. Augustine, Florida, Doctor of Ancient Mythology, Divinity, and Archaeology. Thank you, Doctor Rush."

"Pleasure being here. Be safe."

Matt grunted. He wouldn't have pegged the gawky, creepy man a "Nigel."

Bumper music trickled out of the speakers, so he killed the power and went into the store, grabbing a cart from the rack on his way in.

He sighed at the lines. Nothing provoked panicked spending on things you should already own like an impending snowstorm. People packed aisles half-emptied of staples like bread, batteries, and bottled water, their carts overflowing with more of the same. The hurried, harried crowd made the case for shopping cart traffic laws and still managed to bog everything to a standstill. Matt grabbed a gallon of milk, two packs of diapers, and a forty-pound bag of dog food, then headed for the checkout.

Twenty minutes later and fifty bucks poorer, he pushed the cart out the door. And stopped.

Two men in Titans jackets leaned against the truck, one brown-haired with a smarmy, used-car-salesman's smile, the other a frowning brute, maybe six-three, two hundred fifty pounds, with a purple-and-yellow bruise stretching from temple to ear. Matt pushed the cart to the truck and loaded the groceries in the back.

"Can I help you gentlemen?"

They circled the truck so he couldn't see their hands, or whether they had anything under their coats. Matt leaned against the tailgate and tried to look as nonchalant as possible.

The brute spoke. "We know who you are, Rowley."

"Well that's obvious."

Smarmy lost his smile. "We know what you are." He rounded the truck, hand in his jacket.

Matt raised an eyebrow.

Brute stepped up to sneer down at him, a gesture that would have intimidated Matt a few short years before. The large man struck not the slightest twinge of fear in him.

Matt ignored him in favor of staring down Smarmy. "Okay, so here's how this works. By that bruise I figure you're the assholes who threatened my wife and kid, so that makes me inclined to hurt you. She didn't shoot you, but she's a lot nicer than me and doesn't kill people for a living. I'm not going to throw the first punch, but at the first hint of violence I'm going to cripple you both. And that hand in your jacket's looking mighty violent to me."

Smarmy pulled his hand from his jacket and rested it on his hip.

Matt locked eyes with Brute. "You said you know what I am. Good. I've killed men twice your size with my bare hands and didn't even break a sweat. You ever see what the Hulk did to Loki?"

Brute didn't blink, but he took two steps back.

"That's better." He looked from one man to the other, then stepped forward to stare up into Brute's eyes. "Now what do you want?"

Brute took another step back, so Matt grabbed his jacket and yanked him closer, raising his arm to lift the man to his tiptoes in a lightning-fast show of casual strength.

"You're not going anywhere." His eyes flicked to Smarmy. "You, either. Y'all came here for a reason, so let's hear it."

Brute's smile revealed a chipped front tooth and clean, minty breath. "You think you're hot shit, but you're not. I'm—"

"You all right, Rowley?" Chris Wilcox leaned one arm out of his car window, his massive frame wrapped in a black down coat fit for Siberia.

"Sure. Would you mind calling the sheriff? I'm looking to have these men taken into custody for menacing, attempted kidnapping, and I'm going to guess illegal possession of a loaded handgun without a valid Tennessee carry permit. Meantime, Chris, you might want to clear the area."

Chris's eyes widened. He fumbled with his phone and the clutch at the same time. The car lurched, then rolled out of sight as Matt turned his attention back on his prey.

"Where were we? Oh, right. You were telling me why you're here." He let go of Brute and dusted his hands off.

"You won't get away with this," Smarmy said.

A tiny laugh escaped Matt's lips. "I think of the three of us, only one is on a first name basis with the police force in White Spruce. Y'all come into my town, threaten my wife and child, and—"

"Your child isn't the only demon-spawn." Brute's grin had returned.

Matt squared off against him, putting his back to Smarmy. He felt the impact of the bullet through his skull a half-second before the pistol had cleared the holster. His foot darted backward, crushing Smarmy's fingers against the pistol at his hip.

Brute grabbed his neck.

He spun, pivoting Brute on his hip, and brought him down as hard as he could. The large man's head shattered on the asphalt, splattering blood and brains across Matt's boots. He rolled left, letting Smarmy get off one off-hand shot for the cops' benefit before crushing his wrist against the side of the truck.

Smarmy screamed as the gun fell from limp fingers.

Matt kicked the weapon away, smashed his palm into Smarmy's, denting the truck on the other side, then snap-kicked both knees hard enough to tear cartilage with audible "pops". Smarmy fell on his back, and Matt stomped his right shin, obliterating the bone.

He knelt next to the whimpering blob of meat and spoke, his

voice soft like an NPR host. "I warned you."

A man wailed, a frightened cry of pure sorrow.

Matt whirled.

"Someone call an ambulance!"

"Oh, my God, she's been shot!"

"Call 9-1-1!"

Matt bolted toward the voices.

Bob Morgan's daughter lay on the sidewalk in a ring of people, blood pooling beneath her. The fifteen-year-old gritted her teeth, and tears poured from her eyes. Matt shouldered his way through, dropped to his knees, and jerked up her shirt to expose the wound.

A tiny hole below and to the right of her belly button gushed blood.

Matt wiped his gore-spattered hands on his pants and pulled out his multitool. "Gauze. Now!"

Someone ran for the store, but his life condensed to the immediate. More blood gushed. He couldn't wait.

He tore a strip from his shirt one-handed and passed it to somebody. "Wad that up." The knife sliced across the bullet hole. She writhed, and he begged her to be still. He hacked through her abdominal wall, fascia, and muscle to expose the viscera below, sawing more than he wanted to with the not-quite-razor-sharp blade. She kicked, and he straddled her legs to hold her down. Pushing her intestines out of the way he exposed her left iliac artery, clipped by the bullet on its way through. Hot blood washed over his fingers, but he grabbed the wad of cloth from his other hand and squeezed it around the throbbing, sticky, pencil-thin band.

Shit wafted up to his nose.

He looked up, right into her father's worried eyes. "Bob, I've stopped the bleeding. She's going to be okay, but we need that ambulance, now."

It took eight agonizing minutes—whispering encouragement and squeezing to ligate the artery and trying not to scream at his own stupidity for letting Smarmy fire his weapon—for the paramedics to arrive.

Sarah Mason put her petite, latex-gloved hands over his, then slid around it to grip the shirt. "I got her."

Matt shook his head.

"Matt, I got her!"

"You don't. I've got her artery ligated, but when I let go, she's going to bleed out. You're not strong enough. Nobody's strong enough. You need staples, clamps, something. Now."

They locked eyes, then Sarah nodded. "Okay, Matt. I'll get clamps."

"And her intestine's perforated!"

Sarah gave him a bloody thumbs-up on her way back to the ambulance.

Some time later, they hefted Morgan onto a gurney and put her into the first ambulance. The police stood around the second, eight uniformed officers keeping people away from the scene, waiting for the detectives and lab techs en route. Matt watched the first ambulance pull out, sirens blaring. He wiped his hand on his shredded shirt, smearing blood across his abdomen, and approached the police.

Deputy Broadbent hitched up his belt and reached out a hand. The black-haired, skinny twentysomething shied back when Matt held up his own, still wet with the Morgan girl's blood.

"Tell me what happened here, Rowley."

Matt looked down at the human filth who'd threatened his wife. Brute couldn't get any deader, and paramedics swarmed Smarmy's unconscious, sedated body, his legs twisted at odd angles on the dark gray pavement.

"These men attacked me. I defended myself."

Broadbent squirmed in place. "Cory says you had that guy by his jacket before he called."

Matt nodded. "I did. The other pulled a gun when the big guy tried to strangle me. I reacted."

The interrogation lasted ten minutes in the parking lot, the car ride to the police station, and then another three hours. He recounted every detail, exactly, a dozen times, and had to explain eidetic memory to three separate detectives, even demonstrating it with parlor tricks before they let it go.

He only left out letting Smarmy—Brendan Coleman based on his ID and fingerprints—fire a shot to justify his deadly response. They released him without charges at two p.m. and gave him a ride back to the parking lot. He called Sakura on the way to the hospital.

"Yes?"

"Hey. Where are you?"

"Hotel. This after-report on Atlanta is troublesome. I don't know who will believe it."

"Don't spin it," Matt said. "Just report what happened and let the powers that be worry about what's true. That girl those guys found, the one from the boat, she wake up yet?"

"Yes. She's resting still, but vitals are back to normal, no sign of lasting damage. Her parents are there. Quarantine is lifted."

"Good. How's Kazuko?"

"Resting. Why?"

He filled her in, emphasizing what Brute—Joe Klippelt—had said about "demon-spawn." "The only other person I know that fits that bill is Kazuko."

"Probably others. Many Augs have children, but Adam is the only one post-augmentation. ICAP kept excellent records."

"Do we trust these guys to know the difference?" Humans for Humanity ran the gamut from neo-Nazi to fundamentalist Christian to hard-left anti-GMO conspiracy theorists. Only a hatred for Augs united them.

"No," Sakura said. "But I've seen many strangers around the ward and hotel today. I think I'll go to the hospital, sleep on a cot tonight."

"Want backup?"

"I wouldn't turn it down."

"All right. Let me tie things down here, get Monica some protection, and I'll be up."

He booked a flight two hours later, just in time to miss the storm.

* * *

Sakura walked through the hotel lobby, scanning the unfamiliar faces for anyone paying too much attention. Two men and one woman, all Caucasian, sat at a corner booth and paid too little, looking at anything and everything other than her. They'd stopped talking when the elevator had opened, though, and resumed their murmurs with too much haste.

Rowley couldn't get here fast enough. She stopped ten feet from their booth and looked at her phone, and not one of them looked up at her, even after she coughed.

The front door slid open in a blast of frigid air. Sakura had never felt Minnesota cold, except on high-altitude jumps, and the locals assured her the worst had yet to come. She slid across the ice-slicked parking lot, already bathed in orange streetlights despite the time. Visiting hours on the oncology ward ended at six p.m., but the night nurses had made her a permanent exception.

She shivered in the cold until the bus arrived, paid the fare, and sat in the back behind a small man eating pungent green shrimp curry which reeked of grass, citrus, and coriander. A silver Cadillac SUV followed the bus four blocks, then split off west toward the hospital. She ground her teeth through the ride, got off in front of the main entrance, noted the silver Cadillac in guest parking, and stalked into the eighteen-story building.

The lobby smelled of astringent shit, antiseptic and unchanged diaper.

Forty seconds later she walked out of a side entrance, took a picture of the license plate, and uploaded it to Janet LaLonde. Sakura took the stairs. Her phone blipped as she reached the eighth floor.

The Cadillac belonged to Rocky Sweetman, whose daughter Onnoleigh had poured tens of thousands of dollars of her trust fund into Humans for Humanity on her eighteenth birthday two months prior. Onnoleigh's face matched the girl in the lobby, cute and blonde with too much makeup. A quick scroll through "Ona's" Facebook found the other two: David Gerrold, retired policeman, black hair and round face, and Samuel Burns, a bald, surly-looking former gunnery sergeant in the US Marine Corps, now a self-defense instructor in Fairfax, VA.

She took the remaining six floors two steps at a time and hit the landing sweating and breathing hard. Eschewing the dramatic entrance, she listened at the door. She heard nothing, so she cracked it open.

Gerrold sat at the bench in front of the nurse's station, reading manga. How children's entertainment became an American pastime she'd never figured out. His eyes twitched upward when the door moved, and his hand slid into his jacket. She couldn't fight a gun at thirty feet, not anymore.

She let the door close, stood just to the side, and counted. The Psychology of Security Forces textbook she'd penned for the Tokyo Police Department put a curious guard's investigation time at anything under two minutes. After that, they lay in ambush.

A hundred and seven seconds after she'd jostled the door, Gerrold opened it. She put one knife under his chin, just hard enough to draw blood, and the other against his eye. He blinked and winced as the razor-sharp blade sliced his eyelid, deep enough to hurt but not enough to bleed, a paper cut from five inches of steel.

"Step out."

He stepped into the stairwell, eyes wide.

"Remove your firearm with your left index finger and thumb, and drop it on the floor."

It hit the tile with a metallic clatter.

She pulled the blade from his eye a half centimeter, enough to let him blink. He did, eyes watering, and she took the opportunity to body-block him against the wall opposite the railing. The knife remained under his jaw. These Americans stood so damned tall.

"You know who I am?"

"Yes," he said through clenched teeth.

She lifted his chin a little further with the blade. "You know how quickly I can kill you?"

"Yes."

"What is your intent with my daughter?"

He hesitated, so she drew a line down his cheek with the other knife. He hissed as blood welled along the cut, and tears flowed from his eyes.

"What is your intent with my daughter?"

He blubbered. "It's not about you. You're just means to an end."

She lowered the other blade just enough to let him speak clearly. "Continue."

"Ona doesn't care about you. Rowley's the end-game. You're just a stepping stone."

"What are your plans for Kazuko?"

He closed his eyes, hard.

"What are your plans for Kazuko?"

He swallowed. "We . . . we're going to kill you both."

Sakura jammed the knife up through his mouth into his frontal lobe and yanked it out before he had a chance to twitch. He gave her a confused, pained look. She wiped the blade on his arm as his eyes glazed, then she stepped back, letting him tumble down the concrete stairs.

She called Matt. It kicked to voicemail without ringing.

She picked up Gerrold's weapon and racked the slide, snatching a round from the air as it flew from the chamber. A Sig-Sauer P229, the .40 caliber had more kick than she liked, but it beat a knife nineteen times out of twenty. She didn't bother checking the body for extra magazines and instead shouldered through the door, weapon raised.

The head nurse smiled in recognition and then screamed. She ducked behind the desk as Sakura stalked toward her, clearing corners on the approach to Kazuko's room.

Burns poked his head out of Kazuko's room, a confused look on his face. Sakura pulled the trigger twice and the weapon boomed. Red mist puffed out the back of his head and he crumpled to the floor.

Ears ringing from the too-loud reports, she approached the room on the balls of her feet, careful to make no sound.

"Isuji Sakura!" Ona's young voice shook with nervous energy. "I have your daughter."

"Is she alive?"

"For the mom—"

Sakura rounded the corner and took in the scene. Ona half-crouched behind the bed, holding her daughter in a headlock, cheek to cheek, a shaky hand pointing her pistol at the doorway.

"—ent."

Sakura shot Ona twice in the face, the pinprick holes marring her cheek and eye almost simultaneously. Kazuko screamed. Blossom closed the distance, took one look at the gray matter and blood splattering the heating unit in front of the window, and turned the upraised gun to the door.

She picked up the phone left-handed, but before she dialed she looked at her daughter. She spoke in Japanese to avoid any confusion. "Get in bed, keep your hands in sight. The police will be here soon, they will have guns and will be brash and loud in the American fashion. You must not make sudden movements. Understand?"

"Yes, Mother."

Sakura ran her hand over her daughter's head, clumsy with the phone. "Are you all right, my Kazuko?"

"Yes, Mother. They scared me, but I will recover."

"Good."

She dialed 9-1-1 and sat in the guest chair, pistol still in hand.

Hospital security broke into the ward three minutes later. She set down the pistol, pushed it out of arm's reach, and spoke to them around the corner. Eventually a black-haired kid in a uniform too large and too wrinkled drew up the courage to step into the room.

Fingers laced on top of her head, she explained the situation twice, and twice again for the police. They arrested her pending an investigation, but cuffed her out of her daughter's sight, a courtesy Sakura admired and appreciated.

Given one phone call, she dialed Janet LaLonde.

* * *

Matt gripped the armrest and looked at white nothing out the window, his stomach unable to settle in the incredible turbulence. The sixty-seater bucked in the driving winds, and the little girl right behind him shrieked in terror, a continuous keening that made the difficult landing downright intolerable.

Her scream took him back to the Atlanta rooftop, as Bravo Squad slaughtered one another with ruthless efficiency in response to the banshee's wail. Sakura had been right, of course. Nobody believed the report she'd kicked upstairs, that they'd defeated a supernatural threat by giving a mummy a jacket, and a possessed girl three states away had woken up in response.

The terrified shrieking intensified as they slid down the runway, the sloppiest landing he'd ever experienced. He turned on his phone before the seatbelt light clicked off, eyes on the screen to keep from glaring at the still-hysterical child. A message popped up from Janet.

Sakura's in jail. 101 4th Street. Kazuko's okay.
Might be an ambush. Call me.

He pulled her up and hit "Send," then shuffled down the aisle with the sweating, praying, grateful throng. Janet briefed him on the situation: all signs pointed to self-defense, and the Olmsted County Sherriff's office would remand Sakura to his custody as a courtesy to the Department of Homeland Security, but as a foreign national she couldn't leave the country and would have to surrender her passport until they completed the investigation.

"So what's this about an ambush?" he asked.

"Sakura said one of the dead guys mentioned you."

"All right. I'll plan accordingly."

Matt picked up his bags and glanced up at the TV hanging from the baggage claim ceiling. The polar vortex covered half the country, with blizzard warnings from the Dakotas to the Carolinas. The boards next to the TV showed flight after flight changed to "Canceled."

"Not like we're going anywhere anyway."

* * *

Marie rolled her eyes. "You're babbling, Steve. Calm down and try again."

Breathless, Steve Palermo gasped into the phone. "They're dead. Ona, Sam, and Dave. Total freaking disaster, man. Bitch just went psycho on them, desperado-style."

"Did they get her daughter?"

Steve didn't reply. Big K held out his hand for the phone. His soft chocolate eyes flashed in anger as she turned away from him and asked again.

"Steve, stay with me here. Did they get her daughter?"

"No, man. She's okay, I mean fucked with cancer and all, but she's okay."

She reiterated for Big K's benefit. "So Ona, Sam, and Dave are dead, and both Kazuko Sakura and Isuji Sakura are still alive. Could you have fucked this up any worse?"

"I wasn't even there. I was the fucking lookout in the goddamned parking lot."

She rolled her eyes again. "Okay, yeah. You did great, Steve. Rowley's on his way there, which is what we wanted. Pete's guys will handle the rest of this, so you can bug out as soon as the storm is clear."

"So I didn't fuck up?"

She lifted her hand and made a "talk-talk-talk" gesture. Big K kept his hand out, his eyes flashing with anger as she kept talking. "No, you didn't fuck up. You did great."

"Really?"

"Really. See you when you get home."

She hung up.

Big K snorted and wrapped his arms around her. She leaned back into his muscular embrace, rubbing her hands down his dark skin. "Mayo Clinic's a total bust. They'll see what they can do on the way out."

He chuckled. "Wasn't a bust no matter how it turns out. All we wanted to do was lead Rowley there, and he took the bait hook, line, and sinker. Now we hit him where it hurts."

She turned around and rested her head on his shoulder. "It's good of you to do this. Most people wouldn't put themselves out there like this for a friend."

"I'm not most people. You don't get payback, folks will walk all over you your whole life. He fucked with Yardley, he gets payback. It's that simple."

"Most people wouldn't see it that way. You're a good friend."

"The best, babe."

Chapter 7

The baby monitor clipped to Monica's waist squawked, a sound more gleeful than plaintive. Monica leaned the broom against the deck and blew a stray wisp of hair out of her face.

"This is ridiculous."

The walkway down to the truck sat under a quarter inch of dense white crap, and she'd swept it off four times already. The snow fell in massive, heavy flakes, what her daddy called "heart attack snow" from his days up north at Fort Drum. The trees rocked in the roaring wind under a gray sky more uniform than she'd ever seen.

And speaking of uniforms, the pair of state policemen parked at the end of the driveway didn't lift a finger to help her.

The Rowleys didn't own a snow shovel. Nobody owned a snow shovel. White Spruce got maybe two inches of snow a year, on a bad year. Maybe a blizzard in January or February a couple times a decade, a few inches over the course of a day.

The forecast predicted sixteen inches in twelve hours. Schools and most businesses had closed in anticipation, and the local news couldn't quite settle on "Snowmageddeon" or "Snowpocalypse".

"C'mon, Ted!"

Ted looked up, his muzzle white, tail a berserk whirlwind. He ran in wide circles, flopped on his side, and looked at her, tongue lolling into the snow.

"In the house, dog. Let's go."

Ted rolled to his feet and galumphed up the stairs to the deck door. She let him in, kicked the snow off her work boots, and stepped inside to the ever-present sound of *The Wiggles*.

Adam stood in the living room, leaning against the portable baby cage on wobbly legs. He smiled and babbled and shook his hand up and down in what might be a wave.

She crouched down to unlace her boots, but first she waved back, wiggling her fingers. "Hey little brown eyes. Holding down the fort?"

"Da."

Monica smiled, but glanced at the severe weather warning scrolling across the bottom of the screen. "Oh, great, you speak Russian now, little man? Maybe we should have named you Vladimir."

"Da!"

She kicked off her boots, rushed over and swept him into her arms. He reached for the windows and babbled, a string of nonsense that almost resembled real American speech. She looked at the white deck and whitening trees, and rubbed her son's back.

A contentment she'd never felt washed over her, tinged with longing for her husband's company. His job took him away far too often, but it also made their life possible. He loved being the hero, and she loved him for needing to do it, but . . . .

No, they'd had those discussions, time and time again. No buts, no ifs, no could-have-beens. They led a blessed life, and even the horrors of the past year didn't change that. She leaned her head against Adam's soft cheek.

"What do you think? Bed time?"

Adam pouted, as close as he came to crying these days.

"Well, all right. You can stay up a bit. Ain't like we're going anywhere tomorrow anyways."

* * *

Sakura walked out of the cell, her scowl the same as if she'd been slated for execution or had won the lottery. Matt walked next to her as she collected her personal effects—minus her combat knives, now state's evidence—and led her to the rental car, a block away in public parking.

"You're sure she's safe?"

Matt shivered through the insufferable cold, face turned against the biting wind. "Yeah. They've got SWAT crawling all over the building. No one will get within a mile of her."

He gasped in relief as they settled into the comparative warmth of the car. With numb fingers he fired up the engine and cranked the heat. Frigid air blasted him in the face, so he killed the fan to give it a chance to get hot. "This place is insane."

Sakura blew into her cupped hands. "How do you live in this country?"

Matt smiled through a shiver and put the car in gear. "I live in Tennessee. Even with all the snow, White Spruce ain't supposed to drop below twenty-six, and that's just for a day or two."

A few minutes later he tried the blower, and if not warm, the tepid air didn't make his shivering worse. He made a U-turn into sparse traffic and headed for the Clinic.

City blocks blurred past as the car heated to sane temperatures. Sakura sat still as death, neither speaking nor fidgeting, eyes flicking from mirror to mirror.

With Sakura, Matt tried to avoid anything of a personal nature, but sometimes it couldn't be helped. "Are you all right?"

"There's an SUV following us, two blocks back. Ford, twenty-ten or eleven, three targets."

"Okay." Matt only saw anonymous headlights in the rear-view mirror. He turned left, off-course. Moments later a dark SUV turned behind them. "Care for some ordnance?"

"Yes, please."

"Get to the trunk," Matt said. "I checked some bags, just in case."

She unbuckled her seatbelt and pulled herself into the back. A grunt, then a tearing sound as the false ledge behind the back seats ripped away. She leaned forward and slid the AA-12 combat shotgun between the front seats, then turned back. A moment's stretching, her feet kicking against the back of his seat, and she reemerged with the REC-7 assault rifle.

"You checked these?"

He shrugged. "This is America. With the right permit you can check anything."

She pushed his combat helmet onto his head, then turned away.

"They're closing fast. Look for a box."

"Janet, you with me?"

"Loud and clear," she said through his helmet.

"We've got a tail. Contact imminent."

As if on cue, an armored truck trundled out of the next intersection, blocking their path, a man with an assault rifle standing to take aim outside the side door. Matt whipped the steering wheel around and hit the gas, tires shrieking as the car spun. Sakura steadied herself with one hand and whipped around as the car accelerated toward their pursuers.

Confused drivers veered off the road. The SUV kept true.

Matt kept his foot on the pedal. "I can't play chicken with you in the car."

Sakura responded with a burst from the REC-7, shattering Matt's right eardrum in the confined space. The windshield spiderwebbed around a trio of holes. Matt struck it twice with the heel of his palm, bashing the now opaque glass out of his way. He touched his ear, then wiped the blood on his pants.

The SUV skidded sideways. Matt veered around it, processing the blurred image of a driver missing the back of his skull, a man in a black mask groping for the steering wheel. Sakura wheeled around as Matt blew through a red light, fishtailing around for another pass.

The SUV had careened to a halt in the middle of the road.

"Grenades?" Sakura shouted.

Ears ringing, Matt shook his head.

"Right. Checked baggage. Permits." Sakura fired another burst, and another. Men ducked, their fates unknown. The truck screeched up next to the SUV. The side door opened, and boots hit the ground beneath it. Sakura shot the man in the feet, and he fell to the pavement, writhing.

One figure bolted from the car up into the van. Hands grabbed the wounded man and the truck jerked forward, inertia closing the door.

The truck leapt the curb at the corner, skidded over the sidewalk and down the embankment, headed for the expressway. Sakura squeezed back into shotgun. Matt hit the gas, tires spraying muddy snow behind them. Sakura leaned out the window as the truck came back into view. Her REC-7 chattered as the car lurched over the curb, and her shots went high.

The truck turned left into light oncoming traffic.

"Janet," Matt said, "he's going south!"

"Pursuit in progress," Janet said. "52 southbound. Request air support, over."

Matt gunned the gas, his heart catching as they leapt the embankment. They hit the pavement in a skid, straightened, and shot after the truck. Oncoming headlights swerved to the side of the road as snow pelted his visor. His neck burned in the relentless wind beneath his helmet.

Sakura jammed another magazine home and took aim. She swore as the tires slipped on a chunk of slush, the lurch half-throwing her out of the car. She lodged herself in the window with her legs, then slithered most of the way back into the car. "Get closer!"

"I'm trying," Matt said, his foot on the floor. The tires slipped every time they transitioned from snow to pavement and back, jerking the car into a series of erratic skids. They closed in on the truck from the left-hand side.

Sakura half-stood, peering over the top of the car, and opened fire.

A man in a ski mask leaned out the passenger seat window and bullets peppered the front of their car.

Sakura responded with a short burst.

The man slumped. A rifle emerged from the back door, and Matt guided the car behind a plow. Shots pinged off the massive blade and the driver swerved.

Matt braked hard, and the plow rebounded off of the jersey wall. Matt cut left and hit the accelerator, zipping around the huge yellow vehicle, crossing two lanes of traffic and sliding across the snow-covered median before swerving back.

Behind him the plow jackknifed but didn't tip, and traffic screeched to a halt behind it.

"We got them," Matt said as they approached the truck.

Something small fell from the truck's rear window and tumbled across the slushy asphalt. As Matt veered around it, it exploded. Shrapnel peppered his face as the side window shattered. The tires held.

"Steady!" Sakura said.

Matt spared her a glance. Red leaked into his left eye, half-blinding him, and his head hurt. Something had punched straight through his helmet, but had slowed enough to not kill him. "Like old times, yeah?"

"Shut up and drive."

An air horn sounded as he dodged a tractor trailer. Behind him, it jackknifed and slid. He veered right and approached the armored truck. Another grenade clattered out the rear door, bouncing to the curb before detonating.

"Chopper en route," Janet said. "ETA one minute. State Tactical responding."

Sakura slipped inside, traded her rifle for Matt's AA-12, and took aim.

She pulled the trigger.

The back door rocked as another grenade tumbled out. Matt drove right over it. It exploded behind them, pinging off the back of the car.

The truck lurched away from them and three more grenades tumbled out.

Matt slammed on the brakes, sliding haphazardly through the slush. Inertia carried the grenades forward and they detonated in front of the car, rocking his head back into the headrest.

Sakura grunted as gunfire scattered off of the hood.

"You okay?" Matt asked. He couldn't see out of his left eye. Blood drenched his face.

"Yes," Sakura said, her voice flat. "Hurts, though." She returned fire as the truck pulled away. Two microgrenades detonated under the vehicle, to no effect. "Solid tires."

Black smoke rose from the front of the car as Matt accelerated again. "Where's my chopper?"

"Any time," Janet replied. "SWAT is setting up a roadblock a mile or so up."

Flames licked the underside of the hood. Matt kept his foot on the gas and the motor groaned.

The grenadier's head appeared in the window again.

"Kill him, please," Matt said.

Sakura pulled the trigger and the man's head burst. Blood and bone fragments flew out of the truck and scattered off Matt's helmet.

The State Police helicopter buzzed less than fifty feet overhead, a sniper in the door. "Take out the driver," Matt said into his helmet.

Janet repeated the order.

"Affirmative," replied a male voice. "I've got him."

A burst of light erupted from the truck. A trail of smoke circled right and upward and contacted the helicopter. Shrapnel rained down as the burning fuselage fell from the sky right in front of them.

Matt slammed on the brakes and jerked the wheel sideways. Sakura ducked back into the car as they skidded into the tumbling wreckage with a deafening crunch.

The intense heat ignited Matt's sleeve.

"OUT! OUT!" he yelled. His door jammed against the fuselage, he batted at his shirt with his other hand. Sakura limped out as he unbuckled, then she half-dragged him across the seat to the asphalt. They struggled away from the burning mess and dropped to the ground.

Matt tore off his helmet, reached up, and pulled a twisted chunk of metal from just above his temple. It came away with a wet slurp, and blood spurted from the wound. He put a hand over it. The gas leaking from the car ignited in a whoosh of black smoke. Matt turned his face away from the heat.

He examined Sakura in the dying light. A dark splotch stained her pants on her right thigh. He leaned into his helmet without putting it back on. "We need a medic."

"Ambulances en route." Janet's voice carried through the empty space.

Sakura grabbed Matt's head and wiped away a smear of blood with her sleeve. "Through and through. I'll be fine." She patted his cheek. "So will you."

"The truck?" Matt asked. More blood trickled down his face, undoing much of Sakura's kindness.

"No sign of them at the roadblock, Matt." Janet sighed.

He stared at the flames as they flickered in the slushy mess.

"Well, shit."

* * *

Monica slurped her hot chocolate and stared out at the never-ending white surrounding the house. Trees sagged under the weight, their trunks half-visible through the deluge. She patted Adam's back and let out the mother of all sighs.

"Why do you think I got the urge to go places, little man? Just 'cause I can't?"

If Adam understood her he hid it well, wide eyes flicking from flake to flake.

The phone rang. The only people who used the landline anymore lived in town. She put him in the crib, picked it up and cradled it against her shoulder.

"Hello?"

"Monica. Chris Wilcox."

She rolled her eyes despite no one there to see it. "The fuck do you want?"

"I'm at the store. We got emergency generators and whatnot, so dad's got me working straight through, got a couch in the back and every—"

She hung up.

"Pervert."

The phone rang in her hand. She looked at it, shook her head, then answered.

"Chris, you call here again and—"

"I think you might be in danger."

She whirled and stalked to the bedroom. "Explain."

"Ten minutes ago these guys come through in a jacked up Silverado, extended bed, extended cab, big search lights on top. So anyways, they buy me out of shotgun and three-oh-eight, laughing and joking about a 'cunt hunt.' Thing is, Sandy's here, and she said one of them guys is your Cobalt driver."

She turned cold, despite the heat from the furnace. "That's impossible. Matt crippled that guy at the grocery store. He's in the hospital."

He murmured something, then, "Hang on, here's Sandy."

"Hey," Sandy said. "It's the same guy. I'd bet my life on it."

"No, Matt crippled him. He's in the ICU."

"He's not, Mon. He's not."

"The guy Matt took down won't be able to walk ever—"

"Then they're brothers. Maybe twins or something. But there's worse. One of these guys, he's a Trooper."

She looked out the window at the police car, barely visible behind a wall of falling white. "I have two Troopers in front of my house. They've been there all day."

"Honey, you got to get out of there."

"Where the hell—"

Chris broke in. "You know my cabin out back of Walker's?"

Chris and Cory owned an eight-by-ten hunting shack barely fit for the name, not a terrible walk from her house and inaccessible by car. "Yeah, I know it."

"Head there. You can walk it no problem, and in this shit you won't leave no tracks. Take the boy, leave Ted with plenty of food and water. We'll get some guys out to you, make sure you're okay."

She shoved an extra pair of baby clothes into the diaper bag. "I ain't leaving my dog."

"If you can't keep him quiet—"

"I ain't. Leaving. My dog."

"Fine, but you need to get out of there. Do you have a gun?"

She hesitated. "Four."

"Take whatever you're comfortable with. But go."

Shit fuck dammit shit. "Yeah. I'm going."

She hit "End" and buried her face in her arms.

Don't scream. Don't scream. Don't scream.

First things first, she cinched Matt's holster around her waist, the extra weight of the .357 revolver uncomfortable but better than carrying it in the bag. She threw on another layer, then her coat and boots, grabbed the car seat, and stepped into the nursery. Adam lay in the crib, thumb in his mouth, eyes closed, oblivious to the world. She picked him up, dead weight, put him in the seat, and buckled him in.

Oof. Not an infant anymore, carrying him would be a bear. Nothing for it, she hefted the load and . . . stopped dead at the back door, shaking, frozen, unable to move.

She forced herself to breathe, slow, even, in and out, in and out.

Inaction begets fear. Fear begets inaction. Her Sifu, the other Chris in her life, sprang into her mind, his years of confidence and training cutting through the indecision, shattering the cloying panic with calming words. *You become your habits. You are your routine. Take the dog for a walk, one foot in front of the other.*

"Ted."

He trotted around the corner, sad eyes betrayed by a wagging tail.

"Heel."

She opened the door and let the storm swallow her, Ted on her heels.

* * *

Matt schooled his face to careful neutrality as the guard opened their cell. He'd played ball, neither saying nor demonstrating that their bars couldn't hold him, while Janet pulled strings behind the scenes. He helped Sakura to her feet and offered her an arm he knew she wouldn't take.

She limped out of the cell in front of him, gave a sharp nod to the guard on the way past, and struggled down the hall without comment or complaint. He watched her go, smiled at the guard, then followed. The officer shadowed him.

Detective MacDonald, in charge of investigating the attack on Kazuko, met them halfway to booking. Sakura ignored his offered hand and hobbled by, eyes forward. Matt shook it, and MacDonald gripped harder than he needed to and didn't let go.

"You've got some high-up friends, Mr. Rowley."

"Yeah, I've always been the popular kid." Being a sixteen million dollar investment had its perks. Holding the secrets behind ICAP might have helped, but might not have—Matt had no idea how many aspiring immortals hadn't lost their lives when Gerstner rose out of the machine, or what kinds of grudges they held.

Is this a vendetta? By who?

"You and your friend are responsible for fourteen bodies in the last sixteen hours, six of them cops." He squeezed harder. "Do I have to tell you to stay out of trouble?"

"I'm not sure what's going on, but let me make a few things clear: One, those men attacked us, and you've got a dozen-plus witnesses to corroborate. Two, we didn't kill those policemen. Three, to defend her daughter, Blossom would kill every man, woman, and child in Missouri, and on that score I've got her back. Now if you're done trying to intimidate me, you might consider that I can crush a human hand to jelly without even straining myself."

MacDonald let go, put his hand on his hip, then in his pocket, then back to his hip.

Whispers babbled through Matt's mind, an unintelligible argument of murderous hate and something softer, gentle without yielding, tender and hard as stone. They swarmed over and suffocated each other, and through them a picture formed in his mind.

He blinked.

"You okay, Mr. Rowley?" Detective MacDonald's expression held more wariness than concern, eyes tight and too attentive.

"Yeah. I'm good."

He pushed past the detective and rounded the corner into the break room where a crappy 90's-era TV sat next to a filthy microwave, right where the whispers had told him it would be.

A talking head blathered next to aerial footage of White Spruce. Main Street burned, a half-dozen buildings engulfed in flame under skies smothered by dark clouds. Light flashed from the Fish and Tackle store, bursts of white from the second-story window sending lances of worry through Matt's chest. *Weapons fire.*

"I need to get home," he said to no one in particular.

Sakura snorted. "Airport's closed."

"They're flying a helicopter."

She slapped his cheek, just hard enough to draw his eyes from the television. "That's there, not here. Everything's grounded here."

"No."

She slapped him again, a little harder. "Yes. We'll get there, but not today."

"Goddammit."

She rubbed his face where she'd hit him. "Now we agree."

* * *

The tiny cabin shuddered. Snow drifted from the roof, which hadn't seen new shingles in living memory. It joined the dusting of white on the rough pine floor, trampled over with a thousand dog prints, all of them Ted's. In the distance something crackled, like kids playing with fireworks.

Monica rubbed her hands together and held them over the tiny kerosene stove. Her son slept, oblivious to any danger or the change of venue, his cheeks rosy in the drafty shack. She looked through a crack in the wall, no more than a quarter-inch thick, at the hazy orange glow.

Even with the storm past and the new moon, too many trees intervened for her to see the cause. It looked like city lights flickering off the snow, but the four lights around the town square couldn't illuminate White Spruce like that. No stars shone in the black sky above town, but they did everywhere else. It had to be fire.

Ted lifted his head. He cocked sideways, then chuffed.

"Ted, hush."

He chuffed again, something closer to a bark.

"Settle." She raised a finger and stared at her enthusiastic idiot of a pet, eyebrows raised. "Settle."

Ted lay down with a small whine, his head turned toward the door, tail flat.

The wind hummed, and the hum turned into the rumble of engines, at least two, and louder each second. They approached the cabin without lights, so she killed the heater and shifted to sit Indian-style in front of it, hiding the dying glow from the outside.

A pair of ATVs pulled up in front of the cabin, sunk almost to the tops of their knobby tires in the dense white snow. The motors died, and three silhouettes approached the cabin, two of them holding long guns. They walked awkwardly through the snow, lifting their feet too high with every step.

Monica held her breath. She clutched the .357 to her chest, then pointed it at the door. The barrel shook, nerves as much as cold. In the confined space she might be better served by kung fu, but if they opened up with those rifles they'd cut her down before she ever got close.

She rose to the balls of her feet in one fluid motion. Cocking the hammer, she winced at the click, too loud in the muffled silence of the forest. One of the shadows had disappeared around the side of the cabin, and she strained to hear where it walked.

Boots scuffed on the porch, a four-by-four plank deck nailed to an old pallet. The lock rattled.

She pointed the revolver at the sound, tried to relax her grip.

"Psst."

Her finger crept to the trigger. She waited, shaking, heart thundering in her chest.

"Monica," the man whispered. "You in there? It's Chris."

She exhaled, long and slow, pulled her finger from the trigger, and un-cocked the hammer. "I'm here!"

She yanked the door open to reveal Chris Wilcox and Kevin Bartell, decked head-to-toe in camo hunting gear with stout work boots and giant hats with ear-flaps.

Kevin towered over even Chris, a giant teddy bear of a man ever since tenth grade, made bigger by scotch and good food and a life spent in a taxidermy studio. He raised one eyebrow. "Grab the kid. We got to go."

She picked up Adam, hauled the dead weight outside, and stopped. "What about Ted? He can't ride an ATV."

She glared at Chris to shut him up before anything left his mouth.

"I'll carry him." Sandy stepped out from behind Kevin.

Monica grinned and looked from Sandy to Chris and back, trying not to think about what it might mean. Sandy scooped Ted off the ground and sat on the back of Chris's ATV. He licked her face, tail thumping against her thigh.

Sandy crinkled her nose. "You stink, Ted."

Chris chuckled. "Don't get too close to the other end!"

Monica rested the car seat on the rear rack. "You'll have to drive slow. So what's happening? I can't get a signal for shit out here."

Kevin shrugged, a mountain rolling up and down. "Nothing good. Chris called, said there's guys might cause you some trouble. Storm's knocked out the power and cell towers. Hardware store caught fire, spread to the grocery, and it sounds like someone's letting off some ammo, too. That explosion a few minutes ago had to be the main propane tank out back.

"The cops at your place . . . they didn't make it. Somebody shot them, up close, right through the window."

Monica gaped. "Wait. But . . . ain't no one fighting back? They're just letting thugs burn up our town and kill people?"

"People are holed up, defending their homes if needs be," Chris said. "Cory went to Ma and Pa's, took the Mossburg with him. Roads are so bad the firefighters can't even get through from Cottontown, and some jackass holed up above the bait shop started popping shots at the news chopper."

Monica got on behind Kevin, hands wrapped around him, clutching Adam's baby seat in his lap. "Marty wouldn't be that dumb. I mean, he's stupid, but he's not—"

Kevin grunted.

"—that—"

A loud crack cut her off.

Kevin leaned forward, then slid sideways off of the ATV, dragging the car seat out of her hands and landing with a soft thump in the snow. Adam wailed, the sound muffled by Kevin's massive body.

"Shit!" Chris yanked up his rifle and whirled it toward the sound. Blood puffed from his back, followed by another crack.

Sandy screamed.

Monica dove next to Kevin and scrabbled through the snow, trying to move his dead weight enough to free her trapped child, whimpers muffled under the dead weight. Her muscles strained, but she found no purchase in the slippery, foot-deep snow.

Sandy's scream turned into a wail with another crack. She stumbled into view, blood pumping from her left arm. Her neck erupted, the geyser of blood steaming in the snow. Another crack.

Ted howled.

Chapter 8

Matt stalked out of the airport slower than he wanted to, Sakura limping at his heels to the vehicle dominating the pickup lane. The governor had declared a state of emergency and travel bans covered not only Tennessee but most of Kentucky, Virginia, and Maryland. Janet LaLonde had, however, displayed her usual attention to detail: the huge, tan, military surplus Oshkosh M-ATV MRAP came equipped with roof lights and a magnetic decal emblazoned "Tennessee Department of Agriculture—Forestry Division."

He eyed the empty mount for an M240 machine gun on top and wondered if the bear problem had gotten so out of control that the forestry service needed a half-million-dollar vehicle designed to protect its occupants from roadside bombs and small arms fire. Still, it would make short work of mountainous terrain.

He took the offered clipboard from the TDA flunky, signed off on the vehicle, and hefted himself up and inside, tossing his bags on the floor in the cabin. He leaned back in the almost-comfortable seat, a novelty in a military vehicle.

Sakura took shotgun and ran her hand over the dashboard. "One of ours."

Responsible parties had not quite managed to buff the ICAP insignia from the synthetic dash cover.

"So it is."

Sakura looked northwest. Matt couldn't blame her. The government considered six competent bodyguards trained and paid by the Department of Homeland Security overkill protection for her daughter, but they'd agonized over the decision to leave Kazuko for the chaos in Matt's home town.

He pulled away from the curb and turned left out of the airport, toward White Spruce. Monica had answered neither texts nor calls to the landline. State police had requested assistance for a potential hostage situation, with two missing Troopers—Monica's bodyguards—and shots fired at a news helicopter, but storm damage and the aftermath had overwhelmed EMS, State Police, and the National Guard. Roads remained impassable, and the governor had given priority to the major metropolitan areas.

They hit deep snow before the city line. White buried the streets so deep he couldn't make out the curb or the sidewalks, except where business and homeowners had valiantly shoveled, kicked, swept, or otherwise tried to clear the areas around their doors. The fifteen-ton vehicle handled the roads with no trouble, and the travel ban had cleared them to the point that he could do a comfortable forty miles an hour without bothering to stop at intersections.

As city transitioned to country, he had to slow down. His precognition hadn't returned to its old level, and he couldn't quite trust it to tell him where the road ended and the ditch began. A country ditch shouldn't be much of an issue for an MRAP, but some of the culverts ran eight feet deep. Winding Tennessee roads saw the occasional car in the ditch, and Matt's frustration with their speed grew as the gas gauge dropped from full to three-quarters to half a tank.

Just after dawn he approached a woman standing on the shoulder, waving her arms next to an overturned van halfway down an embankment. The whispers shrieked through his brain, their incoherent jibbers urging him to jerk the wheel right and grind her under the wheels. Compassion told him to stop and help. He swerved around her without slowing.

Sakura said nothing, but he felt her judgment, even agreed with it. Everything and anyone that wasn't his wife and child fell by the wayside of the endless churning miles.

"Call that in, please."

Sakura called 911, and in six curt sentences reported the distress.

Some time later they approached White Spruce under clear blue skies marred by a fading pillar of gray smoke. A dull plink rang out, followed by another.

"We're taking fire." Sakura unbuckled her seatbelt, rolled down to her knees, and grabbed the bag of weapons.

"Be careful." Matt snapped on his combat helmet. "We've got some survivalist types up here who might be jumpy after whatever the hell happened last night. I don't want to kill any civilians if we don't have to."

"Are you instructing me not to return fire?"

The MRAP rocked as an RPG exploded next to it, the bang loud enough to set his ears to ringing even through the armor.

"Where?" he hollered.

"I don't know!"

He gunned the gas and swerved in erratic, patternless jerks. Pulling onto Main Street, he passed the burned-out husks of several buildings and took shelter in the shadow of the town hall. He left the motor running, unbuckled, and grabbed the AA-12.

Sakura's knowing look, flat and almost exasperated, raised the hackles on his neck.

"Yeah, so that's a hostile. But I'm instructing you to use heightened target priority. This is my home."

Another bullet ricocheted off of the chassis with a metallic whine.

Sakura nodded out the bulletproof, three-inch thick window. "Bank. Third window in from the right."

Matt spotted the rifle, extended a good six inches past the granite sill. It flashed, and another bullet plinked off of the armor.

"I see him."

Sakura put her hand on the suicide door's handle.

He put his hand on top of hers and shook his head. "I can run. You can't. Do it, before they get another tube on target."

Sakura limped to the front, picked up the REC-7, and fell into the driver's seat. She gunned the gas, headed straight for the bank lobby. Another RPG washed harmlessly over the roof. Matt waited for the next rifle shot to ping off their armor and popped the door as Sakura returned fire. He leapt out the back of the vehicle, using the door to swing around, and hit the ground running.

He fired his sidearm into the plate glass storefront, then

switched to the combat shotgun as he ran through the open space. Whispers urged him to eat the unfamiliar men behind the counter, about to pop up and open fire with semiautomatic rifles. He embraced the unwelcome teeth chewing at his sanity, half-pulled the trigger to acquire range to the counter, then lifted the weapon an inch and fired. The microgrenade passed over the counter and exploded downward.

The whispers cackled at a man's agonized shrieking.

Matt shouldered through the door and took the stairs three at a time, following his weapon around the corners. A rifle fired again as he kicked in the door to find a room full of filing cabinets and dusty stacks of paper. Bullets chipped brick just outside the window.

A silhouette, red and orange in the infrared, took cover next to the window, a long black tube in his hand.

Matt ran forward and put his shoulder down, slamming into the cabinets with full force. The first cabinet caved in, and the entire stack shifted with titanic force. Two men cried out, more alarmed than pained, and Matt let the shotgun hang in favor of drawing his pistol and a titanium alloy combat knife.

The knife left his hand and punched right through the grenadier's face, pinning his leaking head to the brick wall.

"Humans for Humanity!" the unseen man cried.

Matt fired as he stood. A hole appeared in his assailant's forehead, and a small object fell from his hands, a baleful red light blinking. Eyes wide, Matt leapt over the demolished furniture and smashed through the window in one fluid motion. The whispers cooed in disappointment as his leap carried him halfway across the street.

The world turned white, deafening, a sea of pain and vertigo. He hit something, brittle and cutting and not hard enough to stop his fall. Burnt hair and gasoline filled his nostrils as he tore off his helmet with a blackened hand.

Casey's Hair and Nails. He lay amid shattered shelving and hair care products across the street from the bank, clothes on fire, battered and broken and unable to move. He opened his mouth to cry out, but no words came. He couldn't lift his head, couldn't even turn it.

Brown cowboy boots and tight blue jeans crossed his vision, skinny jeans on skinny, athletic legs. He hoped they weren't there to kill him. The whispers tittered in anticipation.

White mist blinded him, cold and choking. White turned to black.

* * *

Monica stumbled through the snow, freezing, Adam clutched to her chest. She couldn't feel her fingers, and wished she couldn't feel her toes, the relentless cold an agony worse than childbirth. Hot ache hobbled every shuffling step, and the world closed in to just moving.

Right foot. Left foot. Right foot.

She followed the stream downhill, the water's happy babble a taunt and a dare. Water meant civilization. Civilization meant people. Her father's lessons came back to her, down to town, down to town, she just never imagined the cold.

Left foot. Right foot. Left foot.

She tried not to bawl. She'd lost Ted in the chaos, and the pathetic yelp of pain minutes later had been too far away to risk. She could only hope he'd made it back home, and she'd find him on the deck when she got there.

Right foot. Left foot. Right foot.

She kissed her son, so calm, too calm, his baby brown eyes taking in the scenery as if nothing in the world could be amiss.

Left foot. Right foot. Left—

Bright new pain shot up her leg, and she fell. The snow caught her, soft and warm. Adam squirmed next to her, murmuring. She had to get up, had to get her son to safety. Had to pick him back up, carry him.

She blinked, and an angel sat next to her, a shimmering man in flowing white, with wings of cruel ice and a halo of the dawn. He stroked her cheek, whispered to her, silver words that flowed across her synapses with the promise of freedom from worry, from pain.

"No." She put her palms on the ground, through the biting cold, and pushed. She made it a few inches, and the weight of her life bore her down. She spit out the snow and swore and snarled.

But his promises enveloped her with warmth, soothing away the aches and pains and worry. *Move, yes. Save your son, yes. But first, you need rest.*

Rest. Just for a moment.

Take in the warmth.

Rest.

She closed her eyes.

And slept.

* * *

Everything hurt, and itched. And hurt.

Bright green eyes, young and pretty, stared down at Matt from a smiling face just a little too made up.

"Hey, Mister Rowley. How you feeling?"

He tried to smile but coughed instead, a wracking, suffocating mix of phlegm and blood that filled his nose and slithered down his throat.

Casey put a cool, damp cloth on his forehead, dabbing at his skin with too much care. It came away pink. "Shhh . . . . Shhh . . . . Your partner, that oriental girl, Miss Blossom? She said to stay still. Said you'd be hungry, wouldn't feel too good with all that healing to do. You hungry?"

A gaping chasm snarled and gnashed where his stomach should be. He nodded, tried again to speak. This time it came out, a rasping, almost human sound. "Yes, thank you."

She helped him sit up, then disappeared around the corner. He wore a terrycloth robe, light peach and frayed, and nothing else. His hands and right leg itched, a few red spots the last vestiges of his burns. His neck tingled, and when he turned to one side pins and needles shot down his whole body. The air bit with vinegar and bleach tinged with mildew and harsher smells, and in the low light his ultraviolet vision took in the details.

A mop bucket sat in the corner, next to shelves upon shelves of jugs and bottles.

He squinted against the pounding in his skull. "Where am I?"

She came back in with a sheet pan loaded with tater tots, and a bottle of ketchup. "My storeroom. Sorry, not a lot of options what with the place all burned up."

"It'll work." He plucked a searing hot tot off the pan and put it in his mouth, chewed once and swallowed. Three more went in next, then a handful already mashed between his fingers. He swallowed long enough to ask for water, then shoved another handful in his mouth with just enough ketchup for lubrication.

He chugged the water she brought him, and the next two glasses as well.

"Where's Sakura?"

Casey shrugged. "Miss Blossom went out with Pastor Joe and that creepy old guy who always stands in front of the flag pole with his uniform on."

He lay back, limbs tingling, restless and unable to do more until his vertebrae healed.

"I need my phone."

She pouted. "Won't matter. Cell service is down."

"Can you get me my goddamn phone?"

She put her fists on her hips. "You blaspheme, I'm going to put you and your phone outside in the melt. Now hold on."

She fished through his half-burnt clothes and produced his cell. He logged in with his thumbprint and scowled at the zero bars.

"Told you."

"Have they said when they expect power back?"

"They?"

"The news? The radio?"

She shrugged again. "All I've got's digital. Don't work for nothing when the power's out."

He sighed. "Can you get me some more food? Something with protein?"

She looked around the storeroom, eyes wide. "Uh, I got some energy bars?"

"That would be great."

* * *

Fully clothed in hand-me-downs, Matt opened the door when Sakura returned an hour later, three men in tow. Pastor Joe, forty-something with sandy brown hair and bright blue eyes, stood with Jed Callaway, the semi-retired handyman sporting an AR-15 in matte black.

Cory Wilcox ran his hand over his bald head and looked from Sakura to Matt with a face twisted with worry, his eyes bloodshot over heavy, blue-black bags. "Hey, Matt. Good to see you looking better."

Matt shook his hand, and they stepped inside. "Sorry about the store."

Cory threw up his hands. "I'm more worried about my brother. He went off to get your wife at our old cabin—the one back behind the Walker place?—but that was last night. Ain't heard nothing since."

He looked at Sakura. "You know what we're up against?"

"I pulled IDs from the dead, but with the net down, no Janet."

Matt looked up on the hill, where a tower stood, the red light on top not blinking for the first time in twenty years. "What do you think the chances are that cell interruption isn't storm-related?"

Jed patted his AR. "What's say we take your partner up and see what's what?"

Cory shook his head, a slow, deliberate motion. "No. I got to find my brother."

"Who else we got?" Matt asked.

"Well," Cory said. "Pastor Joe and old man Finster are outside. Everyone else is sticking close to home, you know what I'm saying?"

Matt picked up his helmet. "Sakura, take Jed, Joe, and Old Man Finster up to that tower. See if you can't get us some comms. Cory and I are going hunting."

* * *

Sakura popped four Advil into her mouth, cracked them with her teeth and washed the bitter mess down with a handful of snow. "Old Man" Finster—nobody had used his first name, even on introductions—eyed her askance as they walked to Jed's pickup. A grizzled farmer-type in stained Carhartts and a John Deere cap, she couldn't place his age between sixty and four hundred.

"Tastes bad, works faster."

He grunted in acknowledgment and hoisted himself over the tailgate, spry enough at any age.

Jed and the pastor got in the cab, and they rolled out toward the logging roads that led up to the cellular tower. As they climbed, the smell from the fire tainted the air, and grew paradoxically stronger than it had been in town.

Finster spat brown-yellow juice into the snow. "You one of them things, like Rowley?"

"No." She nodded at his weapon, a beautiful .35 caliber Marlin 336. "You are a good hunter?"

He spit again. "Best shot between the Blue Ridge and the Mississippi. I can take a deer at three-fifty without—"

"You ever shoot a man?"

He pulled up his sleeve to reveal a red one surrounded by a blue triangle. "Battle of Huế. Took more than my share, and a bayonet to the leg for my trouble. You?"

"Yes."

He waited for more.

"Jed, the Pastor. Have they?"

"Jed flew an Apache in Enduring Freedom. Joe, now, I don't think Joe's ever done nothing like that."

Sakura sighed, slid to the front of the bed, and knocked on the window. Joe slid it open.

"Yes?"

"We stop a half-mile back. You two guard the truck, cover us in case of snipers or retreat. Finster and I approach on foot. Clear?"

In the rear-view mirror, Jed frowned. "You've got a bad limp. I'm figuring that—"

"No. This is not negotiation, not a video game. You will guard the truck, we will advance. When we stop, don't slam the doors. You will wait for us and cover our escape if necessary. Understand?"

They nodded.

She pulled back and sat in the truck bed, the stitches in her thigh throbbing.

They stopped next to a pile of huge logs, enormous trees stripped of branches and stacked several meters high. Old Man Finster slid out of the back, then helped Sakura down. "You sure you're up for this, missy?"

"Yes."

Jed and Joe got out, weapons in hand, while Sakura unzipped her black duffel. Jed let out a low whistle as she pulled the REC-7 from the bag to compliment the Beretta M9 at her hip. His eyes bugged out when she extracted the bandoleer of grenades and slipped it over her shoulder.

"Holy shit! Sorry, Reverend."

The pastor stood dumb-struck as she put on her combat helmet. She dropped the mirrored visor, hiding her face from the world and the world from the murder in her eyes, and triggered the piezoelectrics to turn the mirror into a matte black finish. Joe continued staring, jaw slack.

She stepped up and grabbed his rifle. He tried to tug it away so she slapped him, hard enough to knock his head sideways, and wrest the gun from his grip. He stumbled and grabbed his cheek, tears brimming. "You are a liability. Jed will take your weapon and you will stay in the truck." She turned to Jed. "You will keep the keys so that he doesn't panic and drive away. Get atop those logs and cover us."

She ignored Joe's hurt look as he clambered into the truck, but muttered gratitude in Japanese when he didn't slam the door. "Let's go."

She picked her way straight toward the tower, around boulders and scrubby pine, grinding her teeth through every electric jolt of pain from her leg. The slippery ground took too much concentration and put too much pressure on her thigh. Finster moved through the snow with effortless silence, in slow, methodical steps.

He held up a fist, then cupped his hand to his ear.

The wind carried the jarring, indistinct sound of American 70s rock, reinforcing Sakura's first impression: however well equipped, however fanatical, these men were not professional soldiers. She nodded to show that she'd heard, then indicated via hand-signal to leapfrog forward under mutual cover.

They crested the rise on knees and elbows. The tower sat on a concrete slab capped with snow, a small maintenance shed at its base, door ajar. In front of it two men sat in a massive pickup with an elevated suspension. Smoke drifted up from cracked windows, tinging the crisp winter air with tobacco and marijuana.

Sakura held up a fist, waited, and watched, her Friend or Foe identifier trying to resolve hostile shapes. A few minutes later, light glinted on the hill behind the truck, and the HUD outlined a shape in double red triangles. She zoomed in, noted the scope lens that had caught her eye as the software highlighted the front of the rifle pointing toward the road. As she looked away, the target remained lit up in double triangles.

She pointed to her eyes and then to the target.

"I see him," Finster said through military hand signals. "Stay here and wait for my signal."

He disappeared behind her.

* * *

The M-ATV churned through the mud and slush at thirty miles an hour, the turbodiesel engine slowing not one whisker as they transitioned from hard pack to muddy field and back. Cory clutched his harness with both hands, rifle stowed in the netting behind his seat. They followed the ATV tracks—at least five of them—through the fields, past Aaron Walker's tree farm, toward the Wilcox brothers' tiny hunting shack.

"Do you think he's okay?" Cory asked.

Matt didn't reply. The suicide bomb trap in the bait shop gave him no confidence whatsoever that these people would behave in a rational manner, and his throat closed every time he thought of his wife and son.

"Matt?"

Matt snarled. "We'll find out when we get there."

They approached the shack from the southwest, taking advantage of the tree line to minimize their exposure. The enormous vehicle did not allow for stealth, only concealment.

Three shapes sprawled in the snow, camo coats hiding their identities.

A grating, keening screech erupted from Cory's throat, louder and louder as they drew up next to the bodies. Cory fumbled for the door handle without even undoing his harness. Matt grabbed his shoulder and put the M-ATV in park. Cory turned to him with wide eyes, breathing too hard, his sweaty face drained of color, slapping ineffectually at Matt's hands to get him to let go.

Matt took a steadying breath. "You can't just run out there. This could be a trap."

Cory fumbled with the harness, fat and panic turning his hands clumsy.

Matt's fingers clenched, digging into Cory's shoulder. "I need you to acknowledge that you heard me."

After another moment's fumbling, Cory stopped, breathed in,

and gasped out a response. "I hear you. Okay. I hear you. What do we do?"

Matt spelled it out the best he could.

"We don't know who's out there. They set a trap for me in town, they could have done it again. What I need you to do is stay inside until I give you the all-clear. Got it?"

He interpreted Cory's wide-eyed stare as a lack of comprehension.

"Do you understand me?"

Cory shuddered, squeezed his eyes shut. "Yeah. I got it. Stay here."

"Okay. And pick up your weapon. Get ready to return fire if someone starts shooting. But don't shoot anyone else unless they're shooting at us. Can you do that?"

His head jiggled up and down.

"Do it." Matt popped his harness, hefted the AA-12, and opened the door. The whispers remained silent. He hesitated; he'd grown accustomed to their return far too fast, but found it hard not to trust them.

He stepped down into the snow, next to Chris Wilcox's body. Cory's brother stared with dead eyes into the sky, his mouth open in silent shock. Matt knelt and put his fingers to Chris's neck, feeling for a pulse he knew he wouldn't find.

Judging by her hair, the gray, curly-haired body next to him had to be Sandy Miller, arms spread wide, face a ruined mess of meat and bone.

Ted chuffed. Despite the danger, Matt's heart skipped an elated beat as his clumsy, bumbling hound dog sat up from his place of rest behind the hood of Kevin Bartell's parka.

"Ted, settle."

The dog lay down with a whine and a plaintive look at Kevin.

Bartell lay dusted in snow, head to the side, face just visible around the faux-fur lining, no signs of trauma visible. Matt scanned the trees for any sign of movement, then moved next to the body and nudged Kevin with his boot. Kevin groaned, but didn't open his eyes, even when Ted licked his nose.

"Ted, truck." Matt stepped back to the M-ATV, dog at his heels. Ted hopped in as Matt opened the side door and pulled the first aid kit off the wall.

Cory stared at Matt with bloodshot, haggard eyes. "He's gone, isn't he?"

Matt gave the tiniest of nods. "I'm sorry. Kevin's alive. I need you to drive to town and get the ambulance crew. Load them up in here and get back as fast as you can. Can you do that for me?"

Eyes wet, Cory nodded.

"Say it."

Cory looked out at Kevin, then back to Matt, his face a mask of grim resolve. "I can do that."

"Good. Kevin's life depends on it. And take care of my dog. Go."

Matt stepped out and got to work while Cory pulled away.

He put his hand on Kevin's neck, warm despite the near-freezing temperatures and covered in dog hair. "Kevin, buddy. Can you hear me?"

Kevin's lips twitched, but no sound came out.

"I can't see where you're hurt. Can you tell me?"

He leaned in close and could just make out the answer. "Chest."

"Can you breathe okay?"

A tiny nod. "Hurts, though. Your Ted. He kept me warm."

"Hush. Don't talk unless you have to." He prodded gently, and Kevin didn't react much. "Ted's a good boy. Does that hurt?"

"No more than usual."

"All right. I'm going to roll you over. Try not to scream."

He dug his boots in as best he could, put his hands on Kevin's shoulder and thigh, and heaved. The giant rolled over with a whimpering sigh.

Matt unzipped Kevin's coat to reveal a flannel shirt beneath, a square object in the breast pocket. Buttons flew as he ripped open the shirt, then tore off the white undershirt to reveal a massive black bruise covering Kevin's entire chest, and not a drop of blood.

Matt pulled the object from Kevin's breast pocket, a polished chrome case he had to wrench open. Inside, a tiny bible lay obliterated, the bullet flattened against the back of the container.

"You lucky son of a bitch," Matt said. He gently prodded Kevin's chest with his fingertips, and tears came to the big man's eyes. Kevin hissed and bit his lip, drawing blood, as Matt assessed the damage. His ribs shifted far too much. A quick check of Kevin's extremities gave him a better assessment. "You want the good news or the bad news?"

"Good." The word came out as a gasp.

"You're a fat bastard and you're well dressed, so between the coat and the dog hypothermia doesn't seem to be an issue. The parka and the gloves protected you from frostbite on your extremities, and I think we can blame Ted that you might have just a touch on your left ear, but that's it." He held up the bible and box. "The Good Book saved you, deflected the bullet and absorbed a lot of the impact. You're going to be fine."

"Bad?"

"Your sternum's shattered. You're likely going to need surgery and won't be up and about for a good while. You need to stay nice and still until the ambulance gets here. Now for the great news."

Kevin lifted his eyebrows. "There's great news?"

Matt grinned and held up a syringe. "This is morphine."

* * *

Light flashed three times. Sakura zoomed in to see Finster lying where the sniper had been. He drew a line across his throat, then positioned himself to draw down on the truck.

Sakura bolted down the slope, feet plunging into the scree under the snow in a series of tiny avalanches. She hit the road at a full sprint and whirled around as she skidded to the front of the truck. Her thigh burned, and red wetness spread across her jeans.

The men inside freaked, the driver diving out of sight, the passenger clutching for a pistol on the dash. She pulled the trigger twice, sending two three-round bursts through the windshield into his center of mass. He twitched and jerked, but Sakura yelled her next command before his dead body had a chance to settle.

"Hands up! Now!" She punctuated the command with a burst into the radiator.

The driver's hands shot up to the roof of the cab.

"Keep them there. I will not warning shoot." She limped up to the side, sneering around clenched teeth. "Now with your right hand you will open the door and step out. Your hands will be in sight at all times."

He got out, a scruffy man in his twenties, eyes wide, cheek spattered with his companion's blood. All color had drained from his face.

"Who are you?" A tickle worked its way down her leg, warm blood trickling down to her ankle and into her sock. She kept the weapon trained on the driver.

He puffed up his chest. "I don't answer to vermin."

An engine revved behind her, and tires skittered across gravel. She stepped back and turned to keep the scruffy man and the approaching vehicle in view, and a shot rang out.

The man twisted and fell to the side, his hand still on the pistol tucked into the back of his jeans.

White-knuckled, Pastor Joe gripped the wheel with both hands, careening to a stop in front of the body. He gaped out the window at her leg. "You've been shot!"

Sakura looked down at the dark stain spreading across her thigh, then back up at the idiot. "And you were instructed to stay back and cover our retreat! Now give me the keys."

"I heard gun—"

She choked up the REC-7 and drew a bead on his face. "Give me the keys. Now."

He yanked the keys from the ignition and held them out. She snatched them from his outstretched hand and lowered the weapon just as Jed Callaway rounded the corner below, slogging up the snowy road with his AR-15 cradled to his chest. She shoved the keys in her pocket and limped into the maintenance shed.

The generator sat idle but intact. A minute's tinkering got it running. Ten seconds later her phone beeped, showing full service, so she stepped out, closed and re-locked the door.

Finster had dragged the other body down from his roost, a ragged red line sliced across his neck. They exchanged nods, then Sakura sat on the snow-covered concrete. She pulled out a knife and sliced through her jeans with one expert move.

Her trip down the slope had shifted the bandage and dislodged the gauze, exposing several stitches that had separated in her exertions. It bled more than it should, but not arterial—with a little care she'd be fine. She re-wrapped the bandage, cinched it tight, and looked up.

They'd laid the bodies out in a line. Callaway held three wallets, Finster arranged their weapons on the hood of Callaway's truck, and Pastor Joe sat behind the wheel, hands on at ten and two, face white.

Finster spat. "Sorry about that. I figured you wanted that one alive, but with your back half-turned and him going for that pea shooter, I figured safe's better than sorry."

"You made the right call." She glared at Joe. "His fault, and Callaway's for letting him get the keys, but not yours."

Jed looked from the weapons to Sakura to the dead men. "What now?"

"I'll report their identities and leave two of you here to guard the tower from further incursion. The pastor will come with me back to town."

Joe opened the door and threw up, the messy splatter darkening the snow.

* * *

Jason Rees ploughed St. Martin's utility van through the snow-covered streets and thanked the Lord the snow had finally stopped. His head swam with fatigue and the last vestiges of withdrawal, and most of all with the vision that had stopped him cold in mid-sermon.

Monica slept in a bed of giant brambles, the thorns piercing angry red welts through her skin. She thrashed and they tightened, lifting her into the air, still unconscious. Beneath her Adam sat in a small ring of bare Earth surrounded by feathers of ice, just beginning to melt under a black sun. Just outside the feathers, black wormlike forms writhed and slithered through and over the ground, probing forward and shying back just before contact.

He'd walked out, the ceremony unfinished, and drove south without explanation. He still had none, other than that the love of his life needed him.

Across the state line he turned on the radio, and caught the news of White Spruce. But despite the gnawing anxiety in his gut, he could drive no faster than conditions allowed.

Chapter 9

Light drifted in rainbows across the room, a silent lullaby given form. The angel smiled as Monica opened her eyes, stroked her hair and folded her in its wings of ice. She sighed and returned the smile, sinking into the soothing warmth. She knew its face; it looked like her dad, but had her husband's brown eyes—or maybe Adam's—but flecked with brilliant green.

It spoke to her, a million words and none, a swirling vortex of comfort that held promise but no meaning.

She opened her mouth to respond, and water filled her lungs. She jerked upright, coughing and gagging, sloshing cool water over the sides of the tub.

"She's awake!" The female voice came from the hallway, nasal New England vowels like fingernails across a chalkboard. Monica gagged and took stock of the tiny bathroom, just large enough to fit a tub, toilet, and sink, all in white as stark as the tile walls.

A wood-framed cross-stitch hung above the toilet. "If it's yellow, let it mellow. If it's brown, flush it down." *Gross.* Water conservation had never been that much of a problem in Tennessee.

A brunette stepped through the door into the tiny bathroom, a teenager with dazzling, golden-brown eyes, her high cheekbones and prominent chin lacquered with too much makeup. She uncrossed her arms, revealing a green T-shirt emblazoned with the words *Division*

By Zero in stark white letters. "You had a close call there. Sorry about the bath. Feeling warmer?"

Monica stood from the almost warm water, snatched a towel from a bar on the wall, and wrapped it around her naked body. "Where's my son?"

The girl turned around while she covered herself. "He's okay. My boyfriend's got him. What were you doing in the woods all alone, and after all this snow?"

"I'd like to see him, please."

"Sure. I got you some clothes that should fit now that you're all warmed up. Come on downstairs and we'll get you some tea. You hungry?" She turned around and smiled with dazzling white Hollywood teeth.

The gnawing pit in Monica's stomach weakened her knees. She nodded.

"I'll make you something and meet you downstairs. Take your time."

She dried off, threw on jeans and a man's T-shirt too big by half, and walked out of the bathroom on wobbly legs. She passed a bedroom where a pair of men played cards on a king-sized bed. They ignored her as she walked by, and the hair rose on the back of her neck.

Curved wooden stairs led to a large living room complete with a stone fireplace, the workmanship closer to the American Revolution than the new millennium. The girl sat on a large couch, a gaudy 70's throwback of stylized flowers on faded ecru. On the coffee table in front of her sat a tea tray with two cups and a steaming bowl of grits with butter and brown sugar. Saliva sprang unbidden to her mouth.

"Sit, please." The girl patted the cushion next to her.

Monica sat and shoveled a spoonful down as the girl poured the tea. It burned her mouth, but she didn't care. She used the scalding tea to wash down gulps of hot grits, buttery and too sweet, and didn't stop until she'd finished both. She leaned back, still hungry, and gave her host a thin smile.

"Thank you so much. Now I'd like to see my son, please."

"In a minute." The girl turned so that they almost faced one another. "What were you doing way out there in the woods? Seems a weird place to be during a travel ban."

Monica closed her eyes a moment at the memories, then forced them open, still woozy from the mental and physical trauma. "You heard about the fires in White Spruce?"

She nodded.

"Well some men, terrorists or something, they come looking for me." She held up a finger to forestall the interruption. "They killed my friends, but I managed to hurt one of them and run with my boy."

"So after you hurt this man, you just ran off into the woods? We found you eleven miles from White Spruce."

"Eleven miles? That's not . . . it couldn't have been. I walked, but no way it was that far. Now if you don't mind, I'd like to see my son now."

"Hold on a minute. I'm still trying to figure out if we need to call Child Protection."

"Child Protection?"

"We can't be sure it's your child. Maybe you took him, and that's why you were running through the woods."

"You're out of—" Monica stopped and studied the girl, scrutinized her as Sifu taught her to analyze an opponent. She seemed relaxed at first blush but kept her hands in front of her, her weight shifted toward the front of the couch, ready to strike or run. Even through a haze of shock and hypothermia, Monica recognized the potential for violent action. "Honey, I don't see my son right quick you're going to need a mortician."

The girl patted her hand, and a tingly electric jitter shot up her arm. "We already need one. That man you hurt, he suffocated when you crushed his throat. His name was Ben. Ben Carpenter. He kept bees, ran a store. He'll never see his wife again. Never pet his dog. A good man, dead. Because you killed him."

Monica jerked her hand back with too much effort, too slow. A million words in her defense came to mind: they'd killed her friends, attacked her, burned her town. Self-defense. Defense of her son. She shook off the haze, smiled as sweet as tea, licked her lips, and said, "Sweetheart, I'm giving you two seconds to bring me my son, or I'm breaking your twiggy little neck."

The girl's expression didn't change but for a flash of anger in her eyes. "Your devil-spawn's not here, Missus Rowley. For some reason we found him just impossible to cut up, and I thought maybe you could tell us why."

Monica struck, or meant to. She jerked to the side, snarling, and slid down to lay on the couch.

"Shit," the girl muttered, then leaned down to whisper in Monica's ear. "Yeah, that paralytic in your grits acts pretty fast, so you're not going to be able to do much more than talk, and not even that very well. So let's try this again."

The girl shoved the coffee table with her foot, then rolled Monica off the couch and face-down onto the floor.

Monica banged her head and saw stars but couldn't catch herself or even roll over. Blood stained the floor in a widening pool, a cut on her head or maybe a bloody nose. It didn't hurt like it should, more a vague throb than a concussive blow. The girl's weight on her back felt dull, a vague pressure in her lungs.

"What sick, twisted shit did you do to your son?"

Her defiant scream came out as a groan.

"I asked you a question."

Monica's tongue filled her mouth, thick and sloppy. She tried to swear around it, but nothing intelligible came out.

"Answer me, you bitch!"

"Hey," a male voice said, soft and deferential. "How much did you give her?"

"Two pills."

Monica tried to turn her head to see the man, but her neck wouldn't respond. She strained to stand and kill them both, but nothing happened.

He snorted. "Those are for hundred-kilo sows, and you just gave two to an eight-stone girl. She's not answering any questions. We got to go, anyway. Company's coming."

"Stone" meant ten or twenty pounds or something in England, but he didn't sound English. His accent couldn't be more generic, middle America or maybe southern Canadian.

"I'm not done." Monica felt more than heard the petulant pout in the girl's reply.

His voice lost its velvet glove. "You gave her too much. She won't feel anything anyway, and she won't be able to talk. C'mon. They just called Homeland Security. It's run time."

The girl sighed. "Car thick, you don't *always* have to ball so hard."

Monica tried to make sense of that, but couldn't. She tried to open her eyes, realized she'd closed them, and couldn't do anything about it.

"They'll take care of her. C'mon. Let's go."

"Car thick—"

"Now."

The pressure lifted from Monica's chest. Her next breath came slower, and the next slower still. The world hazed white in the memory of beating wings.

* * *

Matt's helmet beeped as he bolted down the ATV tracks through the woods, chewing up the miles at a dead sprint, his boots sucking mud with every step. "Rowley. Go ahead."

"Service is restored," Sakura said. "Three casualties, no friendlies." She briefed him on the operation as he ran.

"Thank you. Janet?"

"I read you. Nice to have you back, go ahead."

"We have multiple hostiles active in the White Spruce area. At least three civilian casualties, probably more. Suspected Humans for Humanity terrorist cell, heavily armed with personal weapons, RPGs and explosives. Suicide bombing already in evidence. Requesting DHS counterterrorism support, and right now wouldn't be too soon."

"Wow. Sounds like you kids are having fun. You running? Go ahead."

"They have Monica and Adam. I'm tracking suspects through the woods a few miles south of town. If the uplink's working route GPS to my helmet. And get me that backup!"

"Roger. Requesting support."

He ran another several miles through peaceful, white forest, every step a fight against the giant globs of mud that adhered to his boots. He spooked a doe that ran off, white tail bouncing through the thickets, and in the distance a fox stalked a rabbit through the snow. Worry destroyed any enjoyment he might have gotten from the peaceful scene.

The GPS icon popped up on his HUD, so he brought up the map as an overlay.

"Do we have real-time satellite on this position?"

"In Tennessee?" Janet asked. "Not a chance. I can put in a request, but it'll probably have to go through a judge. It'd be a few days, if ever."

"Forget it. Call Arnold. See if you can't scramble a surveillance drone."

"Who the fuck is Arnold?"

"Air Force base, Janet. Southern Tennessee?"

She sighed. "Arnold AFB hasn't had an operable runway since two thousand nine."

"Then call somewhere else, dammit!"

"Yeah, okay. Request for aerial reconnaissance up-going. Hold your nuts."

An enormous farmhouse came into view, red brick surrounded by acres of lawn, with a hundred yards of clear field in every direction. The ATV tracks led to a huge barn, red paint faded and peeled from years of neglect. Matt stopped at the wood line, stepping sideways to deny a clean shot.

"Janet, can you see this?"

"Uplink's clear, go ahead."

"See what you can figure out about this house, please."

"Give me a minute. I'm on hold with the Air Force."

* * *

"Wake up, bitch."

Cruel man hands shook her, grabbed her by the hair and slapped her. Monica heard it, but didn't feel more than a dull heat. She tried to speak around a thick tongue, tried to gasp for water or something, anything to drink. Her throat screamed for relief, but nothing came out her mouth. He hauled her onto the coffee table, sweeping away the tea tray and bowl with her flopping limbs.

He slapped her again, then lifted her head by her hair, so she could see the pistol he held in her face. He put it in her mouth and slid it in and out. She tasted nothing as it passed over her tongue, but she gagged, and retched, and tried to squirm and scream and scratch his eyes but instead just lay there.

"You like that, do you? You slut. You fucking whore. They said to get rid of you, but use you first. I think you've got some oomph left in you."

He dropped her head to the table and jammed the gun in her mouth hard, one hand wandering to his waist to unzip his pants. He squirmed out of them, exposing stained white underwear stretched to capacity by his erection, a wet spot already formed in his excitement.

"See her looking?" someone said behind her. "She really wants it."

"Yeah, you want this, you fucking slut?" He looked over her shoulder and laughed. "Yeah, boys, keep your pants on until it's your turn. Nobody needs to see that."

He let go of the pistol, leaving it in her mouth, and moved behind her.

She moaned around the gun as her belt came off. She willed her hands to move, to grab the gun and shoot his pathetic little balls off. Nothing happened.

His arms came around her waist, and she heard rather than felt her zipper come down. As he tugged her jeans off, she closed her eyes and tried to pray.

Men cheered and joked as a dull pressure pierced her. Her body rocked, seeding a nauseous pit deep in her stomach. She felt nothing else, but as he grunted and gasped, her thoughts fell to the pit, to darkness and death and murder and a lake of unending fire.

Lost somewhere in madness, Monica screamed, but her mouth stayed silent around the pistol.

* * *

The psychic shriek sent white tendrils of thought worming through Matt's mind, heard without being heard, overwhelming the whispers in a deafening silence. A demon of twisted thorns and cruel, slivered nails raked and clawed at his wife, cackling in glee at each line of blood, each strip of flesh. She writhed as it took her, filling her with darkness and loss and unending pain.

Matt bolted for the house, screaming, carried forward on wings of silvery ice, all thoughts of stealth incinerated in white-hot wrath.

He lurched as something impacted his shoulder. The AA-12 fell from his grip. He spun to the right as the whispers warned him of a second shot. He drew his pistol left-handed and fired four shots at the upstairs window to force his assailant to take cover.

He dropped his visor and cleared the porch in one step.

The bay window exploded as he leapt through. He raised the

pistol and fired as his feet hit the floor. Two shots took the man in the corner, another two at the men in line behind his wife, pants around their ankles, dicks hard in their hands. Others scattered.

The rapist stopped, kneeling in mid-pump, his white ass between Monica's slack legs. Matt wrapped his left arm around the man's neck, pulled him up and backward, and grabbed his face with his right hand.

He saw and refused to see Monica, face down, shirt ripped upward to expose her bra, eyes glazed, drool-covered pistol in her mouth.

As Matt's fingers entered her rapist's mouth the man bit down. Matt jammed them deeper into the slimy, writhing heat, and punched his thumb up through the underside of the man's jaw. Hot blood streamed down Matt's wrist, mingling with that from his shoulder.

He pulled, a steady pressure that would not relent. Muscles tore. Skin fissured, split apart with a soggy wet rip, like splitting a rotten log. The jaw shifted outward, gnashing teeth scraping the skin from his fingers. The man shrieked. His jaw came free in a spray of hot crimson mess and an inarticulate, gurgling choke. Matt jammed the separated lower jaw into the man's naked abdomen, and the smell of hot shit filled the room.

He twisted and brought the man down, punching the bone and his fist through the rapist's guts and the pine board floor beneath. He stood, fist dripping gore, and glared at the young bottle-blonde staring slack-jawed in the doorway. Her pistol clattered to the floor, and urine leaked down her leg under her shorts.

Janet's voice broke through his fugue. "I've cut your helmet camera, Matt. Do what you've got to do."

The whispers laughed and tittered and urged him to tear the girl limb from limb. Young, no more than twenty. Pretty, in a girl-next-door sort of way, with teeth not quite perfect. The white tendrils of thought snaked through his soul, the voices of his loved ones pleading mercy, but he drowned them in seething rage. They surfaced and clambered for purchase, rising against the gale of hatred.

Matt took a deep breath. And a step forward.

Another breath. Another step.

And another. He stood inches from her, staring through the

visor at the tears streaming down her face.

She blubbered, then, blubbered and pleaded and the white tendrils thickened and grew bold, defying the maelstrom of whispers. "Please don't hurt me, mister. Please."

He hesitated. The whispers howled their rage.

"Please don't. We didn't mean anything by it."

The whispers shrieked their triumph as his helmet crushed the girl's skull against the doorframe. Her face crumbled and he pulled back enough to let her body fall.

He turned at a noise from the stairs. Halfway up a man pointed a Glock at Matt's chest. He took the steps three at a time, grunting as his armor solidified around the center of mass shots. Arms spread, he wrapped his assailant in a bear hug, shattering bone as he crushed the shooter to his chest. Vomited blood washed his visor in thick red streaks. He threw the body to the side and vaulted up to the landing.

He kicked in the bedroom door. A man scrambled halfway out the window, legs kicking as he tried to fit his gut out of too small an opening, a rifle leaning against the bookcase. Matt grabbed the sill and slammed it hard enough to shatter the glass and his victim's spine. He ignored the screams, picked up the discarded rifle, and fired at both men fleeing across the lawn. They fell, squirming and screaming, bloody guts sprayed out on the snow.

The man lodged in the window tried to turn, tried to reposition. Matt leaned out the window and placed the muzzle against the back of his head.

"Please! I have a daughter."

He pulled the trigger, blowing teeth and blood down into the snow.

Matt cleared the empty master bath and bedroom, then stalked down the steps and past his wife, her eyes not even following as he pulled the pistol from her mouth, emptied it and tossed it to the floor. The kitchen and guest bedroom lay empty, nobody in closets or under the bed.

The cellar door lock shattered with one kick, and someone cried out in the cool darkness below. The wooden stairs creaked under his weight. He didn't bother with the light.

In the pitch black his enhanced vision separated the hot water heater and furnace from the man cowering behind them, ultraviolet picking out details that infrared couldn't, even while his helmet identified no targets.

Matt found his voice. "Come here."

The man cowered and babbled in sobbing Spanish. He held his pants up one-handed, too panicked by Matt's rampage to even button them.

"I said, 'come here.'"

His pistol fell to the concrete, and he kicked it across the floor to Matt.

"Good enough."

The man screamed as Matt advanced, screamed again as Matt grabbed his nose and tore it from his face. Blood sprayed Matt's chest. He ripped away one ear, then the other, then turned his attention lower.

Outside, Matt left crimson constellations through the white powder, none of it his own. Tracks led behind the barn, to a circular area blasted almost free of snow. Propeller wash. He closed his eyes, blocked out the world, and listened. No vehicles, no motors, no helicopters.

He cleared the barn—nothing but an old, rusted-out combine and stalls filled with long-rotten hay.

The hose on the side of the building gushed frigid water when he turned it on. He sprayed himself, shivering under the cleansing blast. Hot blood sluiced off the hydrophobic fabric covering his armor, clear streaks appeared in the red on his visor. He washed it clean, flexing his shoulder several times as he did so. Satisfied with the returning range of motion, he walked back inside to the living room, careful not to make too much noise.

Monica hadn't moved, but now her eyes tracked him, wide and brimming with tears. Her tongue worked in her mouth, an injured snake squirming in defiance of death.

He took off his helmet and knelt, wincing at the pain in his chest and abdomen, and lifted her, turning her gently to lay her face-up on the couch. He put her panties around her feet, pulled them up, and then tugged on her pants.

Next, he checked her vitals for any signs that whatever they'd given her might kill her. Satisfied, he cradled her and kissed her hair, whispered that they'd never hurt her again.

Some time later, Monica shifted and whispered in his ear.

"I love you, baby."

"I love you, too."

He kissed tears from her eyes and held her.

"Matt, they have our boy. You need to find him."

"He's not here. But you're damned right I'll find him."

A voice from outside interrupted them. "Matt? You in there?" The megaphone didn't quite render Deputy Broadbent's voice unrecognizable.

"Yes," he yelled. "All threats have been neutralized. The building is clear. So is the barn."

The hesitation made Matt smile but not in a way his wife would understand. Or maybe she would.

"All right, hold fire. We're sending someone in."

Sakura stepped in the front door, helmet tucked in her elbow, jeans cut from thigh to ankle, leg a mess of bandages and bloodstains. Behind her Jason Rees held a cloth to his mouth, face drained of all color, gray eyes bugged out of his head.

"Is . . . is she . . . ?"

"She'll be all right." Matt stroked Monica's hair without taking his eyes from his former friend.

Sakura looked at the jawless man, naked from the waist down, then at Monica, and then at Matt. Her eyes drifted over the other bodies, pantsless and otherwise, then back to him. She gave a tiny bow of respect and walked out, yelling orders to the deputies and troopers.

Jason rushed forward, knelt in the bloody muck slicking the floor, and put his hand on Monica's head. He murmured prayers in Latin, eyes closed, and Matt let the words wash over them both.

When he'd finished Jason used his thumb to draw a cross on her forehead, then turned his attention to Matt. "I started driving as soon as I heard about the fires. Got into town a couple hours ago. I'm sorry I wasn't here."

Matt looked around at the carnage, absorbed the stench into and through him, and then met Jason's eyes. "This wasn't your kind of job. If you'd been with her, you'd be dead. But I need to go, and she'll be okay. Thank you for coming."

"Sir," a man said from the door, "you can't be in a crime scene."

Jason stood, absently wiping his hands on his long, black coat, ignoring or ignorant of the filth clinging to the edges. "I'm authorized—"

"—to get Mr. Rowley to stand down, which he has. Now this is a crime scene, so you need to go."

Jason looked at Monica, then Matt. "I'll be outside when you need me."

Matt watched him go, and as Jason disappeared out the door the whispers finally ceased their murderous clamor. He slid his arms under his wife and lifted her, cradling her head, then carried her out into the snow. She just managed to rest a hand on his forearm, and her eyes rolled back into her head.

The M-ATV towered next to four SUV's and a county pickup truck. Cory leaned against the huge vehicle, arms crossed, eyes downcast. Matt approached, Monica still in his arms, and bowed his head.

"Cory. I'm so sorry."

Cory looked from Monica to Matt with bloodshot eyes. "Yeah. I'm glad she's okay, man." He opened the suicide doors so Matt could set Monica down in the comparative warmth. Cory wadded up someone's coat for a pillow, and Matt placed her on the cold steel floor as gently as possible.

Ted hopped down from the driver's seat, waddled over, and plopped down against Monica's side, looking at Matt with his sad eyes.

Matt scratched the top of his head then pulled back, closed the doors and grabbed Cory's shoulder. "When the ambulance gets here, make sure they give her a full check. I don't know what those assholes gave her, but I killed some of them mid . . . mid-rape."

"Will do."

They stood in silence a while, watching the police ring the house and yard in crime scene tape, scurrying around the buildings without going inside, waiting for a detective or the crime lab or someone, anyone else, to do what needed to be done.

"Kevin's going to make it," Cory said.

"Good." Matt knew, but no matter how small, he didn't want to take anything away from Cory at this point. "He's a good man."

"Did you . . . did you get the guys who . . . did this?"

"Most. Somebody got away and took my boy."

Cory looked up to the sky. "Jesus, man, can this get any worse? What are you going to do?"

"I'm going to save him. And I'm going to kill them."

Chapter 10

Dressed in a gray suit and yellow tie, Matt knocked on the door to the shabby Manhattan brownstone and waited. The door cracked open to the length of the security chain, and the warm tang of onions and garlic wafted out of the apartment.

The olive-skinned young man who answered kept his blue eyes on Matt's face. "Yes?"

"Ellery Wong?"

His eyes darted up and down the street. "Who wants to know?"

Matt had no badge to show, so he held up a picture of Marie Thill. "Can I ask you a few questions about this girl?"

He dropped his eyes. "I'm sorry, I don't know who that is."

Matt put his foot in the door. "That's an odd thing to say about your fiancée."

"Ex-fiancée," he snapped. Then he sighed. "Yeah, all right, but I got breakfast on the stove, so make it snappy. What do you want to know?"

"This is going to be longer than snappy. May I come in?"

"Are you a cop?"

"No."

"Legit?"

"I'm not a cop, and I don't give a shit what drugs you have in there."

He looked up and down the street—not that he'd be able to see much through the crack and around Matt—undid the chain and opened the door. Matt stepped inside the apartment and made no comment on the stacks of shit-brown, plastic-wrapped bricks on the coffee table, marijuana by the look of it.

Ellery cut right, into the kitchen, where he had peppers, onions, and garlic in a cast iron pan on the stove. "You want some eggs or something, man? Easy enough to double the recipe."

"It's Matt. And I already ate, so just whatever you can tell me about Marie."

"All right, Matt, where do you want me to start? She's a crazy bitch with a hot temper, likes bad guys, big dicks, and fast cars. She fucks like she fights, and a couple years in the bullshit's piled so high you can't take it anymore." He cracked three eggs into the pan, tossed the shells eight feet into the open garbage, and whisked.

Matt leaned against the doorframe, sliding his hand between the refrigerator and the wall, pushing the magnetic bug as far back as he could. "Current address?"

"Shit, I don't know, man. I've gone out of my way to not know." He sprinkled a big handful of cheddar cheese over the congealing mass in the pan. "She used to have a place in Boston but sold it when her mom died last year. Could be anywhere."

"If you were going to get a hold of her, what would you do?"

"Why the fuck would I want to get a hold of her?" He dumped the scrambled eggs on a plate, turned off the stove, and carried his breakfast to a small table in the corner. "Sure you don't want some?"

Matt waved him off, so he tucked in with a bottle of hot sauce.

A few bites in he looked up, as if remembering Matt's presence. "So, man, yeah, she started hanging with some uppity bitches, then dropped off the planet when her mom died. Fucking Houdini, you know?"

"You have names?"

"Of Houdini?"

"Of the uppity bitches."

He grinned. "Nah, man. Just a bunch of groupies, chasing dick at drag races and street fights." He took another fork full, smothered it in hot sauce, and shoved it in his mouth. "So she's in some deep shit, am I right?"

"She's dead."

Ellery dropped his fork, stared at his eggs. "Aw, fuck. And you want to find who killed her? Not that I'm saying someone killed her—"

"I know who killed her." He relived the crunch as his helmet caved in her skull. "I want to know who she was working with. Do you have contact information for next of kin?"

He pushed his plate away, half-eaten. "Who killed her, man?"

"I did."

Ellery froze.

"She watched as a line of men raped my wife, then told me it wasn't personal."

He exhaled, long and low. "That's fucked up."

"Next of kin?"

"She didn't have any, not that she ever talked about. Her mom left her a bunch of money, but she never even knew the sperm donor. No siblings, no aunts or uncles. Pretty lonely. What tied her up in that shit?"

"She got involved with some bad people. Did she . . . was she associating with anyone who might have criminal connections? Maybe a lot of money?"

He held up his hands. "I don't know, man, she wasn't hurting, and some of those racers pour serious bank into their cars. Got to get it from somewhere, you know?"

"Criminal connections?"

"Well, racing and fighting aren't legal, and all kinds of bookmaking goes on. Good place to distribute, too, if you got cover. Not that I know, right?" He looked down at his lap and then back up at Matt. "Wouldn't surprise me if the gangstas and gangsters are running protection, taking their piece."

"Anything else?"

He sagged, a half-collapse deeper into his chair. "Nah, man. What a thing."

Matt produced one of his new business cards and put it on the table, pinning it there with his index finger covering the Department of Homeland Security logo. "You think of anything, please call me."

As he headed for the door, Ellery spoke. "Holy shit, man, you said you weren't a cop!"

Matt paused. "I'm not, and like I said, I don't care about your dealing. But I'm going to find these people, and when I do I'm going to burn everyone who helped them to the ground. Call me if you think of something."

He left the apartment and waited until he'd walked around the corner to put in his ear bud. "What have we got?"

"Nothing yet," Janet said. "No calls, no conversations, no nothing."

"Dammit, these guys are laying low."

"We'll find them."

* * *

"Well?" Matt scanned the bank of monitors and tried not to grind his teeth.

Sakura pulled up a string of police records and photos. "Operational security is tight, but several of the deceased were either current or past Humans for Humanity members or had donated to political action committees friendly to Humans for Humanity. Look at this."

The monitor showed video of a drag race, nighttime, some city Matt didn't recognize. A chopped Bentley screamed past the camera, followed by a late-model Ferrari. Flags waved, the crowd went berserk. Amidst the cheering, money exchanged hands, and a trio of fire dancers moved out onto the street, whirling flaming balls on metal chains, the light illuminating their distinct lack of modest attire.

Sakura paused the feed and zoomed in, running a filter to compensate for the low-quality cell phone video. "Subject on the right is Onnoleigh Sweetman, middle girl is Marie Thill."

"Who's on the right?"

"We don't know," Janet said. "Brown hair, between five-five and five-eight, one-ten-ish. She's cute, and younger, but no hits on facial recognition. Still, it's weird."

"What's that?" Matt asked.

"These young girls getting tied up in something this dark. It's not something you'd expect."

Sakura snorted, but Janet pressed on.

"Not in American culture, not girls with money. Sure, sometimes they might court the bad boys, but this . . . this speaks 'man' to me."

"What does that mean?" Sakura zoomed out, scanning the crowd as Janet answered.

"It's . . . loud. The fire, the murders, the kidnapping. Women—American women—we expect them to be more subtle, more in the background. Especially the rich kids. Someone got to these girls, made them this way."

Matt grunted. "So Sweetman and Thill both inherited a good chunk of money in the past year, and both gave to H4H. What say we try to dig up any other trust fund girls with sympathies?"

Janet spoke without taking her eyes from the screen. "It's a start."

* * *

Matt put his keys on the kitchen counter, bent down to scratch Ted on the forehead, and joined Jason Rees on the couch.

He kept his voice low. "How is she?"

"She slept most of the day, ate a little. Cried herself to sleep on the couch."

"And you?"

Jason rubbed his eyes. "I'm here, man. You guys have my support, whatever you need."

"And what you saw?"

They locked eyes. "I can't say I condone it. But I can't say I don't."

Matt gave him a curt nod. "Thanks, padre. Has she talked, yet? About any of it?"

Jason nodded. "Yeah. We talked a long while. She's terrified and heartsick and angry, so angry. She . . . said she envies you."

Matt sat back. "What do you mean?"

"She heard you, saw you, kill those men. Take vengeance—no, she called it retribution. She wanted to hurt them so bad, and you got to. She said their screams gave her comfort, and she's ashamed and grateful at the same time."

Matt hadn't given them a second thought. "They needed to die."

"All of them?"

"Yup. Every goddamned one. And you're not my shrink, and this ain't your couch."

Jason chuckled. "Thank the good Lord for that. I'm still having nightmares from what I saw in that room. I can't quite wrap my mind around that level of viciousness, from either end of it. I don't know how to help someone cope with doing something like that."

"Who says I need to cope?"

"I'm just talking, here. Don't get defensive."

"If I get defensive you'll know. Probably from the impact of your face on the driveway."

Jason looked at Matt, then the driveway, then rolled his eyes back at Matt. "Yeah, yeah, tough guy, I like my teeth where they are. So what's next?"

"Any word?"

They both turned at Monica's haggard voice. She leaned against the doorframe in her pajamas, huge bags under puffy, red eyes, her hair a tangled mess, clutching Adam's stuffed ostrich to her chest like a long-lost talisman.

"We have some leads, baby. We'll find him."

"They can't hurt him," she said.

"If they do—"

"No." She shuddered and rubbed her arms. "They can't. The girl, not Marie, the other one, she said so. They wanted to cut him, hurt him, said they couldn't. She called him devil-spawn, tried to get out of me why, but drugged me too good for it."

Jason narrowed his eyes at Matt. "That doesn't make sense."

"I know," Monica replied. "But I hope it's true. I think he has an angel watching him, maybe watching me a little, too."

Matt locked eyes with her. "Wings of ice."

"No shit, baby. You, too?"

"I don't know how to explain it. When I ran to the house I felt something driving me forward, bringing me to you. It tried to stop me . . . stop me from killing those men. But I didn't listen, didn't want to listen."

Jason turned to Monica. "Tell him about the mugger."

She sat next to Matt, winced at his hand on her knee. He withdrew it, but she grabbed it and put it back with a defiant glare at nothing in particular. "Those men that came after Adam and me before, after kung fu. Adam just touched the guy and he went all wishy-washy, staring off into space, a half-smile on his lips. I never seen anything like it."

She stopped Matt with an upraised finger. "And I saw that same angel in the woods, lying there with Adam, and again when I woke up in the house. He kept me safe, kept me from freezing, brought me out of harm's way much as he could."

They both looked at Jason.

"All right, Father Rees," she said. "Angels and ice. Enlighten us."

Jason dropped his head into his hands, palms against his forehead. "All I've got is Dante, and that's not something you want to hear."

Monica reached over and poked him in the chest. "What's Dante say?"

"That in the ninth circle of hell, Satan is trapped in Cocytus, a lake of eternal ice, and that as he tries to escape, the beating of his wings blasts everything in eternal cold winds, creating a million million frozen cells for those who betray and commit treason."

"My boy's angel saved me. He's no Satan."

Jason looked at her over his fingers, hands stretching his lower eyelids down, exposing the red flesh beneath. "I didn't say he was. And it doesn't fit anyway. Lucifer doesn't have wings of ice."

"Besides," Matt said, "Dante's the middle ages, right? That's way too new for all this stuff. We're talking Old Testament here."

Jason frowned. "Older."

Monica leaned into Matt, resting her head on his shoulder. "So what's it all mean, baby?"

Jason leaned down and rubbed Ted's belly. "It means your boy is very special, but we don't know how or why."

* * *

Janet smashed a fresh stick of cinnamon gum between her teeth and pulled up another dossier. These H4H assholes came from all walks of life, though knowing what she knew she felt hard pressed to blame them for their attitudes. Religious psychotics or not, when it came down to brass tacks on some level they had been, in fact, right about the dangers of Gerstner Augmentation. Right down to the demonic influence.

I wonder what fanatics do when their enemy finally falls? If Matt died they'd have won, wholly, eliminated their enemies root and stem, at least until her brother—

She jerked a hand to her nose. It came away streaked with blood.

"Shit."

She plugged her nostrils and hurried to the bathroom, ignoring the concerned looks and comments from the DHS employees—strangers all—who had taken over most of the ICAP Tennessee offices in the name of the Special Threats Bureau. A spasm twisted her as she kicked the door closed and locked it.

A look in the mirror told her too much. Bloodshot eyes stared back at her, blazing bright green. She coughed and leaned over the sink as the Jade Cross tattoo on her back smoked, filling the room with the delicious, sickening aroma of cooking meat.

"No," she snarled. "Not here. Not now."

In response, black wings, the flesh cracked and bleeding from a thousand pus-filled wounds, unfolded from her reflection.

Her hand clutched the cross at her throat, and through bloody phlegm she choked out words, ancient spells and abjurations that bound her spirit to her body, cemented the connection, and drove out intruders.

Dawkins wailed in her mind, a pitiful, hopeless cry of starving despair, begging for succor, mercy, basic human warmth.

"No, brother. Not this way. I am not the vessel of your return."

A shard of jade thought wracked her body, slammed her against the stall door. In the mirror, ropy tendrils of hot red blood streamed from her eyes, nose, and mouth, battered at the mirror, writhed across the surface, seeking cracks.

"Your time will come, brother, but it is not now, and it will not be me." A sob escaped her, and she crushed mercy, empathy, anything that might bind them closer. "No. I abjure you. By the blood we share and the eternal compact, I abjure you. I abjure you, I abjure you, I abjure you. By blood and pain I abjure you. You will never enter this way."

In the mirror her reflection shrieked and lunged, clawing at the glass as it turned gray-brown and crumbled to dust.

Janet closed her eyes, then opened them. A normal reflection stared back at her, a spot of blood under her nostrils, dress rumpled. She cleaned up with a brown paper towel off the roll, touched up her makeup, adjusted her clothes, and walked back to her office.

A DHS flunky in a suit, cute in a geeky Jew-fro sort of way, cut her off at the door.

"Hey, Miss LaLonde, uh, Janet. I, um, was wondering if you were free on Friday?"

She drew a fake green fingernail down his jawline, leaned in and put her lips to his ear. "Oh, I am. And I'm still going to be. Now get the fuck out of my way before I cut your balls off."

He flushed and stepped to the side, hand rising to his ear. "I'm sorry."

She stepped into her office and turned, his eyes not quite leaving her ass fast enough. "I appreciate the thought, buddy, but I don't date work. Ever."

She slammed the door in his face, sank down to the floor,

covered her face with her hands, and bawled.

* * *

Matt opened his eyes and groped for the ringing phone. Monica shifted, her tiny form huddled in a fetal position against his side. He kissed her neck as he brought the phone to his ear.

"Rowley."

"Hey, it's Janet. I just got a call from Ronald Kellett, president of Humans for Humanity. He wants to meet."

Matt rolled over and stood. "Did he say why?"

"Extensively. Seems he's keenly interested in distancing his organization from the events in White Spruce, says he might have a lead you'll find useful."

He grunted. "All we've got so far is circumstantial, but if it quacks like a duck . . . ."

"Yeah, he sounded pretty nervous. No bluster, no threats, no squadron of lawyers. He wants to meet 'man to man' and 'hash out what this is all about,' quote-unquote."

"Man to man. So I should sic Sakura on him?"

"That'd teach him. Or kill him."

Monica stared up at him, dark eyes glinting in the moonlight from the window.

"Yeah. Set it up."

"Your chopper leaves at oh-eight-hundred."

Chapter 11

The Humans for Humanity corporate offices annex to the Martonville megachurch complex would have been impressive anywhere but in the shadow of the enormous modern cathedral that dominated acres of parking lot. The massive edifice could give any NFL stadium a run for its money and took in far more on a yearly basis, tax free.

As their government sedan pulled up to the marble steps, Sakura checked her pistol one last time.

Matt tried not to chuckle. "You really think that's necessary?"

"Could be a trap."

"They'd have to be awfully stupid to invite us here into a trap. DHS knows we're here, so if anything happened to us they'd all go to jail."

She holstered the weapon. "You're supposed to be smart, on paper anyway, but you expect religious zealots to act with reason."

"There is that." He pulled his Glock from the glove box and holstered it at his waist. For the meeting they'd both chosen jeans and black ICAP T-shirts, flaunting instead of hiding what H4H hated so much. He grabbed the manila folder off the back seat. "Okay, let's go."

They got out simultaneously. Matt slowed his ascent to accommodate Sakura's limp, which had improved but not as far as it would have if she'd let it heal without stressing it.

A large black man in a light gray suit eyed them up and down as they approached the door, his muscles stretching the fabric beyond what the tailor would recommend. His deep bass voice resonated across the open space. "You'll have to leave your guns."

Sakura crossed her arms in a parody of his stance. "We're federal officers and invited. We're keeping the weapons."

He moved his hands to his hips, puffed up his enormous chest a little bit more. "I'm sorry, then, you'll have to leave."

The door opened and gray-haired Ronald Kellett stepped out. Tall, clean-shaven, thin and dapper in a thousand-dollar suit, he smiled and extended his well-manicured hand. "Ronald Kellett. You must be Isuji and Matt." His accent mingled British English and Texan in a blur of cultural paradigms.

Matt shook. Sakura kept her arms crossed and frowned at his offered hand.

Kellett looked from his hand to Sakura. His smile never faltered as he reached for the door handle. "Well, if you would, right this way."

They followed him down a hallway more Vatican than central Texas, with ornate statues, biblical paintings in gilded frames, and a plush carpet in royal purple. He turned left, past a dozen rooms—doors closed—into an office fit for a banana republic dictator, complete with a giant painting of the office's occupant above the oversized mahogany desk.

Whispers slithered through Matt's mind, insidious and seductive, flayed skin and eyes crushed to jelly and bones cracked to suck the sweet marrow within. He sat in a giant, cushioned chair and accepted a glass of ice water—with coaster—from a smiling redhead in all white, with perfect teeth and four-inch heels. Sakura declined both the chair and the water, without speaking, and stood just behind the door.

"Mister Rowley, thank you for coming. We seem to have some common ground on this matter that your colleague Janet and I spoke about."

"Commonality, anyway." Matt tossed the folder across the desk. "Of at least twelve people involved in an assault on my town, and the kidnapping of my wife and son, four are confirmed members of Humans for Humanity, two are convicted felons and confirmed members of Humans for Humanity, and six, well, we have no idea who they are and neither does anyone else. Add in the three that attacked the Mayo clinic, you've got two terrorist cells comprising a membership half confirmed to be members of your cult."

Kellett's lips pressed together at the word "cult," and his ears flushed red. "Mister Rowley, I invited you here in a common spirit—"

"Bullshit. After years of agitating violence to your minions, they've finally gotten brave enough to carry it out. You're exposed and don't want your neck on the chopping block. I couldn't be happier at the thought of you hanging from a rope—this is Texas after all—so why don't you cut the crap and tell us what you can about these people so I don't have to drag you in for questioning?"

Face red, Kellett flipped through the folder, separating out three pictures, none of whom had been in the room with Matt's wife, all of whom Janet had tagged as H4H members. "You have to understand that this is an enormous organization, comprising thousands of chapters worldwide. I can hardly be expected to know everybody . . . ."

"But," Matt said, pointing at the papers.

"But, these three men were sanctioned and expelled for fomenting violence against the augmented. You must understand that we do not and never have condoned violence—"

Sakura snorted.

"—and in fact actively counseled those who wished to attempt such. Not only would it have been foolhardy, it would have been unchristian. We are not a violent church, nor a violent people, and while Christ flipped tables and chased people with a whip, he did not direct his physical ire into harming people, and nor will we."

Matt leaned forward and put his elbows on the desk. "Am I

people?"

"Of course." He didn't miss a beat. "We've never hated the augmented, only their augmentations. Which leads to the question of how you maintained yours, when the Almighty stripped all others of theirs."

"No, it doesn't."

Kellett furrowed his brow. "Pardon?"

"It doesn't lead to the question. I don't owe you an explanation and didn't come here to give you one. We came a thousand miles and so far you've told us things a secretary could have confirmed on the phone. So either you cut to the chase, or we're leaving."

He squirmed in his seat. "I need complete assurance that you are not recording this conversation, and that you will not report any of this to the authorities or the press."

Matt held up his hands. "Frisk us."

"Thank you." Kellett pushed a button on his phone.

Sakura rolled her eyes to Matt, and Matt made no attempt to hide his contemptuous snort.

The whispers babbled of the opening door and blood falling like rain from Matt's fist as he obliterated the guard's head.

Instead, Matt stood, placed his pistol on the desk, and turned, hands at his side. The door opened and the bouncer from outside entered. Matt kept his hands raised and suffered a thorough pat-down. He picked up and holstered his weapon before Sakura removed hers. She raised her arms and glared at Matt through the frisk, and while he left no area unaccounted for, for his part the big man remained professional throughout. With a nod to Kellett, the guard left.

Re-seated, Matt raised an eyebrow. "You're on."

"The reason we ejected these men is because they had hired another man, a Mister Peter Salomon, to fire-bomb Jade houses throughout the southern United States. Despite the drug's terrible hold, they sought to punish those poor souls who had fallen to its seduction. We have our differences, Mister Rowley, but I am and always have been a man of peace. We neither supported nor condoned these actions, and cast out these pariahs the moment their actions became known.

"But these are not men of means. They would not have had the wherewithal to hire personal assistants, much less finance a party of anarchy-minded hooligans. No, someone, an ally, backed their scheme and with rather a lot of money for men such as that. It seems likely that whoever hired Mister Salomon before has done so again. Find him, and find their backer."

Sakura looked up from her phone. "Lots of Peter Salomons. We need more."

"He's a bald man, perhaps fifty or so, a little over six feet tall. He runs an import/export business out of New York, a couple miles from LaGuardia."

"This is a front?" Sakura asked.

"It appears to be legitimate, though I confess I haven't investigated it beyond cursory PI work. Our interests extended as far as removing these men from our flock, nothing more."

Matt clucked his tongue. "It didn't occur to you to, say, alert the authorities?"

Kellett frowned. "The authorities did not take a strong view toward our cause, Mr. Rowley. Our ministries have suffered years of harassment by the IRS and the FBI, and both local and state law enforcement showed more interest in investigating us than helping. They saw your organization as a necessary evil and not the abomination it was."

Matt spoke over Sakura's low growl. "Is there anything else you can tell us?"

"I'm afraid not. Remember, this conversation did not happen. Nobody saw you here, and no cameras have recorded your presence. I cannot be seen assisting you, even if it serves a common and very important interest."

Matt stood. "If that's all, we'll find our own way out."

Kellett watched them as they stalked down the hallway, and when they turned the corner they found the bouncer standing at the end of the hall, arms crossed. He held the door for them and watched them until they got in the car and drove off.

Matt called Janet and gave her the information. Twenty minutes later they had tax records and blueprints for Salomon

Imports, a wholesaler and pawn shop with more warehouse than retail space. Salomon kept his nose clean, at least as far as the IRS knew, and did a brisk business in firearms, jewelry, and personal electronics.

Matt noted with some interest that Salomon had no experience with the armed forces, nor with prison. Mediocre scores in high school, a community college degree in accounting, and twelve years doing the books for an upscale restaurant before transitioning into the pawn and import business didn't look like the résumé of a professional mercenary.

"Do you see what I see?"

Sakura nodded. "Something here doesn't add up."

"How about dinner? I'm thinking pasta. In Manhattan."

* * *

New York City shimmered in the evening fog as the Apache touched down atop the MetLife building. Rotors cut through the moisture in a thousand continuous whirlwinds, catching the lights from below and throwing them into a refracted cacophony. The stink hit the moment Matt stepped out of the helicopter, and as it lifted off, the beat of the rotors yielded to the beat of the city—honking horns and the wind-like whoosh of constant traffic.

"Welcome to the Big Apple," Matt said.

"I've been here before." Sakura walked down the steps to where a man in a cheap suit waited, walkie-talkie in one hand, the roof access door held open with the other.

Matt gave a nod to the doorman and followed Sakura to the elevator. They rode down sixty stories, exited the lobby into the crush of late weekday traffic, and walked right into Grand Central Station.

The underground platform smelled of stale urine and body odor, far too hot despite the cool evening, and they suffered through two train arrivals and departures before they managed to catch the third, the press of bodies writhing with impatience every time the doors opened anew. With standing room only, the jerky M train whisked them downtown to 23rd street.

They bounded up the stairs into the cool, comparative darkness, and headed on foot toward Gramercy Park.

Gadadi's defied the stereotypical red checkered tablecloth, with huge windows tinted gold under the orange streetlights revealing a spacious interior more at home in a mansion than a pasta place. Oak tables polished to a mirror shine scattered throughout the dining room under an enormous chandelier, half electric, half candles, just enough light to illuminate without dispersing too many shadows. The bar, a solid slab of lacquered redwood at least eighteen feet long dominated one wall, backed by mirrored shelves holding all manner of liquor. Matt opened the door to a mouthwatering aroma of seafood, garlic, and fresh-baked bread.

The maître d's smile collapsed as he turned to greet them, hands clasping and unclasping in front of his black suit as they approached the podium just inside the door. The short, skinny man's eyes scanned from scuffed sneakers to jeans up to their T-shirts and back down, flicking from detail to detail with a brutal efficiency that Matt expected from professional bodyguards. "I'm sorry, but the gentleman will require a jacket and . . . different . . . trousers. The lady . . . I . . . I don't know where to start."

Matt tried not to smile at the Brooklyn tough-guy accent peeking through the upscale put-down. He opened his mouth but Sakura cut him off.

"He's not a gentleman." Sakura put her hand on the podium and leaned in, her tone cold. "And I'm not a lady."

The five men at the bar, all in suits, turned around on their stools, and the bartender's hands dropped beneath the counter, all traces of joviality gone in an instant.

Matt smiled. "I'm not looking for trouble. I was hoping to talk to Mr. Gadadi and maybe get a bite to eat."

A man at the bar pushed through the back door into the kitchen, but the suit in front of Matt didn't budge. Instead, he made a show of twirling his finger and then pointing out the front door. "If you two aren't looking for trouble, maybe you wants to not look for it someplace else."

"We came a long way." He put his elbows on the podium and leaned in too close. "And that clam sauce smells delicious." Then he waited, aware of but not looking at the other men, whose conversation had stalled in favor of watching the altercation.

The maître d' neither flinched nor blinked, despite Matt looking down at him from eight inches up. The whispers slithered through and around the man's voice as he spoke. "Buddy, you're a thousand miles out of your league, here, so why don't you take your little chink girlfriend and find another place to eat, huh?"

Matt put his hand on Sakura's arm before she could punch the little rat in the face. "Blossom, we're not here to hurt these people."

The men at the bar stood and spread out. Matt assessed their stances and dismissed them as dangerous thugs without any real training, but almost definitely armed with small-caliber pistols.

Sakura jerked free and put her fists on her hips. "Maybe not at first." Her fist snapped forward and stopped a hair's breadth from the little man's nose. She held it there just long enough for him to see it, then returned it to her hip.

He stumbled back, mouth wide. She glowered, but deflated enough for Matt to feel comfortable taking his attention off her.

"I'd advise against racial slurs until we get to know each other better. If you want to keep your head attached or whatever."

The maître d' looked from Sakura's flushed, angry face to Matt's, pointedly avoiding the armed men at the bar. "Who did you say you were again?"

"Homeland Security, Special Threats Bureau. We came a long way to ask Mr. Gadadi a couple of questions about a guy who used to work for him. So if you wouldn't mind . . . ?"

"I've never heard of the Special Threats Bureau."

Matt shrugged. "You're a maître d'. I can't imagine why you would have. Mr. Gadadi, please."

"What kind of questions?"

Matt had to admire the little pipsqueak's composure, even if he wanted to pop his tiny head off. "The kind of questions that Mr. Gadadi might answer. Are you Mr. Gadadi?"

"You got a warrant?"

"I didn't figure I needed one. Because if I, you know, needed one or something, I've got enough probable cause with all the heat in here to get one wired to your FAX while we wait."

Muttering in Japanese, Sakura cut around them and headed for the kitchen door. The four men at the bar moved to intercept, hands going into their jackets. The bartender lifted a shotgun to his shoulder and racked the slide. No shell came out, which meant he'd kept the chamber empty so he could rack it for effect.

Matt hollered to draw their attention and raised his hands. "Hey! I don't want to hurt anybody. I'm just here to talk. Sakura, stand down." He wondered how often she forgot that while an incredible martial artist with stunning reflexes, she possessed a shadow of her former abilities. Standing in the middle of a kill box, arms at her sides but not relaxed, she wouldn't take down more than two of them before they shot her to death.

Still, he couldn't help but admire her courage.

Sakura relaxed, stepped to the side, and sat, hands folded between her knees. The suit nearest the kitchen door waved Matt to him. Bloodthirsty whispers warned him before he stepped forward, so, hands still in the air, he smiled at the little man at the podium.

"You try to club me with that blackjack it'll be the last thing you ever do. You saw how fast she is. I'm so much faster. I've got no beef with anybody here."

The maître d' pulled his hand out of his jacket and placed the blackjack on the podium.

With a nod of approval, Matt turned away and walked over to stand next to Sakura. One hand on the back of her chair, he leaned just enough to look off-guard and raised his eyebrows at the sandy-haired guy who'd waved him over.

The man sized him up. "So you're feds."

Matt nodded. Close enough. "And you guys are damn touchy for happy hour. Just for the record, I don't care who any of you are, or who you work for, or what you're up to. I'm looking for information on a man who used to work here. That's all."

"We don't talk to cops."

Matt held up his hands. "I'm not a cop. She's not a cop. We just have some questions regarding a personal matter."

"And this guy you're looking for, who might he be?"

"Guy who did your books, now runs a pawn shop in Queens."

"Petey Salmonella," someone said.

All eyes turned to a young guy at the bar, his black hair slicked back with too much gel, his suit a little too big. He blushed and looked down, digging his toe into the floorboard.

Matt reached out his hand to the sandy-haired man, pulling his attention away from the kid. "Matt Rowley."

"Chris Gadadi. My uncle owns the place, but he doesn't know nothing you want to know." He jerked his head toward a small side room, with a single table set for twelve. "Lew, get us some clams and bread."

The bartender gave him a thumbs-up as they followed Chris into the private dining room. The other three turned back to the bar. Chris unbuttoned his coat and sat facing the door, leaning on the table to expose a shoulder holster with a small revolver, the mother-of-pearl grip inlayed with polished silver. "What do you want with Salomon?"

Matt pulled two chairs out from the table, then sat in one. After a moment's hesitation Sakura sat with him, seats turned forty-five degrees so they could keep an eye on the door. Nervous energy poured off her, every muscle tense, eyes blazing with promised violence.

Before Matt could answer, Chris spoke again. "You're an Aug."

Matt nodded.

"Nobody's augmented anymore. All that shit stopped working."

Matt's shoulders twitched, the barest hint of a shrug. Chris looked to Sakura, who sat too still for a normal human, then back to Matt. Matt waited. Chris broke first.

"Yeah, all right, your business. So what do you want with Salomon?"

"He's got an interesting résumé."

"You hiring? I don't think he's looking for work right now."

"We're trying to figure out how a restaurant accountant turned import/export tycoon got into hiring out mercenaries and weapons to extremist assholes."

Chris snorted at "tycoon" and his face lost all expression at the mention of mercenaries, his cadence taking on an artificial cast. "We have not been affiliated with Mister Salomon for a number of years, in the restaurant or in any other business venture. I'm afraid I can't help you regarding his current professional exploits."

Lew came in with a giant white platter, loaded with enough linguini in white clam sauce for ten people. Steam rose from the pasta, filling the room with the smell of garlic and clams and heavy cream. Behind him a young man in a stained white chef's coat carried a basket overflowing with crusty baguettes, sliced partway through, steam rising from them in soft clouds.

Matt helped himself to a huge serving and tore off three chunks of bread. Sakura took one slice and put a little sauce on her plate. They both declined the offered bottle of wine in favor of ice water.

Chris took nothing, but sat on the edge of his seat while they ate, drumming his fingers on the table and staring past them.

Sakura tore a bit of crust from her bread, dunked it in the sauce, and held it. "You nervous, Mister Gadadi?"

"Nah." Chris stopped drumming. "I got a lot of energy, and the attention deficit. How's the clams? Best in the world, am I right?"

"Delicious." She popped the bite in her mouth and half-turned so that she could more obviously face the door.

"Well," Matt said around a mouthful of linguini that somehow tasted even better than it smelled, "can you tell me anything about his transition from this job to his current one?"

Chris raised his hands. "Not so much. He made some business contacts—we get a lot of high-profile people in here, you know?—and built his current operation up slow, bringing stuff in and out of the country for people who want it. All on the up and up, totally legit, nothing the cops would even blink at. Started making so much money he quit."

Matt glanced down at his water and blinked, the illusion of a half-melted feather gone as soon as it had appeared. He looked Chris in the eyes. "Is he made?"

Chris chuckled and ripped the end piece off of a loaf. "You watch too many movies. There's no—"

"He hired men to rape and kill my wife and kidnap my son. I'm asking you if I kill him whether I'll have problems with your organization."

Chris leaned back, frowning, and set the bread on the table. "I'm very sorry for your loss."

Matt shook his head. "I interrupted them. My wife is okay, mostly, but I'm looking for my son. He's my only lead."

"You got a picture? I can put some feelers out."

Matt put his fork down, his hunger strangled by grief and rage. "Yeah. Give me a number I'll send you one. Thank you." He dabbed his mouth with the napkin and set it down. "Now what about Salomon?"

Chris grimaced. "The guys like him. He's been a fixture a long time, a lot of us grew up with him." He stole a sauce-soaked chunk of bread off of Sakura's plate and popped it in his mouth. "But he is not under our protection."

Chapter 12

The pawn shop stood on the corner, a squat brick building painted white with iron bars across safety-glass windows and a blazing neon sign stating WE BUY GOLD. Salomon Imports took up the rest of the block, a maze of warehouses and cargo containers stacked six high, all surrounded by a chain link fence topped with razor wire. A guard shack stood next to the only gate, just large enough for one bored-looking attendant half-asleep at the switch.

"You sure?" Sakura asked, her breath billowing white in the night air. "He'll recognize you."

"I'm sure." Matt jerked a thumb at the fence. "You want to play Minotaur while I see if Mister Salomon is in his office?"

"At eight o'clock at night?"

"He's self-employed. These entrepreneurial types work long hours. We'll meet in the middle."

Sakura sighed in a theatrical blast of frosted air, then ducked out of sight. Moments later a shadow slithered through the razor wire, over the top, and down the other side into the darkness. Matt pulled his jacket tighter, stepped over the curb to the pawn shop door and pushed his way inside.

Bright and clean, the interior boasted several rows of glass cases brimming with glistening watches, necklaces, rings, and other jewelry. Electronics lined the left wall, TVs and game consoles, laptops, and tablets. The right side boasted an impressive array of paintball equipment, guns of all sorts, plus helmets, bandoleers, holsters, and camo outfits. Behind the cash register swords hung on a giant pegboard rack, cheap katana knock-offs and huge Scottish broadswords made to imitate movie props.

"Excuse me, sir."

Matt turned to the enormous man perched on a stool next to the front door. His bulging chest and pecs threatened to burst out of the extra-large NY Jets jersey. Light blue eyes stared out from a face bearing not the slightest trace of fat.

"Oh, hi." Matt had seen him from outside, but played clueless. "I'm just looking."

The bouncer grabbed Matt's arm before he could step away. "No weapons permitted in the store."

"Oh." Matt pulled his pistol out with two fingers, flipping it around to hold it by the barrel. "It's loaded." He handed it to the bouncer, who put it in an otherwise-empty cardboard banana box on the counter next to him. "Any others?"

Matt pulled back his jacket and made a pirouette. The bouncer nodded in approval, so Matt wandered along the display cases, trying to do the math on how much merchandise Salomon kept up front. A couple hundred thousand dollars, give or take. Which meant security came in more flavors than "enormous Jets fan."

He approached the cashier, a chubby redhead, mid-forties with black lipstick and clothes to match. "Hey, is Peter here?"

She sized him up, a lingering wander of the eyes that a farmer might use to assess cattle. "Who's asking, beefcake?"

"Matt Rowley. He knows who I am."

She looked at her nails. "Lucky him. You a cop?"

"Only sort of. Can you tell him I'm here, please?"

"He expecting you?" She yawned over his reply.

"Doubt it."

She plucked the phone from its cradle, pushed a button, and stared out into the street. The other end rang four times before a male voice said, "Hello?"

"Yeah, boss, this guy's here to see you. Says his name is Matt something. Rolly. Looks like a cop. Talks like a cop. Says he's only sort of a cop."

Matt didn't catch the reply.

"Yeah, he's standing right here, looks kind of pissed off. No, Pooley's got his gun." Her voice raised in agitation. "Fuck, I don't know." She rolled her eyes at Matt. "Just a sec, I'll ask." She covered the receiver with her hand and raised her eyebrows at him. "You here to kill him?"

"That depends."

She took her hand off the receiver. "He says it depends. Yeah. Yeah. Uh-uh. 'Kay." She dropped the phone in the cradle and smiled up at Matt. "Top of the stairs. Third door on the left."

He turned to go but she stopped him with fingers on his palm. He turned. She leaned forward, plucked a matte black business card from her cleavage, and tucked it in his back pocket. "I'm Patty. And I'm free all weekend."

"Nice to meet you, Patty." He held up his left hand and waggled his ring finger at her.

She pouted.

Matt cut left through the only door up the narrow stairwell to a long hallway that had to bridge between the pawn shop and the warehouse adjacent. He walked down the hall to the third door, the only one open, the only one with a light on.

Peter Salomon sat behind a cheap desk, a .45 pistol disassembled next to his laptop, his fingers on the keyboard. A bronze, bald, spotted egg with prominent ears, his nervous, twitchy eyes betrayed the calm he tried to project with his easy slouch. "Come on in."

Matt stepped in but didn't take the only other chair. The room smelled of old lo mein and cigarettes. A shattered statue leaned in the corner, a white plaster angel in a dozen pieces, her face staring up from the floor by her feet.

"You got some balls, Rowley, but before you do anything stupid let me say a little something." He looked up to the security camera in the back corner, pointed right at the door, right at Matt. "First, that feed goes to the cloud, and the cops already know you're here, so you do anything stupid you're going to jail. Second, I didn't do whatever the fuck you think I did. This business with burning your town, with your wife and kid, I don't know nothing about it."

"But you know about it."

Salomon raised his hands, a plaintive gesture. "Yeah, Kellett and I don't like each other much, but he gave me a heads-up, professional courtesy like, said you might be stopping by. I didn't think you'd make it up from Texas so fast, but hey, you got your kid to worry about, am I right?"

"So you're saying I'm wasting my time." His phone beeped. He looked down, sent a quick reply to Sakura, and put it back in his pocket.

Salomon pulled open a drawer, produced a bottle of scotch, a pair of glasses, and a fat manila folder. "I didn't say that. I got a boy of my own, just went off to college. When I heard you might be showing up I put together a little something for you." He poured them both a couple fingers, apologizing for the lack of ice, while Matt looked through the folder.

Of the sixteen dossiers, Matt separated out the eight he recognized: Monica's rapist, the fat man he'd killed in the window, the three identified by Ronald Kellett, the man from the basement—the whispers cooed and tittered in remembered joy, drowning in shrieks of sweet agony and gushing fountains of hot blood—plus Gerrold and Burns, the two men who had attacked Kazuko's hospital room with Onnoleigh Sweetman.

Salomon finished his scotch, poured another, and nodded in approval at the pile. "All dead men."

"Who are the others?"

"Employees of mine who took some time off with these guys."

"Meaning?"

"Meaning my boys went freelance, in direct violation of their contract."

"Who hired them?"

"Don't know." Salomon downed his glass in one huge gulp, cleared his throat, and stood. "Let's go ask."

* * *

It came for Kazuko on wings of Jade, a billion crystalline feathers that drank the light. An IV of saline and morphine stood next to a beeping machine and both faded to unreality as it approached. A musky scent filled the room, like incense and wet dog, and old leaves under ancient, primal skies. It wore her mother's face, but Kazuko saw through the simple lie; Sakura Isuji did not smile, not like that, not even for her daughter.

"*Daitengu*, why do you come to me with the face of my mother?"

It scowled, an expression more familiar but somehow too deep and not deep enough.

Kazuko giggled, tried to put her hand to her mouth, but lacked the strength. "Your nose is so small. The legends say it would be much larger."

It spoke in all tongues and none, its voice a majestic symphony. "Are you not afraid, child? All fear death."

The ache took her, an ocean of pain where she floated in each waking moment, as familiar as breathing, dulled by the narcotics but ever-present. "I do not want to go, but no, I am weary but not afraid."

The wings enveloped her in a cocoon, a prison, eternal and cold. A bitter wind whipped straight through her, a maelstrom of unending screaming madness. It filled her mind with a million voices, whispers of pain and death and a false joy at pain and death.

Kazuko laughed. The bright joy couldn't coexist with the darkness, and proved far stronger. The wings shattered like glass, the symphony faltered in a groaning whine, the wind died and the whispers turned to dust.

"I know you, demon. My mother did not know you and so gave me to you to save my life. But you cannot take me for what you have not given, and you cannot take what I have not offered. I am Sakura Kazuko, my mother's child, not something you control. And I deny your power. I will go in peace, to peace, and you cannot have me."

The wind threw her, but she closed her eyes and did not resist. It couldn't move her. Powerless to take her even in death, the storm raged like the unending alarms of hospital equipment, like frantic arms pumping on her chest, but she ignored it, and them, and slept, and died.

* * *

Kazuko sighed, a gasp of relief and loss and contentment and sorrow.

Matt heard it as plain as Salomon's footfalls in the gravel.

The whispers shrieked, shredding his mind in a seething, petulant lament of sadism denied. The white thoughts settled the Jade, and Kazuko's voice joined them in compassion and calm, iron couched behind down. Still the whispers raged, but muffled and sulking in their powerlessness.

"You all right?" Salomon raised an eyebrow.

No. "Yeah. Why?" He took his hand off his pistol, returned to him before their excursion into Salomon's compound.

"Because you stumbled and look like you saw a ghost. Anything I need to worry about here?" His .45, reassembled, hung on his hip, but while he eyed Matt's hand, his thumb stayed hooked in his belt loop.

"No, I'm okay." Matt kept his eyes on the warren of cargo containers, blurred with unbidden tears for a girl he barely knew, and a mother who wouldn't cry, at least not in his presence.

They approached an open-air hangar. Fourteen mobile homes, single-wide trailers circa mid-1990s, parked in neat rows underneath an enormous skeletal frame of aluminum and plastic panels.

"They live here?"

"Sometimes, if they want to." Salomon ran his hand over his bald head. "Some of these guys prefer to live off grid if you know what I mean. This is easier and cheaper than cash at a dive motel."

"Are they armed?"

"Probably. I keep the heavier stuff locked up, but most of these guys carry, and I'd be surprised if all of the hardware made it into the lockers like it's supposed to."

"Noted."

They approached the third trailer. Salomon banged on the door. "Hey, Bill, get out here a minute, would you?"

More bedraggled than his dossier photo, Bill Mcloud opened the door. A wiry man in plaid boxer shorts, a cigarette hung from his lip as he looked from Salomon to Matt and back. "Shit, boss. This looks like a 'pants' meeting. Give me a minute."

Whispers slithered through Matt's brain. Salomon grunted as Matt body-checked him out of the way. The shotgun blast took Matt in the right shoulder, spinning him sideways in a spray of hot red meat. He stepped into the turn and spun, Glock in his left hand, and fired three shots through the wall.

"He's here!" Mcloud yelled. "Rowley's here!"

Matt fired again, a double-tap just below the voice, and then burst through the door, shredding the cheap hinges on his way through.

Mcloud clutched his neck, arterial blood gushing between his fingers, eyes wide and pleading.

Matt kicked the shotgun away, then looked at his shoulder.

The point-blank slug had shattered his scapula, the force snapping the clavicle so that his arm hung down in an unnatural slouch. Muscles writhed, cells crawling together, but too slow for the coming fight. He gritted his teeth against the pain and dropped to one knee in front of Mcloud.

"Tell me who hired you, and I'll see to that wound." He kept his eyes on Mcloud but listened for hostiles outside.

Mcloud coughed blood and his hands went slack, eyes glazing over in death.

"Or not."

He turned from the dying man without standing and peeked through a bullet hole in the wall. Five men approached the door in various states of dress, every one of them in Salomon's folder. Poole and Schick carried pistols, Nichols had a chef's knife, Chung a machete, and one black-bearded monster in a long trench coat, Loveland, hefted a four-foot length of rebar, rusted orange.

Salomon sat Indian-style, his palms bloody from where he'd caught himself on the concrete. Even seated, he projected calm authority. "What's going on here, boys?"

Matt stepped outside, pistol pointed at the ground.

"Not your concern, boss." Chung waved him to the side with the machete. "This is between him and us."

"Man here says you took his son, came around to my place of business looking for you. That kind of thing makes it my concern."

Gritting his teeth through the maddening itch in his shoulder, Matt kept his finger off the trigger. "Nobody else needs to get hurt here. I get my son, you all can walk away. You have my word."

Poole rolled his eyes. "Oy, fuck this." His pistol made it halfway up before a small "pop" rang out from behind Matt and a small hole appeared in Poole's forehead. "Oy." He sat down, and his hand went up to the wound, his face scrunched in bewildered confusion. "Watermelon crab people." He fell over, pistol clattering to the ground.

Chung, Nichols, and Schick bolted for cover. Loveland charged. Matt put three bullets in him center-of-mass before three hundred and fifty pounds of 'roided-up muscle crushed him into the wall, blasting the air from his lungs and the pistol from his grip. Matt ducked past a head-butt and screamed as Loveland bit down on his injured shoulder. He punched left-handed, aiming for kidneys, then solar plexus, but his fist hit kevlar backed by metal plates. The monster shrugged off the blows and bit down harder.

Ragged muscle tore further as Loveland crushed Matt's arms to his sides and pulled. Matt's clavicle shifted, the muscles around it shredding. Screaming, Matt lifted his feet from the ground, planted them on the trailer and pushed off, launching them both toward the ground.

Weapons' fire accompanied their tumble. A bullet caught Matt in the foot, white hot pain searing straight through. Loveland hit his head on the concrete and it dislodged his bloody teeth from Matt's shoulder, but he laughed and squeezed harder. Matt couldn't suck air into his lungs, couldn't get enough purchase to—

Sakura bolted past, her pistol barking twice, straight down. Loveland's upper jaw sagged, the bones shattered from the double-impact. Matt head-butted him, caving his weakened face in with an eggshell crunch. His arms fell slack.

Matt rolled to his feet and looked around. Nichols and Schick lay sprawled on the ground, bleeding. Loveland twitched, his face a shattered, blood-soaked mess.

It hurt to breathe. "Where's Chung?"

Sakura flicked blood from her knife and sheathed it. "Running."

"Let's go." His stumble turned into a limping run, Sakura keeping pace only by virtue of the bullet in his foot.

"Adam's not here."

"But you took care of their bags?"

Sakura nodded. She'd found the bug-out bags in the back of an SUV in the motor pool, and at Matt's direction had stripped them of all cash and identification, and slid several GPS trackers inside the pockets. By the time they reached the car Matt no longer limped, but his right arm still hung useless.

He got in, started it up left-handed, and put it in gear. "What have we got?"

The car flew down the street as Sakura looked at the tiny screen on her phone. "They drove fast. Already at the airport. In the parking garage. Four bags moving."

"They're either switching cars or taking a flight. They'll need cash, and will figure out they have no IDs pretty quick."

The phone vibrated in her hand. She pushed "Talk" and held it to her ear. "Sakura. Yes. Explain, please." Matt pushed the car to ninety miles an hour, trusting precognition to navigate through red lights on the half-empty streets. Sakura listened for a long while, thanked the caller, and hung up.

"Who was that?"

"Doctor Clines. Sakura Kazuko is dead." She closed her eyes. "My daughter is dead." She looked at the screen, said something in Japanese, and then, "They are exiting the parking garage and entering the ticketing area."

"I'm sorry." Matt swerved around a delivery truck, cut across two lanes of traffic and took a hard right into the airport. They squealed up to the curb and got out.

As Matt walked around the car, a short black man in an airport security uniform turned to him. "Sir, you can't leave your vehic—holy shit!" He fumbled for his weapon and radio at the same time. His hand slipped off the radio, and the pistol fell to the sidewalk. He crouched and re-triggered the shoulder microphone at the same time. "Medical emergency at dropoff, potentially hostile."

Matt glared down at him. "I'm fine." He made it two steps toward the revolving door.

"FREEZE! HANDS ON YOUR HEAD!"

Matt turned, his left hand raised. "I'm injured. I can't raise my right arm." He looked at Sakura. "Get them. I'll handle this." He turned to the security guard. "I'm with Homeland Security. If you'll let me get my badge—"

The guard tracked Sakura with his weapon. Matt stepped forward, and the gun jerked from the doors back to him.

"Not another step, buddy. HEY! GET BACK HERE!"

As the guard shifted his attention again toward Sakura, Matt lunged. He caught the weapon by the barrel an inch from his chest and yanked it out of the guard's hand. A shell flew as he racked the slide against his chest and ejected the magazine, which clattered to the ground. He held the weapon out by the barrel.

"Take it, but you try to use it and we're going to have a problem."

* * *

Sakura identified the mercenaries on a pair of benches off to the side outside the secure area, clustered around a laptop, flustered and angry. She removed her phone from her pocket, absently sliding from screen to screen, pretending to surf the web as she worked her way behind them. She took a picture. The 80 megapixel, infinite depth-of-field camera allowed her to zoom straight to the screen and read it.

She took four more pictures at a dead run, on the balls of her feet to minimize noise on the tile, for what little good it did in combat boots. Her feet left the ground six feet from them, phone already in her pocket, and she slammed the tall African American in the spine with her heels a moment later. She brought her coupled fists down on another then dropped to the floor, gritting her teeth against the searing heat in her injured thigh.

As the first two collapsed, she leapt. Chung stumbled back. His companion reached for a nonexistent pistol at his hip, and she rewarded him with a steel toe to the temple. He crumpled, the laptop clattering to the floor. Someone screamed.

Chung advanced, blocking two strikes and ducking inside her kick. The small man's reach stretched no further than hers, so she backpedaled away from his strike to her belly, the taut muscle absorbing the hit with a twinge of discomfort.

She dropped low and swept his legs. He backflipped and then sprang forward, striking as fast as she could evade. The small man hit like a hammer, so she flowed with his strikes, limping back until she hit the windows before dropping to the ground.

His fist rebounded off the reinforced plate glass. She used the split second of his flinch to knife-hand strike him twice in the groin. He dropped to his knees but used the momentum to drive his elbow into her injured thigh.

She rolled right, gasping in pain, cursing the slow, feeble shell her body had become. She put weight on her leg, fell to the tile with a gasp, tried again.

A boot smashed her to the floor. She snarled, rolled, and lashed out, snapping a knee with her hands, breaking someone's arm, hyperextending an elbow.

Strong hands lifted her. She struck with palms, elbows, knee, all weapons meant to cripple or kill. They met unyielding steel. Arms enveloped her, yanked her into an unwelcome, unwanted embrace. Pain poured out of her, a raw wail without recourse or end.

* * *

Matt kept his arms around Sakura as her killing strikes faded to ineffectual struggling, the ragged sound from her throat resolving into haggard breaths. She kept her arms between them, a shield against human contact, but he pulled her close and held her nonetheless. He cradled her body as she collapsed to her knees.

Two of the mercenaries writhed on the ground, while the others didn't move at all. A TSA agent clutched his knee, screaming, while another nursed a forearm bent at ninety degrees, his breaths short and sharp, face pale. Others surrounded them, wide-eyed and twitchy, weapons raised, fingers on triggers.

A redhead glared at him over the barrel of her rifle. "Lay on the ground and put your hands on your head."

"I'm with the Depart—"

"I SAID LAY THE FUCK DOWN!"

With deliberate motions, Matt let go of Sakura. They both lay flat on their stomachs. Wincing at the tearing sensation, he dragged his hands up and folded them over his head. Sakura lay with her head facing away from him.

Sharp pain jolted through his injured shoulder as rough hands twisted his arms behind his back and cuffed them. He waited for the redheaded security officer to read him his rights before speaking. "Ma'am, we're with the Special Threats Bureau. As I've said multiple times, my ID is in my wallet. These fugitives we just apprehended are armed and extremely dangerous."

She pulled his wallet out of his pocket, scanned over his ID, and pinned him with her eyes. "We'll have to verify this."

Sakura turned her head to them. Her mask of resolve had slammed into place, but the evidence of her outburst still lay damp on her cheeks. "We need that laptop. No time to lose."

Matt nodded. "Call the Federal Building in Nashville—"

"—you're hell and gone from Nashville—"

"—and ask for Janet LaLonde. We have jurisdiction here."

She looked down at them and shook her head. "Not sure what part of 'remain silent' you didn't get, but this is the airport, so TSA jurisdiction supersedes whatever the hell you said you're from." She turned to another officer. "Get all six of them to holding, separate cells, and tag everything. This is a crime scene now, so treat it like one."

"Ma'am, paramedics are en route. This man's dead."

Matt couldn't see who they were talking about, but the whispers muttered their approval.

"Then call the coroner. But search him first. The TSD is on his way. And bring me that laptop. I want to know what all this is about."

"Yes, ma'am."

Chapter 13

The chains linking his wrists to the table allowed Matt just enough freedom to put his head in his hands and try not to pull out his hair. The single naked bulb hanging from the ceiling clashed with the modernized airport so hard that Matt couldn't help but think it intentional. It complemented the metal table, folding chair, and two-way mirror perfectly. He didn't know how long they'd been detained, but long enough for his shoulder to have healed.

And every minute took his son farther away.

Transportation Safety Director Harry Cooper asked him the same question for the millionth time in three hours. "Why did you come to the airport?"

Matt spoke without looking up. He'd seen enough bushy mustache and square-rimmed glasses to last a lifetime. "I have answered this question. Those men—"

"—say you were hired to kill them, Mister Rowley, and that they were running for their lives."

"We work for the Department of Homeland Security—"

"—yet committed assault on four men in my airport, killing two, without the slightest provocation, without the slightest attempt to arrest them. Being a government employee doesn't give you—"

"For the millionth time, my jurisdiction supersedes yours."

"Whose blood is on your shirt, Mr. Rowley?"

Patience exhausted, he looked up. "There's been more than enough time to verify our identities and credentials, which means you're either incompetent or stalling."

Cooper stuck his finger in Matt's face. "This is my airport, you uppity shit, and I can hold you here as long as I deem necessary."

"I'm done." Matt jerked his arms, snapping the steel chain that bound his wrists.

Cooper backpedaled toward the door, eyes wide, his chair tumbling across the floor. Matt beat him to the exit, jamming it closed with his foot. Cooper gaped like a fish, then looked in alarm at the mirror.

Matt grabbed his chin and turned his head. "So let me be clear how this is going to work. You're going to let me and my partner out within the next five minutes, or I'm going to take you into custody for aiding and abetting a terrorist organization. If you somehow doubt my ability to follow through on this promise, I suggest you review the training procedures your men went through to deal with augmented threats. I'll bet they're out of practice and don't have nearly enough ordnance."

"There are no Augs—"

Matt let go of Cooper's chin and telegraphed his punch enough to give the officious little prick time to duck. Chunks of cinder block exploded into the air as he jerked his fist back. He held up his hand, unharmed but for bloody, broken skin, and flexed his fingers. "You sure about that?"

Fingers itching as new skin crept over the wounds, he stepped out of the way. As the door opened he called out one last warning.

"Five minutes. Then you're under arrest."

Cooper scampered out and returned three minutes later with Matt's sidearm, phone, and wallet in hand. "Mister Rowley, let me apologize personally for the delay."

Matt snatched the key to the handcuffs out of his hand and shouldered past him into the hall, where two security officers stood with hands on their sidearms. He unshackled his wrists and tossed the broken cuffs on the floor at Cooper's feet, followed by the key.

"Where's Sakura?" Matt heard Cooper's excuses before he said them and stalked down the hall to the next door. Sakura sat inside at a table, a massive bruise covering the right half of her face. Matt opened the door over Cooper's protests. "We're leaving."

She stood and held out her wrists. "These men beat me."

Matt unlocked her manacles and ran a gentle hand over the bruise. "And they'll pay for it."

She winced as she stood, and limped to the door, favoring both legs. He stepped into the hallway, locked eyes with Cooper and put his phone to his ear.

Janet answered after the first ring. "About time, Rowley. You're at the airport?"

"I need all security feeds from LaGuardia International Airport, including the holding cells. Now would be good, before they have a chance to delete them." Cooper turned to leave. Matt grabbed his shirt and pulled him close, fingers tangling in the director's red tie as he gave Janet further instructions. "I'd like a call to internal affairs or whatever the TSA calls it to review the tapes. Agent Sakura appears to have sustained some injuries while in custody, under the direction of LaGuardia TSD Cooper. In a few minutes we should have something else for you."

"On it."

He hung up, and leaned in to within an inch of Cooper's face. "You're going to want a lawyer. Meantime, where's that laptop?"

"Let go of—"

Matt twisted, cutting off Cooper's breath, and turned to the closest security officer. Cooper beat at his wrist and clawed at his hand while Matt spoke. "I'm relieving TSD Cooper of his command on authority of Homeland Security Director Lawson. Call his office right now and verify with today's authorization one-one-two-six-three-nine-five-one." He turned to the other officer. "If you want to keep your job, get me that laptop. Now."

He let go, and Cooper dropped to the floor.

"And put this piece of shit in chains."

* * *

Minutes later he found himself in Cooper's office, standing by the door while Sakura worked with Janet to pull information out of the mercenary's computer.

"So what prompted the attack?"

Sakura typed a moment before looking up. The massive dark splotch spread from her temple to her fat upper lip, and bright red bled across her eye. "Money transfer. Fifteen thousand dollars from Banca Privada d'Andorra. I wouldn't get the account code and password before he'd finished, so I prevented him from finishing."

"Okay. You all right?"

"Yes."

"You sure?"

She typed something, then clicked the mouse. "No. But I will act as if I am all right up until the point I cannot. At that time I will recuse myself of duty and stand down."

Instead of a reply he checked the window to the hall, where Cooper sat manacled to a folding chair, hands folded in his lap, head down.

"You want to press charges?"

"I hurt their colleagues because I lost control. It won't happen again. And no, I don't want to press charges, I want to apologize to the men I hurt. Now be quiet."

Matt left to see to the prisoners, but both had been sedated and transported to the hospital. Three hours later, they transferred Cooper's case to TSA oversight and flew home, while Janet brought the full might of the NSA to bear on the money transfer.

* * *

Monica pushed her way through the aisles of Walmart, a forty-minute drive out of the way, but the closest place to get diapers since the grocery burned. The .357, too big for a concealed holster, felt strange on her hip, but stranger still that it had company. It seemed every third person carried pistols in plain view while pushing their carts and giving strangers naked appraisals.

The government had assured all the towns and counties around White Spruce that the terrorist threat had been eliminated, that the criminals were in custody, that the streets were safe. In typical Tennessee fashion, they'd take a while to accept such a pronouncement.

And in the meantime, they'd arm themselves.

Monica wouldn't allow for the possibility that they wouldn't need diapers. Doubt skittered across her brain, water on a hot skillet, there but unable to settle, to penetrate. She'd made the drive to Walmart because of course they'd need diapers.

Her phone rang. She dug in her purse and pulled it out, just in time to miss the call.

Matt.

She called back and spoke before he could answer.

"Did you find him?"

"No, baby, but we will. We're getting closer. You busy?"

"Just shopping. You home soon?"

"Just landed. Can I send you a couple pictures?"

"Sure." She hefted two packs of diapers onto the cart, atop a couple of shirts and jeans for Matt and three new blouses, then headed for the grocery section.

"I think we have a lead, thought maybe it's the girl who drugged you. She's got an affiliate named Karthik"—he spelled it for her—"which sounds a lot like your 'car thick'. It's a real common name in India, not so much in the USA. Here, I'll send them."

Her phone blipped, and she looked at the pictures.

The girl's hairstyle varied from shot to shot, and Monica couldn't pick out the eyes, but she looked like the right person. High cheekbones, prominent chin. She gasped at the fifth picture, the girl—no older than thirteen or fourteen—standing with a large group of teens in front of some strange metal contraption the size of a washing machine. The machine and every kid wore the same color green, it and their T-shirts emblazoned with *Division by Zero.*

Panic seized her, but she let it flow through and out of her, channeling the nugget that remained into pure rage. "Who is she?"

"Is that her?"

"Yes. I'm positive."

"We've got a match," he said to someone else. "Thanks, baby. See you when I get home."

"But when—" The phone clicked dead. "Dammit, babe."

* * *

Matt met her at the door. They made gentle love and talked about things that didn't matter and slept, and in the morning he left again to find their baby, and the fifteen-year-old who'd had her raped and tried to have her killed.

She'd tried not to shudder at her husband's touch and prayed he hadn't noticed. A long shower helped but couldn't kill the filth that crept through her body. For the millionth time in a week, shudders wracked her for want of a fix. She dropped to the floor of the tub and wept under the hot streaming water.

* * *

Janet handed out dossiers to Matt, Blossom, and Shane Keene, the Assistant Special Agent in Charge of the FBI's Boston headquarters, a grizzled man who but for his clean shave, looked like he'd be more at home on a Harley than in a suit in a meeting room, complete with dark glasses propped on thinning gray hair. Janet's four inch heels clacked on the tile floor, and as she passed, Agent Keene's eyes crawled up her short dress in the most brazen and least appropriate manner possible.

She whirled around—an impressive feat in those shoes—and looked Keene right in the eyes. "All right, kids, here's what we've got. The Andorra account is held in trust by Liaguno, Morton, and Wood for a Libby Kamen, fifteen years old going on Lindsay Lohan thirty." The projector flashed a picture, a pretty young woman with dark brown hair and eyes almost gold in the sunlight of an autumn day. "Miss Kamen is the sole heir of her parents, Angela and Winston Kamen."

"Wait," Matt said. "Winston Kamen of Kamen Industries?"

Janet clicked the remote to advance the slide. A middle-aged couple leaned against an immaculate plum-purple Bentley Continental convertible with tan leather interior and Massachusetts plates parked in front of a meticulous tulip garden. The ocean dominated the background, a lighthouse off to the right.

Keene let out a whistle, long and slow. "Nice car. What's that, a quarter-million-dollars?"

"More or less," Janet said. "They own the garden and the lighthouse, too, which cost a bit more. Kamen's parents both inherited eight-figure sums from their respective parents as teenagers, met at Yale twenty years ago, and got married shortly thereafter." She flashed through slides of yachts, jets, skyscrapers, and banks. "In a few short years they'd spun their fortunes into businesses worth tens of billions of dollars and have donated vast amounts to charities all over the world, not to mention politicians in dozens of countries . . . ."

She flipped to the next slide, a funeral at a massive synagogue packed to standing-room only with people in expensive black suits and dresses. Matt recognized several celebrities, businesspeople, and politicians, including the Vice President of the United States.

". . . and both died on the same night last year."

Wary of the direction of the conversation, Matt let Keene take the lead.

"Foul play?"

Janet shrugged. "They stopped breathing on the same night, but two things point to murder being unlikely. One, forensics couldn't find a cause of death for either of them, though the missus had consumed a good amount of alcohol. Two, Angela was at a party in Barcelona surrounded by dozens of her closest and richest friends, and Winston was asleep in a well-guarded penthouse in Los Angeles. She dropped on the spot, unresponsive to CPR, and his assistant found him the next morning."

Keene couldn't know that Angela and Winston Kamen had died not only on the same night but at the same exact moment that Gerstner had stepped off the machine. They hadn't been able to determine the couples' true age at time of death but had narrowed it down to somewhere around eighty. On the day of their deaths, neither had looked a day over forty, yet the funeral had been closed-casket, ostensibly at their request.

"I think I remember this." Keene waggled his finger at the image. "Didn't a bunch of conspiracy sites pick this up, turn it into some Bilderberger-Rockefeller-Illuminati thing?"

"Yeah," Janet said. "Late night radio went nuts with it. Bunch of prominent folks died within a day or two—all unrelated, of course—and the tinfoil hat crowd positively exploded over all the possibilities."

Keene's enthusiastic nod jostled his sunglasses from his forehead. He folded them closed and set them on the table next to his pen. "And the Jade market dying at the same time, all the Augs failing. Some kind of mystery poison or cure or whatever, and no one knows why." Keene avoided looking at Matt so hard that he might as well have been staring.

"I know why," Janet said. When Keene widened his eyes she winked and shot him with both hands. "I'd tell you, but I'd have to kill you."

He smirked. "Right. So about her parents?"

She leaned forward and pinned down the folder in front of him with her index finger. Face full of cleavage, Keene kept his eyes trained on hers as she spoke. "It's all in Libby's dossier, including a comprehensive psychological evaluation by your office. She lives wherever she wants, but her legal address makes her squarely your purview."

She stood back to her full height and turned around with a wink to Matt. As Keene blinked, Matt tried not to smirk too much. Janet knew how to play men and had never been shy about doing so.

"So for the past few years, Libby Kamen's been tooling around with this guy." The slide showed a large, dark-skinned man in a Toronto Blue Jays jersey and huge sunglasses. "A Canadian of Indian descent, Karthik 'Big K' Kana-something-really-long, you'll have to read it, twenty-two years old, is a real 'playah' on the MMA scene." She flipped through several pictures of the pair at bouts, street fights, celebrity events, and drag races. The last picture showed Big K and Libby standing with former MMA superstar and ICAP agent Murdock Yardley at a promotions table. Yardley had his arm around a busty young blonde holding a martini glass the size of a salad bowl. She boasted a highlighter-yellow bra, short shorts, platform heels, and nothing else. Matt pegged her at mid-teens.

The last time Matt had seen Yardley, he'd been lying on the floor of a hospital, spine severed, his back a mass of raw meat from a point-blank grenade Sakura had strapped there, but still alive and regenerating. Matt wondered what had become of him after his Augs failed, what convalescent home he'd ended up in. There's no way a post-Aug bonk of his size could move under his own power. He made a mental note to look Yardley up and ask him about the girls and Big K.

"Sweetman."

They all turned to Blossom.

"Girl with the drink. Onnoleigh Sweetman, the girl who attacked my Kazuko in the hospital."

"Yes, it is." Janet flipped through several more photos of the four of them. "It seems that Sweetman and Kamen met at one of Big K's unregulated fights and hit it off. Kamen was barely eleven and accompanied by several bodyguards, Sweetman almost fourteen with a twenty-six-year-old date. The three of them became fast friends—

only friends as far as I've been able to suss out—attending dozens if not hundreds of bouts over the past several years."

Matt frowned. "That was a heck of a martini for a fourteen-year-old."

"Sixteen in that picture. Sweetman and Kamen have both been arrested on many occasions, sometimes with but most of the time without Marie Thill. The charges range, mostly disorderly conduct and possession of controlled substances, speeding, driving without a license, noise ordinance violations, that kind of thing. Typical behavior for kids with way too much money and inadequate supervision. None of the charges ever stuck."

Matt leaned forward. "So where do we find Kamen?"

Janet shrugged. "At last count she has seventeen homes, nine in the United States, five in Europe, one each in Beijing, Hong Kong, and a private atoll near the Maldives. But she spends most of her time here." The screen clicked to an aerial photograph of a large city with a lot of swimming pools. "In a cozy nineteen-thousand-square-foot pad in Los Angeles. She's not there now, but that shouldn't be a big surprise. Big K has a bout in Rio de Janeiro tomorrow."

Keene frowned. "I don't have any jurisdiction in Rio."

Matt shrugged. "We do."

* * *

Monica stepped out of the store into the lights of a camera crew.

A bottle-blonde in a light blue skirt-suit shoved a microphone in her face. Her smile didn't reach her eyes, and her crow's feet showed that instead of Botox, she just didn't mean it. "Missus Rowley, is it true that the attack on White Spruce was directed at your family?"

Monica opened her mouth, closed it again. The police hadn't released the fact that Adam had been taken, and Matt had warned her not to share that information with anyone.

"Missus Rowley?"

"No. I don't know what you're talking about." She pushed the cart past the reporter and stepped around the camera man.

"Where is your son, Missus Rowley?"

Monica turned. It would be so easy to break her pert little nose, and in White Spruce she could have done it and gotten away with it. "I don't know where you get your information, but you leave me alone."

She ignored a barrage of questions—and the growing crowd—as she loaded the truck. Finished, she pushed the cart out of the way. Ted raised his eyebrows as she got in, then settled back down, his tail thumping against the floor mat. She revved the engine, put it in gear, and lurched forward.

The cameraman rushed toward her, blonde in tow, as she reached the stop sign at the edge of the parking lot. Tires shrieking on the blacktop, she merged into sparse traffic with the gas pedal to the floor, blinking away tears in order to see the road.

A quarter-mile later she slowed to within five of the speed limit. Ted chuffed up at her with his sad Bassett eyes.

"I don't know, Ted. But if I find out who told them, I'll kill them."

* * *

Sakura shifted in her seat, trying to get comfortable.

Matt hung up, unplugged the satellite relay from his cell phone, and turned thunderous eyes to her. "Somebody leaked that Adam's missing. A reporter ambushed Mon outside a Walmart."

The NSAIDs dulled the pain but couldn't eliminate it, and she refused narcotics as a matter of course. She raised her voice over the drone of the private jet's engines. "Any ideas?"

"It didn't come from my office," Keene blurted, his hands raised in a defensive gesture.

"Why would it come from your office?" Sakura said.

"It wouldn't."

"Then why did you say that?" She ignored his frown to press the point. "If you had no worry of leaks then you wouldn't leap to defend your colleagues."

Keene turned to Matt. "Your partner got a problem with the FBI?"

She managed not to snarl.

Matt snorted. "My partner is better at reading people than anyone I've ever met. Do we have a confidentiality problem?"

"No." He didn't hesitate, but his eyes flickered as he said it.

Matt looked at her, one eyebrow raised.

"He believes but is not one hundred percent confident in the assessment."

Matt closed his eyes and leaned back in his chair. "Great. Just great."

"Now wait just one fucking minute—"

Sakura put on her headphones, turned up the white noise, and went back to sleep.

* * *

The plane touched down at Galeão–Antonio Carlos Jobim International Airport just after noon. While not as hot as Matt expected, the humidity still slapped him across the face as he stepped down to the tarmac. A salty, nauseating odor permeated the soupy air: unwashed bodies, unflushed sewers, and rotten fish.

Keene put his hand to his nose, drawing a glare from the sweating porter unloading their luggage.

"Guanabara Bay," Sakura said. "You get used to it."

Keene rubbed his face with both hands. "That smell is exactly why I never had kids."

Sakura ignored him and approached the waiting car, a light blue late-eighties Caprice Classic with a dented fender. She got in the driver's seat.

Keene flashed his eyebrows at Matt. "Personal chauffer, huh?"

"Get in the car before she hurts you." Matt didn't wait for a reply, and Sakura hit the gas before Keene had a chance to close his door or buckle up.

Sakura led them down a long highway that smelled even worse than the airport, right through rolled-up windows. She took an abrupt turn, then another, and in moments Matt found himself looking across an endless slum of multistory concrete buildings sprawling across a steep hillside. She wound through the streets, higher and higher, without a hint of hesitation.

"Fight is here," she said. "This favela has some tourist attraction for such things. No rules street fighting popular with Yakuza and others with the means to travel for it. Kasahara-san lost his Codecasa to an American here."

"Cod-a-what?" Matt asked.

"Yacht. Very big, very expensive."

Keene's forehead wrinkled down. "You know a lot about this."

She nodded, once, without taking her eyes from the road.

"Who was this Sahara guy?"

"Kasahara-san is Yakuza, very important in the global heroin trade. Though now in prison he is thought to control at least sixty percent of the global market, including almost all exports from Afghanistan and Mongolia."

"And you know him how?"

"I was his enforcer, bodyguard, and mistress for three years in my later teens. My testimony put him in prison."

Keene gaped like a fish, looking from Sakura to Matt and back.

Matt turned his gaze out the window at the passing slums. Keene's presence transformed their usual comfortable silence into a taut string, so by the time they'd arrived at the venue his nerves had rubbed raw.

They parked several blocks away and walked through a growing crowd of dark-skinned people in bright but threadbare clothing. On the far side an artificial railing cordoned off a line of fancy cars, Ferraris, Corvettes, and chopped Mustangs glinting in the fading sun in brazen defiance of the squalor around them. Matt had, against everything he expected, gotten used to the smell of rank humanity, but now it mingled with a spicy, not-unpleasant aroma reminiscent of Christmas cider and grilled chicken.

The roar of the crowd reached a crescendo as they approached. In the center of the throng, a black iron cage hung thirty feet above the ground from a rusty crane, and on the floor a man lay on his stomach and twitched, one arm dangling over the side. Underneath him a drizzle of red splattered the crowd, and they cheered for it.

"These guys don't fuck around." Keene nodded toward the wall of muscle guarding three black limousines, each boasting an array of computers in their open trunks. As money changed hands, a bevy of well-dressed goons circled through the crowd and back to the cars, where small men in expensive suits hammered away at the keys.

The cage crept toward the ground and the crowd parted beneath it, a frantic struggle against the surge of humanity to keep from being crushed by the massive weight. A couple of bruisers opened the door and let the victor out, a topless mid-weight fighter with streaks of blood down his face and chest. The loser they carried, his head lolling as they pushed through the crowd.

Matt scanned the throng for signs of Libby Kamen, but Sakura beat him to it.

"There."

He followed her gaze to a crowd of large men near the cage, conspicuous more for their expensive black suits than their Caucasian skin. In front of and ignoring them, Kamen chugged from a giant belled tube of green plastic. Pale liquid spilled down her white tank top, soaking it to expose the construction-crew orange bikini top beneath.

Her laughter drowned in the crowd noise, a flash of white teeth under a mop of dirty-blonde dreadlocked weave. Matt tried to reconcile this carefree, spirited girl with a monster who would order men to rape and murder. His mind balked.

"They see us." Sakura gave them a princess wave, her face a flat, indifferent mask.

"What the hell are you doing?" Keene said.

She shrugged. "They saw us. No reason to play coy. I'll plant the tracker."

The crowd roared as Big K stepped into the cage, upraised fists wrapped in strips of black leather. His opponent stood six inches taller, a well-tanned brute in a black leather mask and ridiculously tiny white shorts. An announcer babbled in Portuguese, introducing Big K and "Rancoroso."

They couldn't move in the sudden press, so Matt watched Karthik as the bell rang. The smaller man slid forward and feinted with a left jab. Rancoroso stepped into it and cuffed Karthik on the side of the head. Karthik rolled with the blow and brought his own knee up into the side of Rancoroso's.

Matt eyed the sloppy work with feigned interest. Neither man exhibited much discipline, and both used street fighting techniques that could benefit from serious honing by a true master of the martial arts. But Big K's ferocity matched his speed, impressive for an unaugmented man, and Matt took pause.

Big K telegraphed moves he shouldn't have, took hits with too much anticipation, and didn't press the advantage as much as he could. *He's playing around.* The crowd cheered at the theater. Matt tried to push closer, earning him nasty glares and more than a few elbows to the midsection.

He looked down at a sharp sting in his side. A young man had buried a thin knife into Matt's kidney. He smiled a vicious killer's smile that turned to ash under Matt's unwavering gaze.

"Ouch." Matt plucked his wallet from the pickpocket's hand and smashed his forehead into the bridge of his assailant's nose. The would-be thief collapsed in a spray of blood and the crowd swallowed him.

"Be careful. A pickpocket just knifed me," he said for the benefit of the microphone in his ear bud.

"Acknowledged," Sakura replied.

Karthik spun inside a haymaker and smashed his elbow into Rancoroso's solar plexus. The big man hunched over and stumbled back, but Karthik pressed the attack, kicking and kneeing in a haphazard series of strikes that could have opened up a vulnerability, but didn't.

Definitely on purpose.

Matt turned his attention to the girl.

Libby watched with rapt attention, eyes wide, body leaned forward in anticipation, a wall of muscle in dark suits separating her from the crowd. Her bodyguards looked in every direction, save the one who kept his eyes trained on Matt.

With thousands of people jammed to standing room only, Matt gave up trying to close the distance. He leaned his head to the side to be heard over the noise. "You got her?"

"No," Sakura replied in his ear bud. "Need a few minutes to make the cars."

In the cage, Karthik stepped to the side in a fluid dodge and kicked Rancoroso in the temple. The bigger man dropped to the ground, and Karthik fell on him, driving his full weight onto his elbow, which impacted Rancoroso's throat. The crowd exploded in cheers and boos.

Matt watched the larger man writhe on the steel floor. "Fight's over. You'd better hurry."

Chapter 14

Sakura drifted the rear end, downshifting and punching the gas just before they hit the intersection. Their lumbering vehicle skidded through the turn, tires throwing gravel as the back end fishtailed around. The 5-liter V8 roared, throwing Matt back against the seat again.

In the far distance, Kamen's bright yellow Corvette disappeared around the mountain curve.

"This is bullshit," Keene said, his face a jaundiced green-yellow.

"Oh?" Matt asked.

"If they made us at the fight then there's no way they don't know we're following them, and this shitbox can't hold a candle to a Camry much less that Z06, especially on these roads."

Matt's opinion of Keene ticked up just a hair. "Right."

"So they want us to follow them, which means it's a trap." Keene lifted his sunglasses to look Matt in the eyes.

"Right."

"And you're following them anyway."

They blew past a man leading a burro down the side of the road, the wind from the vehicle ripping his hat from his head. Sakura jammed the car into high gear and the four-speed whined in protest. She glanced in the rear-view mirror. "You want out? Jump."

"I'm not saying that. I'm just saying it's a trap."

Matt responded by patting his AA-12 combat shotgun. "It is, but not their trap. Four miles up ahead the Brazilian military has a checkpoint, and they're on the lookout for that little hot rod."

Keene grunted. "So you're flushing them out."

Matt shrugged. "If they're unarmed, we have a nice chat and take them into custody. If they're packing illegal hardware, the Federales do it for us."

Sakura rolled her eyes. "Policia Militar. The Federales are Mexican."

Keene pulled out his phone. "Let me call for backup. The CIA—"

Matt cut him off with an upraised hand. "The Shop has already been informed and are embedded with the PM. Just sit back and let Sakura play sheepdog."

Keene looked from his phone to the road to Matt, sighed, and put it away. "Woof."

A half-mile later the road broke into a small village, a collection of a dozen concrete homes around a central square. The hand-pump well combined with the rectangular, two-story buildings to give the area a depressed Eastern Bloc feel. Chickens scattered as they approached, and a young boy led goats down an alley between two buildings and out of sight.

On the far side of the square, the Corvette sat sideways in the road, blocking passage with the help of a pair of Korean War-era Jeeps. A bodyguard stood behind each Jeep, using the engine block as cover, pistols drawn and resting on the hoods. Armed men lurked on the balconies on either side of the street.

A man by the jeep pulled up a long tube and pointed it at the car.

"Plan?" Sakura asked without taking her foot off the gas.

"Follow the goat," Matt said, grabbing the door handle.

"Oh, shit!" Keene hunkered down as far as he could manage.

Sakura whipped the wheel counter-clockwise, throwing Matt against the passenger-side door. They disappeared behind the building as the RPG streaked toward them. The explosion obliterated the far wall of the alley as the car slid sideways into the narrow space, blasting them with deafening noise and heat and chunks of plaster.

Matt popped the handle and used his momentum to carry himself around the door, and pushed into a hand-stand before launching himself upward onto the top of the car. They crunched sideways into the wall at speed, slamming the door and destroying the side-view mirror in a spray of concrete dust.

Matt hit the wall feet first, already at a run that carried him straight up the side of the building. He grabbed a window sill one-handed and launched himself inside, training the AA-12 through a girl's faded pink bedroom before blasting through the door to the upstairs hall.

A woman screamed. Sharp pops from the men's pistols met the characteristic chatter of Sakura's REC-7. Matt leapt over a charging Doberman onto the front balcony and shoulder-blocked a gunman over the railing. The man cried out in startled terror and landed with a wet thud on the dusty street.

Matt slammed the door then opened fire, sending a pair of fin-stabilized fragmentation grenades into the man one house over. He stumbled backward and looked down in stunned confusion, then his chest exploded in a steaming red mess that sent gobbets of flesh raining down to the street.

Whispers rejoiced at Matt's bloody brains splattered against the wall, so he took the warning and dropped to the floor. Puffs of concrete erupted from the wall above his head. Prone, he ignored the rifleman shooting at him from across the street, found his range and fired another grenade, this one triggered to explode upward.

It skimmed over the dead man on the adjacent balcony to the next, passing between metal railings straight between a gunman's knees. Without waiting for the explosion he sprang up and leapt across, following the grenade to draw fire away from Sakura and the car.

* * *

Sakura dropped behind the car as bullets punctured the engine block. By the sound, the shooters held low-caliber hunting rifles—what Matt would call a varmint gun—which plinked as they hit the metal, and at least one medium weapon, maybe a 7.26 mm with two hundred grains behind it. She looked under the car but saw no feet, so she flashed her hand up and whipped it back down just as another barrage pinned her in place.

A quick scan of the alley revealed little of use—a rat skeleton, a rotted-out plastic garbage barrel, and the shattered remains of the side-view mirror. She snatched a piece of broken mirror and pulled it to her chest. Readying the REC-7 with her right hand, she raised the mirror in her left.

All three balconies across the street had men on them, at least four armed combatants. Keene huddled in the back seat, covering his head with his hands. The glass shattered in her hand. She whirled left and fired a burst around the side of the car before ducking back.

"Keene! Now!"

He didn't move, didn't open the door, nothing.

She swore, rolled to the wall, and popped up again. The shooters reacted, but she shot first. One man stumbled back, his weapon tumbling to the street. Sakura streaked left with her finger on the trigger. As bullets sprayed their position the gunmen ducked for cover, so she backpedaled down the alley and ducked behind the building.

Slamming another magazine home, she ran to the back door and yanked it open even as an unarmed man burst through, wide eyes white behind dark skin. She struck him in the throat hard enough to stun, stepped forward and hooked her leg behind his, using her body to knock him to the floor as she moved past. A woman huddled in the corner of the kitchen with two small children, their heads pulled against her bosom.

She glanced out the window without disturbing the curtain. A man shrieked in the street, clutching a leg that had twisted sideways on impact. His rifle lay forgotten behind him. The men across the way continued to shoot at the Caprice. Sakura raised the REC-7, gauged the height, and then fired three quick bursts, rotating between them to change targets. The first and last hit home, the targets twitching and dropping out of sight, but the middle gunman kept firing.

Cursing her frail, inadequate form, she turned back to the man on the middle balcony just as he opened fire. She grunted at the impact below her right breast and stumbled to one knee, falling to the right as another round thudded into the wall. Each gasp of breath brought fresh waves of agony.

She touched the point of impact and her hand came away wet with blood. The piezoelectric gel in her vest softened as the kinetic energy from the impact dispersed, so she tore at her shirt to survey the damage. The bullet had scattered between two ceramic plates and punctured the carbon nanofiber backing, the lead mangled to an unrecognizable form. She plucked out the mangled slug with numb fingers, coughed, and wiped her mouth with the back of her hand.

Bright red blood smeared across her index finger.

She reached for her fallen rifle but her right arm wouldn't obey.

"I'm hit." It came out a gasp.

"Bad?" Matt asked.

"Yes."

A wall hanging shattered behind her, followed by the report of the rifle. She struggled to breathe through the white-hot agony, coughed and spat blood onto the worn, beige carpet.

Matt's shotgun boomed, and the rifle didn't fire again.

Her pain faded, and though she fought the dullness with all her will it closed in around her. A girl stepped around the corner, with dark brown hair in a bowl cut and a cute blue *doresu,* and around her the world blazed white.

Sakura knew her, and knew the impossibility of it. Still she asked, "Kazuko?"

Her daughter bowed and replied in Japanese. "Yes, Mother. The *daitengu* came for me with your face and emerald wings, but I am my mother's daughter and saw through its tricks. It could not take me."

"How can you be here, my Kazuko?"

"I am not there, but you come too close to where I am. I can feel your love and shame as physical things, Mother, so strong, too strong. There is much yet for you to do. Open your eyes, Mother. Open your eyes and fight."

Tears streamed down her cheek. "But my Kazuko, I have always fought for you. Why do I fight now?"

Kazuko closed her eyes and bowed. "You fight because it is who you are, Mother. You fight because some cannot. Now get up."

Sakura's eyes snapped open just as the frying pan came down. She reached up, grabbed the descending wrist and jerked. As her attacker stumbled, off-balance, Sakura leapt to the balls of her feet, taking cover behind the concrete wall, and threw. The pan rebounded off the now-fleeing woman's head with a dull thud, and she dropped to her face.

Frowning, Sakura rubbed the wound, sore but manageable under the bulletproof vest.

A mystery for another time.

The door burst open. She pulled her strike but Matt whirled and caught her hand anyway. She sneered, furious that after all her training he could beat her speed.

"I thought you were shot."

She shrugged. "I was. Now I'm not. Status?"

"Guards are dead or run off. The police came up their six and they scattered into the jungle. Kamen's unconscious. You?"

She shrugged again. "Well enough. Keene?"

"Fine. Shook up. A bullet grazed his shoulder, but fine."

* * *

"Yes?" The voice on the other end of the line rasped, a rumble both too deep and too ragged for a human throat.

"You son of a bitch," Karthik said. He grabbed his hair with one hand, pulled, let it go, grabbed it again. "You told me augmentation failed when Jade died."

"It has, except for his. You knew he was dangerous. I warned you to be careful."

"We were careful. Nine men are dead because you didn't spill. What the fuck do you think you're—"

"Don't presume to question me. He'll come for you, him and that sycophant Yakuza bitch, and you need to be gone before he does. Kill the baby and send me the video."

Sweat broke out on Karthik's forehead, sweat that had nothing to do with the mountain air. Words wouldn't come. He swallowed, breathed in, and tried again. "I—we can't."

"It's too late for can't. Tell her to obey me. Her ego is too tied to our approval for her to disobey on something this hot."

"No, that's not it. We tried to kill him and can't. Every time we go to do the deed we . . . just can't. I don't have an explanation, you know? It's like some Golden Child shit or whatever." Karthik looked down at the toddler, blissfully unaware of anything in his drugged sleep. An intense feeling of paternal love squeezed his heart the moment he reached for the pillow, as happened to anyone who tried to harm Adam Rowley.

"That doesn't make sense. Put Libby on the phone."

"Yo, you can't use her name on an open line—"

"PUT HER ON THE GODDAMNED PHONE."

"I can't, *Murdock*. They took her."

"No."

"The fuck yes they did. They took her, and killed Steve and Jeff and their whole motherfucking crew. They set an ambush and Rowley tore them a new asshole. You should have told us the guy was augged, man. This whole shit's falling apart."

"I did tell you. You chose not to believe. Now close your mouth and open your ears, and I'll tell you how to get her back."

Karthik listened. When he hung up, he turned to Mark, a racist redneck shithead he could barely trust with his wallet much less his life, yet somehow the most trustworthy of his surviving companions in Brazil. Mark looked at him with wide, rheumy eyes, both hands thrust into the pockets of his overalls, fondling with all their arthritic might.

"Mark, we got to skip town, now. Grab the kid, I'll call the chopper."

Mark grinned, exposing toothless gums. "The Master approves?"

Karthik rolled his eyes. "This ain't a cult, moron. He ain't your master, just my boss. And you work for me, so hop fucking to."

* * *

Jason sat in the tiny motel lobby, reading an exegesis on his tablet, which in turn rested on the owner's black and white cat, its grotesquely fat, furry body stretched out in his lap. Between the cat and the blazing fireplace he drowned in his own sweat, and wished he owned something more comfortable than a black clerical shirt and collar. The snow had melted to residual piles of slush in the darkness outside, and at two a.m. the world lay quiet.

He couldn't sleep without drowning in violence and blood, and his haunted dreams had started creeping into his waking thoughts.

Eyes closed, he prayed, for peace and protection and healing, for himself and the love of his life, but as the firelight cast shadows through his eyelids he saw only the ground smoldering beneath a forest of cruel thorns, blood, and dark worms writhing through a protective ring of icy feathers, melting under the black sun.

* * *

Matt frowned at Sakura.

She sat on the bed in her bra and combat pants, admiring the fading bruise under her breast without the slightest sign of modesty. The bruise on her face had faded to a jaundiced yellow, far faster than it should have.

The room contained little more than a bed, a filthy mirror, and a nightstand with the veneer obliterated by generations of cat scratches. Libby Kamen lay spread-eagled on the threadbare comforter, each limb tied to a different bedpost with nylon rope stretched taut.

"That looks a lot better than you led me to believe," Matt said.

Sakura gave him a curt nod. "It punctured the vest. One moment I coughed blood, the next I felt only mild discomfort. The bruising will be gone by morning at this rate."

"You're regenerating."

She rolled her eyes. "I never understand why you waste time on the obvious." She cut him off with his mouth half-open. "How long between regeneration and the return of the whispers for you?"

He hesitated. "Half a year, maybe a bit more."

"Then let's worry about this in six months." She nodded to Kamen's unconscious form. "We have better uses for time."

Sighing, Matt leaned down and patted Kamen on her unbruised cheek. "Hey. Libby. Wake up."

Her eyes fluttered open, revealing blue-gold irises and dilated pupils, then closed again. Her head lolled to the side, exposing the massive bruise left by Matt's boot when she'd tried to shoot him with shaking hands and zero discipline.

"Concussion," Sakura said. "She'll not think straight a while."

Matt held up a finger to silence her, then turned back to Kamen and held a picture of Adam in front of her face. He snapped his fingers. "Libby, I need you to wake up and look at this."

She opened her eyes again, lolled back and forth, then squinted in the dim light. And then she giggled.

The whispers surged through Matt's consciousness, mingling with his own hopeless rage, urging him to crush the life out of the pathetic excuse for nothing lying before him. Before it happened, he basked in the glorious crunch as his fist obliterated her cranium, and shoved eager fistfuls of steaming brain into his mouth, luscious and creamy like pate and brie.

He blinked, remembered the present, and stayed his hand. "Why are you laughing?"

"Because you're too late, Rowley." Her words slurred around a thick tongue. "They're going to parade your boy in front of the world like the freak he is, the freak you made him, and then when they figure out his tricks they're going to cut his tiny little throat." She giggled again.

Matt took a conscious step back to distance himself from the subhuman beast masquerading as a fifteen-year-old girl. Now the consuming desire to crush her skull had nothing to do with Gerstner Augmentation, nothing to do with whispers or possession or a psychotic break. The purest hate wound its way around his heart and squeezed, smothering compassion and humanity.

Sakura stepped forward, put her hand on Matt's chest and pushed him back an extra step without turning away from the bed. "This boy has done nothing. Why punish him for what his father is?"

"He's an abomination. A sin against life and God and human decency. Like all sin he must be denied before we can enter the Almighty's kingdom."

"How can a child be a sin?"

She laughed again. "I wouldn't expect you to understand."

"Try me."

Kamen's eyes rolled into the back of her head, then flipped back and concentrated on Sakura with obvious effort. "My head hurts. You got anything to drink, bitch?"

"No."

Kamen snorted. "Neither did your kid, there at the end."

Matt saw the blow before it landed and stepped forward, but couldn't get there fast enough to stop it. Sakura's heel-of-her-palm strike to Libby's mouth burst her lips. Blood splattered the pillow and streamed from Sakura's hand as she pulled it back. Libby reeled with a cry of anguish, turned to the side and spat out several teeth. Matt caught Sakura's retracted arm and hurled her away from the bed.

She crashed against the wall, flipped to her feet, and scowled, but cast her eyes down in shame.

Choking on the blood leaking from her shattered nose and mouth, Libby squealed, a pathetic wail that brought Matt back to the roof in Atlanta, to the banshee children keening at him as his act of mercy robbed them of their power and form. He tilted her head to the side to let the blood drain somewhere other than down her throat, and ran his hand over her head in compassion he didn't feel.

"Dammit, Blossom," he whispered through clenched teeth. "I need her to talk!"

Sakura held out her palm. Teeth marks marred the heel of her palm under streaks of blood. "It's healing." She rubbed it on her thigh. "A little."

Matt ignored her and looked down at Libby, now bawling, her tough-girl facade as broken as her mouth. He knelt to put himself at eye level, though with her lids squeezed shut she couldn't see him.

"Hey, I'm not trying to hurt you. I just want my son back. Please."

Blood streamed from Libby's mouth as she smiled and spoke with a new lisp. "I will set my face against all those who turn to mediums and necromancers who commune with the dead, to prostitute themselves by following them, and I will cut them off from all people." Her eyes flashed bright green, the light blazing through her flesh to expose her dark skull beneath. "Your soul is forfeit, and your son's and his progeny to the last generation."

The light disappeared as fast as it came, drowning the room in cold shadow. Libby sagged into a defeated, broken slumber.

Matt turned to Sakura, and her wide eyes said that she'd seen it, too. "What the hell was that?"

Sakura stared down at Libby's unconscious form. "There is something very wrong here."

Matt nodded. "Necromancers? You believe that?"

She replied too quickly. "The dead are dead. All else is myth."

"Yeah. Somehow I don't believe that quite as much as I used to."

Sakura looked up, closed her eyes, and took a deep breath. "We need to talk. But first, sedate her."

* * *

The Brazilian government brought Matt, Sakura, and Keene by helicopter to Libby Kamen's retreat deep in the mountains, a villa more than a mansion, almost quaint compared to her palace in Los Angeles. They found it abandoned: no guards, no servants, no sign of occupation. An empty crib sat overturned in an abandoned hallway, the yellow flannel cold.

The house had no landlines to trace, and internet came via satellite.

Matt frowned down at the bedding and spoke into his helmet. "Janet, call the NSA, please. Get me whatever you can about activity on local cell towers in the past few hours."

"On it."

* * *

Three hours later Janet had identified seven calls from the remote area, two from the same phone: a charter jet service operating out of the Zona da Mata airport, and a cell phone in rural Maryland. Zona da Mata confirmed a jet registered to a subsidiary of Kamen Industries taking off that night with a flight plan to Atlanta. It never landed.

Matt, Sakura, and Keene took the helicopter to Brasilia and hitchhiked aboard an embassy jet home. The flight staff paid so little attention to Libby Kamen's battered, unconscious body that they may as well have tattooed "CIA" on their foreheads.

Out of earshot, Keene leaned in to Matt. "When we touch down my office can take her. We've got a rendition site secure enough, it won't be a problem."

Matt exchanged glances with Sakura. "Nah. I've got a better idea."

Keene raised an eyebrow.

"Go back to Boston. We'll be in touch."

"Are you serious?"

Matt closed his eyes and leaned back. "Yup."

Chapter 15

"You've got to be kidding me." Janet stood behind the screen door in light blue flannel pajamas, her hair up in a bun, toothbrush in hand. "You brought her *here*?"

She opened the door to let them in off her side porch. Matt carried Libby Kamen's drugged, limp body into the living room. Sakura followed, eyes scoping out the corners as if in anticipation of an ambush.

"What possessed you to bring her to my house?"

Matt raised his eyebrows. "Guest bedroom?"

"Couch." God knows what he'd do if he saw the guest bedroom. After her brother's death she'd removed the bed and replaced it with a giant pentagram she used to commune with him. It kept the headaches from blossoming into full-on migraines, and kept her nose and ears from bleeding with the strain. The longer Dawkins remained on the other side, the worse it got—but the bedroom made it bearable.

Matt set Libby on the couch with more care than necessary given her snowed-out condition.

"Why did you bring her here?"

He shrugged. "You traced the call to Maryland."

Janet rubbed her forehead with her fingertips, buying time to figure out how to play the situation. "Yeah, to Baltimore, not Fulton.

The only thing you're going to find here is turkeys."

Matt leaned against the wall. "Yeah, I remember that smell from last time. Not sure I understand the appeal."

Janet shrugged. "Keeps the yuppies out. I like my space. I'm not a big fan of Jehovah's Witnesses or Mormons or coworkers walking up my porch unannounced—especially if they're carrying underage drugged celebutante zillionaires they kidnapped from Brazil. She is drugged, right?"

"Yes," Sakura said. "Regular soporific injections to keep her down. There is something off about her and we do not want her waking."

Janet's fingers returned to her scalp. "Off, how?"

"She quoted the Old Testament to us and her eyes glowed green."

"As in, like, Jade green?"

Matt gave a curt nod in her peripheral vision. "Same color as the cross on your back."

Janet shifted under her PJs, the giant tattoo itching as if aware of their attention. The ward against possession had kept the last of the Nephilim out of her mind, but did little to stave off her brother's desperate attacks. "So that means what? Gerstner is back? Growing stronger? Cue the Darth Vader music and all that?"

Sakura scowled. "Is everything humor to you?"

Janet stared her down. "I haven't found much funny in the past ten or so years, no. Certainly nothing today. And you're never funny." She turned back to Matt. "So what are we talking about here?"

Matt shrugged. "We don't know."

"But you came here because there's something you want to talk about but not over the airwaves, right? Or are you just trying to make me an accomplice in a revenge kidnapping?"

"That's not what this is—"

She cut him off with an upraised hand. "Tell it to the judge. The Kamen family owns entire cities and eats politicians—and judges—for breakfast. The cops show up, that's going to be the story no matter who knows different. Now quit wasting time and spill it."

Janet almost smiled at the rarest sight of her recent life: uncertainty crossing Matt Rowley's face. Sakura's blank expression could mean anything or nothing or both, but a sledgehammer like

Rowley uneasy, that sent a thrill of worry and excitement up her spine.

"Umm. What do you know about the afterlife?"

"That's kind of a 'priest' question, isn't it? I'm just a computer gal." The flippant response bought her time to recover from the pointedness of the question. *How much did they know?*

"We both know that's not true," Matt said. "You're way more than your job. Did Dawkins—did your brother ever talk to you about life after death? Ever find anything concrete in his research?"

She weighed the value of additional flippancy and decided against it. "Why are you asking me this?"

Sakura licked her lips. "My Kazuko came to me, surrounded by white light. It felt very much like the whispers of Gerstner augmentation but exactly not. Mercy where they are cruel, sadness where they find joy."

"So you're crazy."

Matt shook his head. "I've felt it, too. The whispers are back, but there's something else with them. I can feel people I knew, Akash and Garrett and even Adam sometimes, before they took him. Even you. I've only ever felt Augs and Jade users, and sometimes it feels like they're all there."

"I'm in your head?" She considered running, but knew she'd never make it more than a couple of steps, if that.

"Just a vague impression. You and lots of other people, all tied up together, indistinct, swimming around like a . . ."

"Maelstrom."

He grunted. "Exactly. A maelstrom of people's thoughts."

"My brother?" She watched him for anything, any sign that he knew Dawkins could step through the veil, no matter how little. Matt's face held no guile, and he'd always lacked the imagination to lie with any success.

"Now that you say it, no. I've never felt your brother in . . . whatever this is. Lots of other people, some long gone, but never him."

"Never?"

He held up his hands. "I'm sorry. I don't have an explanation."

"Who else? Who else do you feel?"

He ran his hands through his hair. "Everyone?"

"Explain."

"It's like they're all there, millions of people swimming through my head." He gave Sakura a small bow. "Kazuko joined them. Blossom and I compared notes. Her daughter passed the same moment, half the world away. I can't explain it, I don't know what it means, but there's something here, something that remains of these people. And I think it's because of Gerstner. She's the only common denominator."

Sakura pulled off her T-shirt.

Janet bit back an obnoxious comment, suppressing the defense mechanism she'd built over so many years in the enemy's nest, and leaned in to examine the faint, puckered scar beneath Sakura's black, no-frills bra.

"Looks old. Get it yesterday?"

Sakura's eyes flashed. "How did you know?"

"COM traffic. You were hit, bad enough to admit it, which must have been pretty damned bad, and then you were fine. Didn't take a genius to figure out something weird happened. Matt said they'd beaten you at the airport, but here you are, no obvious bruising. So there you have it, functional Gerstner regenerates. And if I know it, the assholes at DHS know it."

Matt ran his tongue across his front teeth and tried not to sneer. "We are the assholes at DHS."

"Yes." Janet raised a finger. "But not all the assholes. Not by a long shot." She turned to Sakura. "They've been keeping a close eye on Matt, but are too afraid to touch him, mainly because they're not sure if they can take him without Aug support. You can bet they'll have a stethoscope up your ass before the week's out."

Sakura pulled her shirt back on. "They wouldn't dare."

Janet switched gears. "So your daughter dies—I'm so sorry—and you're saved in a genuine, Vatican-thinks-it's-cool miracle."

"I'm not Christian."

Janet ignored the objection. "So you regenerated. Generation two or generation one? Any mutations? Funny growths?"

"No." Sakura ran her thumb over the scar. "It's much like before, not quite so good."

"Well that's a plus." Second-generation regenerates improved on the first in almost every way: faster, without weird mutations or increased risk of bonking out, it had revolutionized ICAP soldiery. A reversion to first-generation regenerates might be worse than no regeneration at all. "So why do you think this weird shit is tied to Gerstner? It sounds . . . different." She whirled on Matt. "Maybe you're the common denominator."

He shrugged. "You remember Ben Mueller, from almost ten years ago? I've never met him, not before he joined, not as an agent. Never saw the body after he bonked out, didn't go to the funeral. I don't think I've been within a hundred miles of him, ever. But here he is. More like him, too."

"So there's some kind of gestalt hive-mind made up of those exposed to possession by a Nephilim who just decided to live in your brain and give you advice. Seems perfectly logical."

"What do you want me to say, Janet? We're here because we thought maybe you could shed some light on the subject."

She mimicked his shrug. "Sorry. In Janet-world, dead is dead. Nothing in D's research ever said otherwise."

* * *

Matt filled the 0.5-cc syringe, stabbed it into Kamen's shoulder, and injected the sedative. Her eyes drifted lazily behind closed lids throughout the injection, with no sign of having registered the sensation.

"She's lying," Sakura said behind him. "Janet."

"I know. About what, do you think?"

"Dead is dead. She knows something she's not saying."

"Why?" He looked down at Libby, her ruined mouth puffy and bruised despite a hefty dose of anti-inflammatories.

Sakura's shadow blocked the light from the stand-lamp in the corner. "I don't get 'why'. She's a good liar, but there's something she won't tell. You can't trust her."

He turned away from the drugged girl to look at Sakura. Bloodshot eyes over deep bags betrayed her stoic expression, and deep lines creased her forehead. If he didn't know better he'd call her tired, but for Sakura to show that much on her face she must be in exhausted anguish. "I'll keep that in mind."

* * *

The phone rang six times before a female voice dripping with aspartame answered. "AR Promotions, how may I direct your call?"

"Tina Allison, please." Janet matched the artificial sweetness note for note and stared out across her back field. The goldenrod had faded to light brown and had started shedding petals, revealing dusty purple raspberry canes scattered throughout the semi-tamed field. She'd have to hire that kid with the zero-turn to knock it down in a week or two.

"Is she expecting your call?"

"No she's not. This is Janet LaLonde from the Department of Homeland Security Special Threats Bureau. It's of the utmost importance that I speak with her immediately. Interrupt if necessary." She gave her ID number, twice, to give the girl a chance to write it down.

Nothing. Then, "Hold, please."

Six minutes of insufferable pop music later, the line went quiet. A strong female voice said, "Miss LaLonde, this is Tina Allison, sorry for keeping you waiting." Her accent tasted of generic Americana, Las Vegas with maybe a little Denver thrown in.

"I understand that you represent the MMA star Big K. It's imperative that I speak with him."

"Umm, he's out of the country at the moment. May I ask what this is about?"

"I'd prefer to speak to him directly."

"By company policy we don't pass on cold calls, Miss LaLonde. We have a lot of celebrity clients and doing so would jeopardize our business, so I'm going to have to insist."

Janet watched a trio of chickadees frolic through the brush. Their carefree play belied the constant panic of their existence—eat enough to survive the winter or starve. "Okay. He kidnapped a colleague's child, raped his wife, and killed several of his neighbors. I have something he wants and am willing to broker a trade for the boy."

"Excuse me?" Allison's shock sounded genuine enough.

"I didn't misspeak. I can make a trade for the child, or my colleague can use the full might of the United States military to exterminate your client like the useless vermin he is."

"There must be some mistake—"

"There isn't. You can call whoever you want to verify my credentials. Pass on the message, please." She gave the number for the encrypted satellite phone.

"This is unbelievable."

"I agree, it is. Your client is a success in his own right who up until recently had a long life ahead of him. His decision to fuck with the most dangerous man on the planet is, to be blunt, completely insane, and the best he can now hope for is life in prison, though I give his odds of surviving this self-made clusterfuck less than one in fifty. I hope you're well insured. Anyway, have him call me at his earliest convenience. Thank you, buh-bye."

She hung up, ran her fingertips over the countertop, and turned around.

Matt sat at the kitchen table staring at his hands. She leaned in to draw his attention. "Well, that went about how I expected."

He looked up. "What do you think? Is she in on it?"

Janet touched the space bar on her laptop to wake it up. "I don't think so, but it's hard to say, especially over the phone. I'll bet we're about to find out."

She turned up the volume on the external speakers. Macklemore blared through them for a moment, then Big K's phone kicked to voicemail. "Yo, you've reached me. Do it."

Tina Allison's voice shook. "Karthik, it's Tina. I just got the weirdest fucking call in the history of ever from some girl who says she's with the Department of Homeland Security. You need to call me as soon as you get this. I'll text you, too. Call me right away. This is serious. Bye."

The phone clicked dead.

"Okay," Janet said. "So we've got his number. Let's see if we can't sniff it out." She pecked at the keys with her too-long nails, then hammered ENTER. "Okay. UPSTREAM's got his phone traveling west on Interstate 80 just outside Joliet, Illinois."

Matt moved behind her and looked at the map. He smelled of gun oil and Old Spice, a noxious, overly-masculine brew that reminded her of NASCAR and pro wrestling and noodling catfish on the bayou.

The map showed cellular locations traveling west from Chicago, a series of quasi-hexagonal regions, each centered on I-80.

"So that's Big K's phone, looks like a clean seventy miles per hour. Loading CO-TRAVELER." Janet clicked again, and thousands of vectors joined the first, turning the screen into a writhing mass of multicolored, digital tendrils. In large groups and then small, they faded and disappeared until only two others remained.

"Who are they?" Matt asked.

"First is a Verizon phone, 217 area code. Let's see . . . Jeff Rock, Decatur, Illinois address. No record, no priors. Second is . . . also Verizon, 312 area code. Issued to FedEx Chicago, Lake Street, downtown."

"On it." Matt called the Lake Street FedEx and verified that the second phone had been issued to one of their long-haul drivers, Jeff Rock, who often ran ground shipments from Chicago all the way to Sacramento and everywhere in between.

A phone call and a few minutes later, the Illinois Department of Justice dispatched the State Police to apprehend Rock, who cooperated fully after surrendering a tenth of an ounce of weed and two rolling papers. A half an hour after that they found Big K's phone, turned on with GPS enabled, in a sealed cardboard box en route via ground transportation to The Venetian hotel in Las Vegas.

Matt frowned at the picture of the label on the box. It had shipped from Baltimore.

"Nice try, you tricky bastard."

At Matt's urging, they let Rock off with a warning.

* * *

An hour after dark, Monica pulled into the driveway and killed the truck's engine, blocking in the unfamiliar maroon car. Dried mud spattered the weatherworn Camry's wheel wells. She killed the lights, drowning everything in green afterglow, then got out, helped Ted down, and pulled the pistol. Nine steps brought her to the car, and her eyes hadn't fully adjusted.

She placed her left hand on the hood. Cold. Whoever drove it had been there a while. She took shelter behind it, blinked away the last of her night blindness, and called out. "Hello?"

Dark shadows shifted on the porch, and the porch swing chains creaked in their mounts. She wished for the millionth time that Matt would get around to installing the motion lights.

"Identify yourself!"

"Mon." Jason's voice carried over the susurrus through the trees, just loud enough for her to recognize it. Ted chuffed and bounded for the steps, tail wagging.

She holstered the weapon and marched forward. "Shit, Jason, you scared the crap out of . . . are you okay?"

Dark bags dwelled under his eyes, and he hadn't shaved in days. And he stank, like old eggs and milk gone sour. Jason sat on the step and the dog shoved his nose in his crotch. Jason scratched Ted's ears and the Bassett flopped down on the spot, tail drumming an enthusiastic tattoo on the pine boards.

She put her hands on her hips. "You look like shit."

His head bobbed, the barest hint of a nod.

"You *smell* like shit."

It bobbed again.

She waited, he said nothing. His eyes wandered across the railing and through the brush, down to Ted and up almost but not quite to her face.

"Well, shit, you know you ain't supposed to be here. Maybe you and Matt patched things up a bit, but that won't stop him from pulling your arms off and beating you to death with them if he finds you talking to me when he ain't home."

"Is that what he said?" Jason's voice carried a ragged note that matched his current appearance. "That we patched things up?"

"Well, not right as rain, but you helped him with some old thing down Atlanta way, and again with me. He's grateful for it. Said you saved his life, right?"

He sighed and lay back on the porch, eyes turned up to the stars. "I did, and maybe even Blossom Sakura's and that little girl's, and brought some long-sought rest to some who needed it. I did all that. But that doesn't make us friends."

"Oh, come on. I know he's stubborn as a mule, but—"

"It's not him. It's me. He has something I want and can never have, and I can't forgive him for it, not for taking you and keeping you, and not for bringing you back into my life last year." His eyes sparkled but didn't turn to her. "You've broken me, and I can never heal."

Her heart lurched in her chest. She put her hand on the railing. "I think you need to go."

He squeezed his eyes shut, pressed the heels of his palms to his temples. "No, no, that's not even why I'm here. I'm here because I love you, but I'm not here for you or because of you. I came here because of Adam."

She shivered in the crisp mountain air. "What do you know about my boy?"

"I've been dreaming about him, about the people trying to hurt him. Only this time he spoke to me. He's so much older than his years. There's something in him, like the void between the stars, you think it's empty but it's not."

She fumbled with her cell phone, thought about calling 9-1-1. "You're not making sense."

He gave a vigorous nod of agreement. "No. But that doesn't mean it's not true." His eyes snapped open, wide, mad. "We have to help him!"

"Matt's doing everything he can. Adam will—"

"Not Adam. We have to help your husband!"

"Jason, you listen to me." She cleared her throat. "You don't start making sense real soon, I'm going to kick your ass six ways to Sunday and call the county to haul you to the drunk tank."

He put up his hands. "I'm not drunk. Haven't had a drink in weeks. I'm . . . enlightened. I can see past here and now, to a string of endless unrealities. I—"

She leaned in and delivered an open-palm slap, hard enough to wrench his head to the side without the leverage necessary to knock him unconscious. Ted barked at her. Jason carried on, so she slapped him again. "Last warning. You can't bring shit around me. You can't."

He took a deep breath, letting it out like a drag off a cigarette. "I assure you I'm quite sane and not under the influence. Your husband is in grave danger, and we need to help him."

She frowned down at Ted, tried to hide her sudden craving in his soft brown eyes.

". . . which is something my son told you. Adam, who's barely even said his first word. In a dream."

"In a dream." He flinched and threw up his arms in a defensive posture. "Please stop hitting me. I know it sounds crazy. I thought I was crazy. But it's not, and I'm not. I swear on the cloak of St. Martin that I'm not."

"Is that blasphemy for you folks? I don't know about you Catholics and your saints."

"No, it's not blasphemy. It's a miracle."

"So, what, Adam comes to you in a dream and says his daddy's going to get killed?"

Jason shook his head. "No. His daddy is going to kill someone, and in the process lose his soul. We have to keep Matt from going bonk."

Monica stared at him a long moment.

Ted looked from Jason to her and back, trying to decide who might have treats.

"I'm listening."

* * *

In the darkness, Jay Z blared at Tina Allison. She fumbled for the console next to her bed and hit "Snooze." Unabated, it dragged her reluctantly from sleep until she sat up, grabbed her phone, squinted at a screen she couldn't see without her glasses, and hit 'Talk."

"Hello?"

"Yo. I need my accounts."

"Karthik?"

"First thing in the a-to-the-m, got it? Every penny."

She couldn't tell if his usual intensity had ramped up to something more, but that he didn't ask for more information about her last message brought a tightness to her chest. "What the hell is going on?"

"What's going on is I need my accounts transferred."

"Are . . . are you in trouble?"

"Nothing I can't handle. You ready for the number?"

"Give me half a second." She got up, shuffled to the desk on the far side of the room, and pulled out a pen. "Hit me."

She wrote the number on her hand and read it back to him.

"Soon as the banks open, babe."

"You got it, K. Be safe."

"I always am."

She hung up, opened her laptop, and pulled up Janet LaLonde's number.

* * *

Matt put on his tactical helmet and double-checked Sakura's chute. He gave her a thumbs-up, so without hesitation she leapt from the open door of the small airplane. He followed her out, and the vista of Baltimore on a late fall night opened up twelve thousand feet underneath him. Oriented over the Gwynn's Falls hiking trail, a twist of his upper body shifted his path of descent toward the rooftop of a large industrial building leased by Liaguno, Morton, and Wood.

Big K had used a burner—a prepaid phone with no contract and no linked accounts—but with the number they'd managed to narrow his cell location to Baltimore, and put out a discrete APB. Eyes-on by an astute beat cop from the Baltimore Police Department pegged Big K at the warehouse below. A task force of FBI, BPD, and Maryland State Police had quietly cordoned off the area with orders to detain anyone attempting to leave the building, but due to the likelihood of at least one hostage—eleven months old—come in hot only if called by Matt, Sakura, or Janet.

The aerial entry had been Sakura's idea, a way to get inside the perimeter fence and past any guards without drawing any eyes. Mankind had left the jungle too long ago for the average person to consider looking up to scan for threats. Blueprints had indicated roof access via a southern balcony, and a wide-open warehouse area topped by two floors of offices.

Positioned above the building, they dropped in pencil dives, the air whipping past them at terminal velocity. The HUD indicated no hostiles on the roof but two on the ground inside the fence perimeter, walking together instead of on opposite sides of the building. He wondered again if it were a trap, and how far his enemy would go to kill him.

They deployed canopies three hundred feet above the building.

His boots crunched gravel so he pulled in his chute, twisting the fabric to keep it from blowing away or dragging him off the building. Sakura reached the ladder first, her chute already wrapped around a pipe sticking out of the rooftop.

She dropped back on her haunches and signed, *Guards below, two of them, walking east, chatting like sweethearts.* Her American Sign Language outpaced his by a good deal, but he understood her well enough despite the lack of practice since ICAP had ended tactical operations.

Wait for them to circle to the North side, then ignore them.

She nodded her agreement, waited until their voices had faded into the distance, then led down the ladder to the fourth-story balcony.

Matt put his fingers on the glass and pushed up. The unlocked window slid open with ease. Hands bare, Matt took point through the small manager's office and listened at the door. He heard nothing, so he opened it without a sound and peeked out into the hallway.

Doors lined either side, dark save for one, a room at the far end with light peeking under the door crack. Matt approached on the balls of his feet, scanning the floor for loose boards or anything that would betray his presence. Light clacking sounded behind the door.

Matt pulled an endoscope from his kit and slithered it under the door crack. A quick survey showed two dark-haired occupants sitting on an enormous brown leather loveseat. Both wore headphones and played Call of Duty on a giant flat screen TV, their backs to the door. A pair of Chinese AK-47s leaned against the wall next to the TV. Matt pulled back the scope and stuffed it into his kit.

Behind me, take the left, Matt signed to Sakura.

He turned the knob ever so slowly and opened the door. Neither man responded, so he motioned Sakura in, drew a combat knife and stepped forward. They took them together, leaning down in synchronous motion to grab foreheads and drag their knives across unsuspecting throats.

Matt held his target's head against his abdomen as blood leaked from the struggling body. When he lay still Matt let go, wiped the knife clean on the back of the couch, and sheathed it at his ankle. After a quick look out the window—they had an excellent view of the main gates—Matt picked up the controllers one by one, said AFK, and left the game while Sakura disabled the firing pins on the AKs.

The dead men both stared at him, heads leaned together like new lovers at the movies. Brown hair, brown eyes, they had to have been brothers, the older no more than twenty-five. Matt wondered if either had raped his wife, or taken his son, or murdered Chris and Sandy.

They closed the door on the way out and backtracked to the unlit rooms. Dusty collections of filing cabinets and banker's boxes, none held a crib or bassinette, none held his son. They took the stairs to the third floor after checking for cameras or tumblers and finding none.

The well-lit hallway looked identical to the one above it, save that every door stood open, every room ablaze with stark fluorescent light. Matt raised his AA-12, and Sakura switched from her knives to the REC-7. They made it four steps before a man walked out of a far room, eyes downcast, blowing across the top of a steaming mug in his hands. Matt's Friend-or-Foe identifier outlined him in a double triangle.

Sakura stepped into a doorway, taking cover while keeping her weapon trained on the target.

The man froze mid-step and turned, giving Matt a good view of his face. Big K's soft brown eyes widened under his bright red baseball cap, but to his credit he neither panicked nor tried to run. Instead he smiled, blazing white Hollywood teeth behind red gums. With easy confidence he took a sip of his drink. "Your son's not here, Matty-boy. Yardley's got him somewhere you ain't never going to find."

Yardley. What did that psychotic have to do with Humans for Humanity?

"Where is he?"

"Safe, for now. But you so much as muss our hair, your son won't live to see sunup."

His finger on the trigger, Matt shrugged with a nonchalance he didn't feel. "Too late for that. Your boys upstairs won't be finishing their game."

Black rage descended on Big K's face. "If you touched my brothers—"

A twinge of guilt sparked off the whispers, who rejoiced at the heartache and agony he'd caused.

"Too late. You shouldn't have brought them into this."

All sense of toughness drained out of Karthik's body, and in that moment he looked like nothing so much as a scared little boy. His coffee clattered at his feet. "Are . . . are they okay?"

"They're dead," Sakura said.

The whispers giggled and tittered just before two things happened simultaneously: Karthik charged, and someone threw a grenade out the door to their left. Matt stepped forward and turned, using his momentum to swat the grenade back to the room it came from. He ducked under the undisciplined MMA fighter and heaved with his legs, throwing Karthik past the room. Matt just had time to slam the door and turn his head before the explosion rocked him.

Jagged splinters dug into the back of his neck between his vest and helmet. In the deafening silence he picked up weapons-chatter, staccato bursts characteristic of Sakura's efficient, impersonal brutality. Matt turned as Big K struck, his fingers punching right through Matt's visor to shatter his nose.

Matt stumbled back, blocking a series of lightning-fast strikes and kicks. Only his precognition kept him alive as Karthik hammered him with strikes too strong for a normal man, too fast even for Sakura. Matt ducked a wild haymaker and didn't take the bait—instead of closing in to take advantage of the false opening, he took a farther step back and raised the shotgun.

Karthik chopped down on the barrel and Matt's shot hit the floor, but the microgrenade sprayed Karthik's bare ankles with high-velocity shrapnel. He didn't fall, didn't even react except to snap-kick Matt's hand, crushing his fingers between boot and gun.

Matt stepped into the kick and brought up his knee. Karthik turned to catch the blow on his side, but the force slammed him into and partially through the plaster wall. Matt cracked him under the jaw with the stock, and Karthik sent him flying with an open-palm strike to the chest.

His armor solidified around the blow, disbursing the impact, but he slammed into the opposite wall hard enough to snap the stud behind the now-ruined plaster. The shotgun clattered to the floor.

Karthik grinned around bloody teeth. "New game in town, Rowley. Time to die."

Big K covered the distance between them in two fluid steps. Matt fell back to the ground and, as Karthik's knee occupied the space where his head had been, unholstered the Glock and pulled the trigger twice, sending two .45-caliber bullets up through Karthik's groin into his abdomen.

Matt kipped up to his feet as Karthik collapsed to the ground, eyes wide, mouth open in a surprised "O." He fired twice more into

Karthik's center of mass at point-blank range, then swept up the AA-12 and opened the first door, through which he'd batted the grenade.

A mangled body smoked next to an overturned table, and a third clutched his ruined leg and screamed inarticulate madness. The injured man wore a pistol, so Matt stepped forward and kicked him in the side of the head. His neck snapped under the force. Matt turned and stepped back into the hall, shotgun raised and ready.

Sakura took cover in the room across the way. Rifle in one hand, she pulled a flash-bang grenade from her bandoleer, grabbed the pin with her teeth, and pulled it. She nodded to Matt, then gave it a toss. He timed his charge for the split second after the explosion and made it halfway down the hall before anyone had recovered.

A man leaned out from the far room, an AK-47 raised toward where Matt used to be. Matt spun around the barrel and slammed the stock of the AA-12 into his neck. A second stumbled back and shot Matt twice in the chest with a small-caliber pistol. Matt grunted as his armor absorbed the impact, let go of the shotgun, the explosive rounds near-useless in such proximity, and lunged.

He punched through the shooter's torso, shattering the drywall behind, turned, and threw the body at the doorway. Ravaged entrails spilled out of the cavity as Matt's forearm pulled out of the wound with a wet sucking sound. Red meat and rotting curry filled his nostrils, mixed with a sharp, acidic bite. Another man rounded the corner and fumbled his weapon trying to catch the body as it hit him.

Matt leapt, tackling both dead body and living man through the hallway into the kitchenette. Bullets stung his leg on the way through, hot and sharp but through-and-through. He tore out the living man's throat left-handed and with his right, drew his pistol and fired twice, taking the room's sole occupant square in the chest. The shot man stumbled back into the coffee pot then sank to his haunches, blood streaking the cupboards on the way down.

In the sudden silence Matt's right hand burned, and his throat tightened at the stench of bile and stomach acid. "Sakura, status?"

The dead man fell forward onto his face, a pool of red leaking out under his body.

"All but the last two rooms are clear. The three who tried to make the stairwell are down. We can probably negotiate with the rest."

Using a chair, Matt dragged himself to his feet. He couldn't put weight on his leg yet, so he needed to buy a little time. "Alright, I need a minute. Can you cover them if they come out?"

"Yes."

He raised his voice. "Your boss is dead. If you want to live through the next sixty seconds, throw down your weapons and come into the hallway with your hands on your heads. We won't ask again."

He looked down the hallway. The stairwell door stood ajar, the bodies of three women in their underwear lay in a tangle, preventing it from closing. An infrared signature kept just out of sight of normal vision in the dark beyond them.

"That includes you in the stairwell. The building is surrounded, and you're going to jail on weapons and kidnapping charges, unless you prefer suicide by cop, which we're happy to provide. Your choice." He flexed his leg, put a little weight on it, then bobbed up and down on his toes. "You've got forty-two more seconds."

The first man came out ten seconds later, followed by another four.

In the end they had seventeen casualties and five perpetrators in custody, including two more of Peter Salomon's former employees. Matt washed up before forensics moved in to pick through the bloodiest "no-knock raid" in the history of the city of Baltimore. This time their credentials kept them out of custody and put them in the interrogation rooms with the perps.

They talked.

* * *

Standing over Karthik's split-open remains, Matt raised his eyebrows at the coroner, an FBI forensic examiner on loan from Keene. The pasty little man looked up from his calculator, and then at the rib fragment in the graduated cylinder, and cleared his throat. "By my estimation, bone density is three grams per cubic centimeter, not quite double human normal. Based on the luster I would suspect some kind of metallic additive—it looks like honeycomb under the electron microscope."

Big K's organs already lay in trays, for the most part normal, but as the coroner had removed each one, tiny black filaments pulled from them, the combination of strength and tiny size leading Matt to believe they were made from—or entwined with—graphene fiber of some kind.

"What about the brain?" Sakura asked.

He smiled. "Let's take a look, shall we?" He plopped a face shield on his head and picked up the vibrating Stryker saw. The high-pitched whine lowered as it bit into Karthik's forehead and a musty, smoky odor overpowered the antiseptic aroma of bleach. "Difficult, like the sternum."

They waited until the little man had pried Big K's skull cap off, then stepped around to observe the pinkish, shiny blob.

"Seems normal enough," the coroner said. "Let's see what it weighs."

As he worked the brain out, a thousand or more black fibers held it in, and he grunted at the effort necessary to pull the organ away from the skull. They came away like hair, black and wiry, all attached to a tiny bundle at the base of the brain stem.

Sakura leaned in and clicked on a small, hand-held flashlight. "Processor."

Over her shoulder Matt saw the truth of it: the bundle of artificial nerves terminated at a clear box, inside of which a series of small microchips lay on a bright green circuit board.

"Fascinating," the coroner said. He turned to them, bloody gloves raised in the air, and gave a quick nod toward the door. "I'm going to wash up and call in someone who might know what this is, who built it, and how it got into our fighting friend, here."

"Can you trust him?"

He nodded without hesitation. "She and I have worked together on many sensitive issues. We'll get you a report as soon as we have one to issue."

"Thanks."

Chapter 16

Twelve hours of surveillance via satellite and county PD told them enough to go in without weapons: Murdock Yardley's mother lived alone on her seventeen-acre farm and employed neighborhood boys to keep the yards mowed and the cows fed. She'd upgraded fourteen years earlier, after her son had made his first million dollars as a prize fighter, well before he'd volunteered to join ICAP. He held the house in his name, but had never lived there.

They drove up the winding, pothole-filled dirt driveway to the modern McMansion completely out of place in the middle of the Maryland pasture. The brick facade and vinyl siding encased enormous windows revealing an open floor plan with all the amenities—a fake fireplace, marble countertops, bar, Jacuzzi. Sakura stayed with the car by choice, so Matt walked up the porch and rang the bell.

Anita Yardley smiled when she opened the door in a chaotic broomstick dress to make any hippie proud. Her gray hair hung in curls almost to her waist, and Matt couldn't help but admire her beauty. Approaching sixty, she didn't look a day over forty, and the kind of forty that makes boys appreciate women as opposed to girls. "Well, if it isn't Matt Rowley. What brings a gentleman like you down a country road like this?"

If she saw Sakura leaning against the car, she made no comment of it. Instead she stepped back and offered him a drink—which he refused—and a plate of cookies, which he accepted. "You look . . . fantastic. Miraculous. Skin grafts can't do that."

"No ma'am, they can't."

"So . . . ?"

He shrugged. "I can't explain it."

After they'd settled in her immaculate living room, in front of the gas fire, she took a sip of tea and set it down. "So what brings you here?"

"I'm looking for Murdock. I haven't seen or heard anything from him since that day you and I met, when things went south last year." Like so many bonks, Yardley had collapsed under the weight of his own body when his augmentations had failed. Matt had spent far too much time visiting former colleagues in hospitals. He'd met Anita Yardley at her son's bedside when Murdock still languished in a coma and Matt had been covered with burn scars.

"Is this a social call?"

"No, ma'am, it's not."

She waited, so he continued.

"He's either causing trouble or someone's using his name to do it. Either way, I'd like to speak to him about some friends of his who seem to have a vendetta against me."

She took another sip, pinning him over the top of her cup. "Well, he said you really showed him something in some fight or another last year, before, you know, before. He didn't have many nice things to say once he woke up."

Matt remembered it well enough. Yardley had been called in to kill Matt and Sakura and didn't give a damn when Matt proved they hadn't bonked out by trying to have a conversation with him. He'd only stopped crushing Matt to death when Sakura had torn out most of his spine and emptied half a magazine up into his abdomen.

Yardley liked killing people and didn't much care who, how,

or why.

"We didn't really know each other except by reputation. He was following orders, I was doing my job, we ran afoul of each other. Wasn't his fault, wasn't mine. Either way, he's not in the hospital and he's not here. Can you tell me where he is?"

She shrugged. "Lying in a bed somewhere with a machine keeping him alive. Other than that, I'm not sure I'm comfortable ratting out my son to the police. Or whatever you are. Do you have a title anymore? Jurisdiction?"

"My credentials are what they need to be. Where is he, please?"

"I don't know."

"Can you get a hold of him?"

"Not for you, I don't think so." She smiled a sad smile and patted his hand. "He's never been a good boy, but he's still my son."

Matt closed his eyes and took a deep breath. The whispers shrieked and laughed as he tore the flesh from her face and stuffed it into her screaming mouth. He opened them. "He has *my* son, my baby boy. I just want my son back, that's all."

She stood, smoothed her dress down, walked to the door and opened it. "As do I, Matt. As do I. Now if you'll excuse me, I have a book that won't read itself. Good day."

Matt stalked out, fuming. Sakura waited until they got back to the hotel to ask what had happened.

* * *

The heat of the caves helped strip the cold from Murdock Yardley's bones. Ever since his Augs had failed, he couldn't get warm, no matter how many blankets he wore. They said the nerve bundles would help, and maybe they did, but not enough. Not nearly enough. Sweat streamed down his face from the heat radiating through the wall, the fifty-year-old fire on the other side bathing the whole area in blessed warmth.

The phone rang twice in his head. Murdock answered it with a thought, the graphine-coated gold tendrils interfacing his brain and the mechanical suit taking care of the connection with no effort on his part.

"Hi, Mom." His voice reverberated through the natural chamber two octaves lower than a normal man's.

"Hey, baby-cakes. Matt Rowley came looking for you today. Says you've done all sorts of terrible things."

Servos whined as the hydraulic pumps actuated the metal cages that held his legs, carrying him across the room in a lumbering parody of human walking. "How could I do terrible things, Mom? I can't even stand."

"I said as much, but he didn't listen. Made up some story about you being a kidnapper. Just figured you'd want to know."

"Thanks."

"I love you, pookums. Be good."

"Love you, too, Ma."

He killed the connection, picked up a boulder the size of a basketball in mechanical hands that almost mimicked the feeling of human nerves, and tossed it up a few times like a boy with a softball. Murdock looked down at the little man in a suit in front of him. "You're sure they traced the call?"

"My office set it up." Special Agent In-Charge Shane Keene smiled. "Remember the deal—we need Sakura alive."

"As long as I get to kill Rowley, you can have your plaything."

He closed his fist. The sandstone cracked, then crumbled.

Murdock Yardley smiled for the first time in a year.

* * *

Monica met him at the door, her face a mask of I-don't-want-to-tell-you-what's-wrong.

"Hey, baby." He held her and kissed her hair, kicking the door shut with his boot before Ted could sneak out to chase squirrels he'd never, ever catch. "We know he's alive, we know where he is. We're almost there."

"Where is he?"

He thought about what to tell her and landed on owing her the truth. Most of the truth. "Do you remember Murdock

Yardley?"

"The agent who attacked us when I was in the hospital."

"Yeah. Sounds like he's got a vendetta against me, blames me for being in the shape he's in."

Monica squeezed him. "You are to blame for the shape he's in."

"True. If I hadn't destroyed Gerstner's machine he'd have—" He caught himself before using "bonked out" in front of his wife. "He'd have had a psychotic break by now and would have been put down."

"There's that." She held him a moment. "So Yardley took our son?"

"Looks like he paid some people to do it, yeah."

"So what are you going to do?"

"I'm going to get him back, and I'm going to kill Yardley and everyone who's helping him."

She shook her head against his chest. "No, don't do it like that. Let him live. Let him live in that bloated body for as long as God lets him. Let him suffer."

He pulled back to look her in the eyes. "Baby, that's not the person you want to be. Sometimes people have to die, but they never have to suffer, not if you can avoid it."

Again her eyes screamed at him while her voice said nothing.

"What aren't you telling me?"

She looked down, screwed her toe into the floorboards. "Jason came here the other night." She held a finger to his lips to keep him from interrupting. "Babbling all crazy-like about fallen angels and how Gerstner's setting you up. He told me not to tell you, said telling you's the way to screw it all up. But I trust you, baby, and I want you to know what he said."

He pulled her close again. "Okay. What did he say?"

"He said you're going to kill someone and it's going to push you over the edge."

Matt thought about the people he'd killed early that morning and felt nothing but righteousness. They'd taken his son, raped his wife, planned to do more. They'd courted death and gotten what they deserved. "I'm okay, baby. I'll be okay."

* * *

Naked, Janet held the cat to her breast, stroking its head to calm it. The pentagram glowed in the candlelight, the chalk a ruddy mix of red and brown. She lifted the heavy creature by the scruff, held it over her head, and inserted the knife just below its throat. It kicked and writhed, shredding her wrist with its claws, but with one fluid motion she drew the knife down. Blood and entrails spilled from the dying creature, drenching her face and hair, running down her spine and between her breasts.

The blood sizzled where it touched the Jade Cross tattooed across her back, filling the room with the delicious and nauseating smells of cooking meat and boiling blood.

She swallowed everything that fell into her mouth, choking down the hot viscera while chewing as little as possible. Gagging, she dropped to her knees. The cat twitched on the floor, eyes wide, chest heaving, trying to scream with ruined lungs.

Blood streamed from her nose, eyes, and mouth.

IT ISN'T ENOUGH. Her brother's voice battered through her skull, rending sense and sanity, both less and more than it had ever been.

She shook her head. "It's all you'll get, D. I'm not sacrificing children, not even for you."

I can't remain with what you give me. It isn't enough.

"Then take it," she snarled. "Rowley's a walking breach, an open door you just have to step through. I can see the conduits, white and jade. Pick a path and take it."

SHE IS THERE.

Blood leaked from her ears, black and thick like motor oil used too long. In the window the sun went out and wind howled through the room. Struggling to hold on to any vestige of herself, Janet latched onto what defined her relationship with her brother.

With equal parts love and scorn, she laughed. "I never took you for a coward."

You don't understand.

"I understand all too well, D. You're afraid. Well, so be it.

Fade to nothing. Give up everything you've fought for. Surrender to the Pit, let Gerstner have you after all these years, consume your frightened little soul to free another of her precious egregoroi. Wither and fade, give up and die, end life as you began it, naked and screaming and helpless."

The wind died to a whisper.

Sister, why are you so cruel?

"I've given you more than you've ever had a right to. And I will bring you back but not by whatever it takes. I will not kill children to give you the strength. We'll find another way."

* * *

The dark brown motel off Route 61 looked like a mountain cabin had gotten out of hand. A massive gray chimney rose out of the kitchen, offering the broken promise of brick-oven food. It also happened to be the only thing breaking up the flat brown of the roof, siding, and trim. The parking lot smelled like fry oil and diesel exhaust.

"Home sweet home," Matt said.

Agent Keene threw up his hands. "Hey, man, don't blame me. This is the closest place to Centralia with public lodging."

Centralia, Pennsylvania's, only claim to fame consisted of an underground fire in a coal mine that had started in 1962 and spread uncontrollably through hundreds of acres of tunnels, burning ever since. Sinkholes, toxic levels of carbon monoxide, and basements heated to a hundred-plus degrees had persuaded all but a few diehards to take a 1984 government buyout and leave town.

Matt wondered how much Yardley knew, to choose a flaming pit for his hideout.

The sign out front boasted, "Hells Mouth Nacho's $3.99!" and "Seafood Wednesday's are ON!" and "Mt. Carmel Cake with real carmel!"

"This place is disgusting." Sakura wiped a sheen of grease off the chimney on the way by.

"Yelp gave it almost two stars," Keene said. "Compared to

some of the dives I've had to crash in, this is paradise."

"That's unfortunate." Matt followed Sakura, desperately happy it wasn't Wednesday.

The inside had little enough to offer. At three o'clock on a Friday, a half-dozen people sat at the bar, and a young couple occupied a booth in the gloomy, dated dining room. As they walked in, everyone looked at them and then turned back to their food and drinks.

Matt scanned the crowd for anyone from Salomon's dossiers while Sakura ran license plates on her tablet.

They paid for adjacent rooms, one for Matt and Keene, and one for Sakura—the same one used by Anita Yardley on the three occasions she'd stayed there. Matt entered his room and admired the sad, flat pillows, threadbare comforter, and chairs with foam bursting out their seams. At least it didn't smell like cat pee.

They settled in and brought out the computers, using Matt's bed as a makeshift operations suite. They had little to go on—Yardley's cell phone didn't have GPS enabled, and neither UPSTREAM nor CO-TRAVELER could give them a specific location, so they had to settle for "somewhere around Centralia, PA." They'd tracked medical equipment a man in Yardley's condition might need and turned up nothing.

A truck roared by on 61, the thin walls doing little to muffle the noise. With their FOB a Marine Reserves barracks an hour away in Harrisburg, it'd have to do.

"So what's first?" Keene asked.

"Less than six thousand people live in this town. First thing we do is show some pictures around and see if anyone recognizes any of our perps."

Keene looked out the window. "You don't think that might tip them off?"

Matt shrugged. "They're already tipped off. There's no way Yardley isn't smart enough to know that we tapped his mom's phone before dropping by."

The FBI agent gaped like a fish. "So you think it's a trap?"

"Of course it's a trap. He took my son for bait, used easily traceable mercenaries from a legitimate company, and then took a call from his mother on an unencrypted cell phone. It's got exactly the subtlety I'd expect from that sadistic meathead. Thing is, he's always been smarter than he lets on."

Keene stood and looked out the window. "So what if he just blows the place up with a drone?"

Sakura shook her head. "In seven years with ICAP, Yardley never once used a firearm or explosive device. He's a warrior, not a soldier."

Keene furrowed his brow. "I'm not sure I know the difference."

"When war ends, soldiers go home to their lives. Warriors find another war, because that is their lives."

Matt leaned in. "Yardley likes to kill. Loves it. But it has to be up close and personal, brutal and bloody and physical. He may not be able to come for us himself, but he'll at least make it something he can watch. No, the only drone strikes anyone has to worry about are ours."

Keene frowned. "So the plan is to bait Yardley into attacking and then take him out?"

Matt sighed. "I don't care about Yardley. I just want my son."

"Okay, so how do we find him?"

* * *

John Murray frowned down into the crevasse. Hot smoke trickled out of the sinkhole, the smell and the deadly vapors imperceptible through his gas mask. The ground shifted under his feet, so he backpedaled away from the natural deathtrap straight into a tree, leaves withered to a late-October brown.

"Sergeant," Todd Nelsen said.

Murray turned. "What is it, Corporal?"

"This place gives me the fucking creeps."

"Acknowledged." A city boy by birth and upbringing, he found the deep woods freaky enough without pits of fire emerging out of the ground, scattered buildings crumbling between streets overtaken by plant-life. For the sake of morale, he didn't see the value in agreeing with more vigor. "Take your team to the next intersection."

"Rah, Sergeant." Nelsen turned and screamed.

Murray whirled, jerking up his M-4, but Nelsen had already fired his M203. The massive shadow batted away the grenade and charged. It exploded behind the monstrosity.

Twelve feet tall, the humanoid form grabbed Nelsen with a huge claw. The fireteam leader exploded in sprays of blood, severed chunks dropping to the ground as the beast laughed. An M27 chattered behind Murray, the bullets pinging off the burnished metal plates. He fired, backpedaling.

His stomach lurched, the ground disappeared beneath him.

Hot gas seared his lungs, and daylight disappeared. He scrambled for purchase on crumbling rock walls hot enough to blister his fingers. Skin bubbled, his uniform caught fire. Then the high-explosive rounds on his bandoleer detonated.

* * *

Matt held up a fist. Seeing it, Sakura froze. Keene took two more steps, then stopped when she grabbed his arm.

Idiot.

She heard it then, the distinct chatter of automatic weapons, something light like a 5.56mm just at the edge of hearing. The ground shuddered. Matt bolted. She turned to follow, and Keene grabbed her wrist.

"Wait!"

She jerked free as the sound from the explosion reached them, and raised her combat visor to look him in the eyes. "What?"

"Don't leave me out here on my own. I'm not combat trained."

She rolled her eyes and slapped a hand to the side of her neck at a sharp pain. Keene jerked his hand away, flinging something small and glass into the brush. She stepped after him, and her knees gave way, pitching her to the forest floor.

"I have to help Matt," she mumbled. She struggled to open her eyes, to stand up, but her body wouldn't cooperate. ". . . can't do it himself."

He pulled off her helmet and tossed it into the brush. "Sorry,

Sakura. Rowley's not my problem."

Thoughts wouldn't form on her tongue, so they came out a jumble of English and Japanese. Rough hands hog-tied her, but she couldn't feel the bonds, only a vague sense of discomfort as he wrenched her limbs around.

". . . kill you . . ."

"Maybe some other time. Go to sleep."

She did.

* * *

Matt came upon the remains of the squad, a dozen men in hundreds of parts, the foliage painted red with their blood. Huge marks gouged the trees, and something had left tracks strong enough to mar the asphalt as it had crossed the road.

"Sakura, are you getting this?"

She didn't reply, so he switched his HUD to her helmet camera. It took him a moment to resolve the image, an ultra-close view of tree bark.

"Sakura?" Nothing. He followed the tracks of the massive whatever-it-was. "Janet, a hand, please?"

"What's up, Matt?"

"Can you do a rewind on Sakura's feed, tell me what just happened?"

"Moment."

The tracks stopped at a hole in the ground, a crevasse right out of a horror movie. Tendrils of black smoke rose from it, wiggling their way under Matt's helmet to tickle his nose and the back of his throat.

"Can't tell. She watched you run off, then slapped a hand up to her neck."

"She's with Keene. Where are they going?"

"I don't know. She took it off, dropped it on the ground."

"Delta squad is dead. Send Alpha and Bravo after Sakura and Keene, and route Charlie to my position. We've got to deal with whatever did this."

"Will do."

The ground rumbled. He looked into the pit, which glowed bright in the infrared spectrum, maybe a hundred and thirty degrees. "Shit. Janet?"

"Go ahead."

"Belay that order on Charlie. Send them after Sakura. There's no way they'd survive this heat. I'm going in."

"Roger that."

He clambered down crumbling rock into the pit, sweat evaporating as fast as it could spring from his pores. A tunnel wound downward, glowing way too hot. He set off, navigating by ultraviolet which turned the pitch darkness into a blue-black outline as he followed the thing deeper into the caves.

Chapter 17

Monica followed Jason Rees into the pit, rock scree crumbling under her hands and feet. Her Vietnam-era gas mask fogged with her breath, making it next to impossible to see even with the LED lamps on top spearing the darkness.

Jason walked with confidence he had no right to, not in this light, not with never having been here before. "He's this way. Hurry! We have to get there before Matt does."

She stumbled through the rough, hot chambers after him, her faith in him shakier than his faith in whatever-this-was. The walls closed in, black slate and dark gray siltstone, oppressive in their drab majesty. The unbearable heat sucked the energy from her, and the gallon of water she carried on her hips would last only so long.

The ground rumbled, and dust fell from the walls. "We're going to die down here."

He turned and grabbed her shoulders, eyes bugged out behind his mask. "No. You must believe. He'll keep us safe."

Monica scowled. "Adam is not some messiah, Jason. He's just a little boy. A scared little boy who needs his momma."

"Right. Exactly." His tone told her nothing. He turned and scrambled down a narrow tunnel into a wide room, then up into another. With no choice at this point, she followed.

"This place is huge." Her clothes clung to her body, but she didn't yet dare take a sip of water.

"Yes," he said. "There are hundreds of miles of tunnels, only a fraction of which right around Centralia are on fire. The rest rumble and stink but aren't connected to the tunnel that's on fire, at least not yet. In a couple hundred years, who knows?"

"Hundreds of miles of tunnels."

"Yes."

"And you won't get us lost."

"No. We won't get lost."

She followed, a prayer on her lips.

* * *

Jason followed the silver filaments blazing through the tunnels, lighting the way better than any headlamp ever could. They twisted and intertwined like will-o-wisps stretched to infinity, an endless cacophony of joy and mercy and love.

Jade streaked through them, cruel and capricious, but he ignored it, and the single black filament that wormed along with the rest. That way led to madness, and he would not let them touch him.

The vision had no other interpretation. Monica would die if she wasn't there, die and be lost forever, and through her death invite a darkness that had slumbered since ancient Sumer. He didn't care about the world, only about her. Fragile yet so, so strong, she rode a knife's edge that could fall either way.

He wouldn't let anyone have her, not even himself.

* * *

Matt felt it before he saw or even heard it, a deep rumbling cadence that rocked the caves and sent dust crumbling from the walls. He ran faster, lungs burning in the acrid air, hoping against hope that whatever killed those marines would lead him to his son.

He stopped just before a sharp turn, the whispers gibbering their delight at his near death. The rumbling had stopped. He held his breath, listening for any clue as to the beast's nature.

"I know you're there, Rowley." Yardley's voice carried through the chamber, far too deep for a normal man. "Why don't you come out and play?"

The whispers faded. Matt stepped around the corner and gasped.

He could just make out parts of Yardley within the bionic augmentation. The giant machine stood over twelve feet tall in a parody of human form, a collection of thick metal plates and nanofiber mesh, a robotic football player from hell. The helmet depicted a caveman-like parody of the worst of bonks, with a prominent sloping brow and huge serrated teeth through which he could just make out Yardley's eyes. Hydraulic pistons and electromuscle weaved over and even through Yardley's flesh, fusing the suit directly to his body.

"What is this, Murdock? Build yourself a new toy?"

Yardley laughed, a bray more suited to a startled cow carried by what had to be hidden speakers. "Where would I get the funds to make something like this?"

"That's the right question, but I've got a better one. Where the fuck is my son?"

Huge metallic claws like eagle's talons smashed together, then rubbed back and forth. "I'll fight you for him. Just you and me, like nature intended. And this time that bitch Sakura isn't here to interfere."

Matt smirked, projecting a confidence he didn't quite feel against the hulking behemoth. "Why would you think that?"

Yardley laughed again. "'Cause Agent Keene's got her in a van on the way to a black site to find out what makes the two of you so fucking special." He shrugged massive metal shoulders. "Everyone's got a price."

* * *

Sakura snapped awake and tried to sit up.

Metal ties held her to a gurney and sliced into her wrists and ankles as she struggled. The world swam, fuzzy and indistinct.

"I wouldn't bother." A woman appeared in surgical scrubs complete with a mask, her chocolate-brown skin a stark contrast to the bright white of her clothing. "Titanium-reinforced nanofiber. You'll just hurt yourself."

A man appeared on the other side of the gurney, Caucasian, a little too pale and similarly dressed. "An impressive recovery, Miss Sakura. Based on your current physiology we expected you to remain unconscious for at least another few hours, and a normal human wouldn't wake up at all."

The voice shouldn't have surprised her: Keene's coroner, who'd autopsied Big K.

She snarled and pulled. Muscles strained, the restraints dug deeper. She bit her tongue to distract from the pain in her wrists. Bright red blood splattered the woman, and she shied back. Sakura's arm throbbed, and with each pulse of her heart another jet of arterial blood sprayed through the makeshift ambulance.

The bonds neither heard nor yielded to her screams.

The man picked up a pair of gigantic forceps, the ends serrated, a pneumatic tube trailing from it up and out of sight. He leaned in, grabbing her left breast with the cold metal tongs, the teeth pricking her skin in almost a tickle. Only then did Sakura realize that she wore no clothes. He squeezed and twisted. Her cry of determination changed to agony and rage. She swore at him in Japanese, writhed and swore and screamed and kicked as he twisted farther, then wrenched. Her breast came free from her chest with a wet sucking sound.

She dropped back, hyperventilating, forcing her rage to overcome her panic. *I will not despair. Despair is the refuge of the lost. I am not lost. I. AM. NOT. LOST.*

The coroner dropped her breast onto a scale. "Point-two-one kilograms, typical for size." He smiled at his companion, who had changed her mask but still had blood in her hair. "Let's see if it grows back, and how fast."

She leaned in next to him. "Look at the ribs, still fused, or is it fused again?" She turned to Sakura and held up a chisel and hammer. "Let's find out, shall we?"

* * *

Matt dove right as Yardley punched, and the cave wall exploded over his head. Yardley's reach extended at least nine feet, and the crude-looking mechanical body did little to hinder his reflexes. The massive helmet denied Matt the easy targets—mouth, eyes, or neck. Matt took aim on the run and fired, but the next three grenades performed exactly as the first two, impacting on the surface of Yardley's armor with no visible effect.

Lungs tight in the toxic air, Matt processed his options. He drew a combat knife and closed, ducking beneath a haymaker and diving between Yardley's legs to come up behind him. He stabbed for a joint in the armor and hit flesh. Yardley kicked, and the impact shattered Matt's sternum. Blood erupted from his mouth. He hit the wall thirty feet away and dropped face-down.

He rolled to his feet and clutched his arms to his chest as Yardley charged. At the last moment the whispers warned him of the feint, so he leapt. His foot landed on Yardley's knee, and the next on his shoulder. He kicked as hard as he could, hooking his foot under Yardley's helmet. The strap snapped and it flew off, even as Matt flipped to land on his feet facing the ruined section of wall where he'd just stood.

Yardley spun. Matt ducked the first claw. The second caught his right arm. He screamed as the massive hydraulic shears closed, severing his forearm just below the elbow. A geyser of blood sprayed Yardley's mechanical arm.

Matt stumbled back, his regenerates overwhelming the first signs of shock and suppressing the pain to a dull ache.

Yardley grinned, his face barely unrecognizable under the maze of wires and connections. "Problem, Rowley? You might need that."

He swept forward, hunched, talons spread.

* * *

Jason stopped and turned off his light. "There it is."

Confused, Monica killed her own. In the distance she made out a faint fuzz, neither bright nor dark and in that fact different than everything else around her. "What is it?"

He said nothing in the pitch black. Then, "Come on. We're almost out of time."

They stumbled forward, picking their way across the uneven floor toward what resolved into the opening of a much larger cavern. The light didn't flicker but looked too flat, too lifeless, to be sunlight.

Afraid, Monica put a hand on Jason's shoulder. "Sweetie, you need to tell me what's up there."

Jason pulled away and kept walking. "Your son."

She followed.

* * *

"Come on, Matt. How am I supposed to kill you if you won't come out?"

Matt slithered deeper into the crevice, beyond the grasping mechanical claws. Lightheaded from blood loss, he sighed in relief as the spurts from his arm slowed to a trickle and stopped. The itch rivaled only that in his chest as the least pleasant sensation of his existence.

Yardley reached into the entrance of the small opening and dug his claws into either side. With a grunt, a layer of rock broke free. He punched and bashed at the exposed shale, reducing it to chunks and powder. In five minute's time, he'd managed to get three feet closer to Matt with no more than six feet to go.

"This rock is soft, Rowley. Soft and weak, like you."

Matt lacked the energy for witticisms, so he said nothing.

"Come on, Rowley. Where's your sense of fun?" Murdock shredded another foot of siltstone and shale, claws mashing away at either side of the entrance to give him more room to work.

Matt tried to wiggle back farther, but the crevice ended just behind him. His obliterated ribs had almost recovered, but his arm would take hours to heal. He took stock of his inventory: a combat knife, two flash-bang grenades, and a bandoleer of ammo for a shotgun Yardley had crushed against a wall.

His mind turned to Yardley's question. The suit must have cost hundreds of millions of dollars to develop, perhaps as some sort of counter to Augs in the pre-ICAP days. It had the look of a prototype, blocky and inelegant in exactly the way any politician would see as a waste of time. A discarded DARPA or black project, some mad scientist's dream shelved for newer, more elegant options.

Armor covered all of Yardley's vitals, leaving only the occasional bit of meat exposed, but given his past and level of mental instability, Matt put no faith in shock or general trauma for shutting the behemoth down. His forearms and legs were entirely enclosed in vicious talons made of something stronger than steel. It reflected light like steel but demolished the walls of the cavern without any sign of even minor damage.

As the man-machine tore through another foot of rock, Matt formulated a plan.

* * *

A string of LED light bulbs hung from the walls, thirty or forty in all, plugged into some kind of metal box Monica didn't recognize.

She tore off the gas mask and rushed toward the crib with a sobbing gasp. "Oh, my baby!"

Adam stood against the side railing, head halfway above the padded bar, and watched her come with his typical "just woke up from a nap" smile. He looked no worse for the wear, impassive and chubby and healthy. A case of diapers sat next to the crib, alongside crates and crates of 1990s-era MREs.

His smile grew when she reached him and he lifted his arms. She picked him up and squeezed him tight, and he gurgled happily at the contact. "Mama."

"Yeah, baby, Momma's here. And Momma ain't going nowhere anymore."

She turned and frowned. Jason kneeled next to them, head

bowed, hands clasped in prayer. The huge cavern sported sixteen cots and an entrance big enough for a tractor trailer. Shelves lined the walls, loaded with foodstuffs and sundries, toilet paper and paper towels and cigarettes.

"Jason?"

Rees's lips moved. She caught a hint of Latin or Greek or something.

"JASON!"

He started, and looked up at her, eyes far too at peace for their situation. "Yes?"

"I don't think we're alone down here."

He turned and took in the underground barracks. "No, maybe we're not."

"Let's get the fuck out of Dodge."

He shook his head. "We can't. You have to be here."

She carried Adam over to him, held him in front of Rees's face. "Look at him. This is my son, goddammit. We got him. So we need to get the fuck out of here, right now, before any of these psycho bastards come back. I don't care what happens to me, but we need to get him out."

Jason smiled. "I'm sorry, but we have to stay here. This won't end unless we face it."

Monica shrieked.

* * *

Matt pulled a flash-bang from his bandoleer and waited until Yardley could almost grab him. He ducked and rolled, taking the impact with the floor on his right shoulder before throwing the flashbang at the wall.

His regenerates compensated for the blinding light and deafening boom even as he came to his feet at a dead run. He took the passage on the left, and then the left again, each too small for Yardley's exoskeleton to fit.

The passage narrowed until he could just squeeze through, and only then by pulling off his helmet. He left it behind.

Behind him a methodical cacophony hammered his ears as

Yardley reduced the walls between them to rubble with tireless zeal. Matt cringed at the louder sounds, whole sections of decaying rock ripped away under the relentless onslaught. He wriggled farther and farther down the artery, praying it led to an escape.

If it didn't, when Yardley caught him, he'd die.

* * *

"Fascinating." The dark-skinned woman prodded Sakura's breast even as the flesh writhed around her fingers. "Does it work with more sensitive organs?"

Sakura couldn't scratch the unbearable itch, couldn't scream around the rag stuffed in her mouth. The pale man picked up a power drill, attached an eight-inch spade bit, and revved it a couple of times.

"Kidneys, you think?"

The woman bobbed her head back and forth, pondering. "Sure. She's got two, so if something fails we won't lose the specimen. Work from the side. No reason to cause more trauma than we have to."

He rolled his eyes and gave Sakura a wink. Then he plunged the bit into her abdomen and pulled the trigger.

* * *

Adam back in his crib behind a pile of sandbags, Monica pried open another large floor locker with a crowbar. After bats, swords, knifes, clothes, and food, she sighed in relief. "At least one of these assholes has good taste." She pulled the camo-pattern Remington R-15 .30 RAR from the locker, exactly like the one Matt had gotten her for Christmas four years prior, grabbed the only magazine—loaded with nine rounds—and slammed it home with an authoritative click.

"Can you shoot?" She chambered a round amidst a vague memory of Jason and Matt in middle school, coyote hunting on Schneider's chicken farm for ten bucks a pelt.

Jason shook his head. "It's been decades."

She grabbed the .308 Marlin bolt-action out of the locker and tossed it to him, followed by a box of twenty bullets. "Even if you don't hit nothing, you might get people to keep their heads down."

As if on cue, voices rang out down the passageway, laughing and happy. Monica took aim and waited for the first man to round the corner.

A cute brunette with boobs only a teenager could possess slapped an African American man on the shoulder as they walked up the slope into the room proper. Monica fired, turned, and fired again.

The man dropped like a rock. The woman had whirled at the first report, and Monica's second round caught the side of her face. The bullet tore through her cheekbone in a spray of blood, bone, and cartilage, and she stumbled back, hands to her ruined flesh. Screaming, Monica fired again, center of mass, and the girl sat down.

A shadow dashed across the hall into an alcove that hid him from view.

"COME AND GET SOME, YOU FUCKHEAD FUCKERS!" Monica rolled left, then trained her rifle on the side of the door she'd watched the shadow run to.

Spots of light flashed from deep in the hallway, and bullets pinged off her position.

"Jason! SHOOT HIM!"

Jason lay frozen, watching the hall down his scope, one eye closed, knuckles white on the stock. He pulled the trigger and the bullet ricocheted high, but the shooter stopped shooting. Monica sent a round that way for good measure, then rolled again behind another cot.

A rifle appeared around the corner and sprayed bullets. Monica ignored the indiscriminate fire, took aim, and fired. Fingers vanished in a spray of red gore, and the weapon fell to the ground.

Jason fired into the hallway, and someone yelped in alarm.

Monica popped her magazine. One round, plus one in the

chamber. "Jason, you cover me, okay?"

His blank look inspired no confidence.

"When I get up, fire into the hallway. Reload and fire again until I'm up against that wall, as fast as you can. Can you do that?"

Eyes wide and full of tears, he nodded.

"Ready? Go!"

She bolted for the doorway, and Jason fired a round. She'd taken eight more steps before he fired another. Six more and a shadow rolled out into the hall. She fired the Remington twice and the figure rolled back out of sight. Jason fired again as she hit the wall.

Chris Malec's voice rolled over her, her Sifu telling her to be calm even in the worst excitement. She closed her eyes, listened. On the other side of the wall three voices murmured back and forth, all male, all worried but confident.

Jason fired as she rounded the corner. The man training his assault rifle on her stumbled back, blood spurting from his mouth. She kicked a rifle up into the air, spun, and chopped another man in the neck.

She screamed as a knife tore through her foot, a searing pain that jolted straight up her spine. Stepping forward she kicked anyway, jamming the hilt up under the chin of the man who lay on the ground. She gasped and fell as her leg went numb.

Wriggling backward, she grabbed an assault rifle off the floor, pointed it down the hall, and pulled the trigger. It jerked upward on full auto, both blinding and deafening her in the enclosed space.

Jason appeared behind her, grabbed her under the armpits, and dragged her back toward the large room. She fired another several shots down the hall for good measure.

She grabbed for the knife and Jason slapped her hand. "No, wait. If it hit the artery you'll bleed out too fast."

He untied her shoe, looked her in the eyes, and grimaced. "Ready?"

She shook her head. "No."

"Ready to do it anyway?"

She closed her eyes, nodded once, and opened them. "Do it."

She yanked out the knife as he pulled off her shoe. It didn't hurt at much as it could have, and she took the lack of gushing geysers of blood as a good sign.

"Ow, that fucking hurts."

Jason packed the wound with strips of cotton torn from a dead man's shirt, tied it tight with more of the same, and helped her up.

She took a step, keeping most of her weight on the heel. She took another, and though she limped hard it could have been a lot worse. She said as much.

He looked down at the dead men. "I've never shot anyone before." He made the sign of the cross over their bodies.

"I have, once. Now twice." She looked into his haunted, pale gray eyes. "And I never want to do it again."

* * *

Sakura panted because she could do nothing else. The van rolled to a stop and the back doors opened. Agent Keene looked down at her as they wheeled the gurney out the back, his face tinged green.

"Holy shit, you didn't waste any time." He patted Sakura's hand on the way by, and she didn't have the energy to pull away, or the strength to crush his fingers.

The blood-spattered woman ran a finger along Keene's jawline. "This is war, silly. We don't have any time to waste."

He stepped forward as they wheeled her through a bay door into a blinding hallway. "Is she going to live?"

"Not your problem," she said. The doors closed and she wiped sweat from Sakura's forehead. "For as long as we can keep you alive, I suppose, though I don't think you're going to enjoy it."

Chapter 18

Smothered in dog's blood, Janet sliced lines down her forearms, adding her life force to the ancient words spilling from her mouth. "Ereshkigal I invoke you, by the power of blood and the power of pain I beg you. It is for you alone to rule the underworld, in every age and form and name. Ereshkigal, Thoth, Bhaironji, by the power of blood and the power of pain I beseech you."

The candles sputtered, and shadows of shadows danced on the walls.

"Open Neti's gate, by the bond of blood and the womb we shared I call my brother to me. By the power of blood and the power of pain I implore you, return Meseket to the living lands, and carry upon it one soul. By the power of blood and the power of pain, my blood, my pain, and the pain of the conduit, may her spirit find mercy in your embrace, by this power and this blood I command you."

Staked spread-eagled to the floor, Anita Yardley cried out through her gag as Janet knelt. Anita quivered at Janet's touch on her naked body, her fingertips brushing face to breasts to belly to between her legs, and then to the floor, where the bronze knife once wielded by Sargon of Akkad lay. Janet grabbed the hilt in her right hand, put her left on the perfect carnelian in the pommel, and gently, slowly, pressed it into Yardley's belly, leaning in where necessary to force the dull, ancient blade through the wall of muscle without damaging the viscera beneath.

Anita thrashed. Janet sawed downward to her mons pubis, and then up to the base of her sternum, eyes closed, guiding the knife by touch against the quivering skin. Her hands wet and sticky, she ripped the knife left, then right, and peeled open the cavity to expose the organs below.

"By the power of blood and the power of pain I command you. My will be done."

As Anita shuddered and twitched in the throes of shock, Janet opened her eyes, and ate.

* * *

Lightheaded, Matt wiggled through a tiny opening into a larger hall that meandered for miles. The temperature rose, fell, then rose again. A deep throb shuddered through his severed arm. It hurt like hell and itched worse. He kept having to cut flesh away from the bone as it crawled out longer and longer from the point of injury. Matt left a drizzle of blood like breadcrumbs that popped in the infrared, and the first time he crossed his own trail he almost collapsed in despair.

The narrow cavern forked, so he took another path, again and again. At long last he saw light ahead and imagined fresh air and birds singing and an end to endless dark passages. He stumbled faster, ravenous, so when he finally broke into the huge chamber he almost couldn't process what he saw.

"Monica?"

She held their baby asleep on her lap. Standing behind her, Jason Rees stood with a hunting rifle, the barrel pointed at the ground.

"Told you he'd come," Jason said to her.

"You did." She frowned at Matt, too calm. "What happened to your arm?"

Matt looked from Jason to his wife and said the only thing that came to mind. "What are you doing here?"

"Jason brought me, to get our son. We need to go now."

He looked at Jason. "Did you drug her?"

Jason shook his head. "It's not me. It's Adam. He has a calming effect."

The cavern shuddered, and the lights swayed, casting shadows of shadows across the walls. It shuddered again.

Monica's eyes widened to a desperate plea. "You can't kill him, baby. Promise me you won't kill him."

He looked from her to the large doorway to the other exit. "Then run."

They made it five steps before Yardley burst into the room with a deafening roar. He charged, and Matt whirled to meet him head-on, ducking between his claws to impact him square in the torso. Metal crunched and Matt's shoulder exploded in pain. As he fell to the floor he leapt, rolling to his feet behind the monstrosity.

The open chest next to him contained a pile of junk, including an aluminum baseball bat and a crowbar. He picked up the crowbar and rolled left as Yardley's foot came down, obliterating the locker and its contents. He ran for the panel box on the far wall.

* * *

Monica shoved Adam into Jason's hands, exchanging him for the .308. "You hide in that fucking cave and you don't come out until it's dead or we are, you understand me?"

"I can't let you do this."

She stepped forward and threw her shoulder into his, turning him. He reeled, so she put her foot on his ass and shoved, sending him stumbling into the crevice, Adam still in his arms. "I didn't ask your permission. You protect my son."

She wheeled and took aim with the .308, trying to ignore that her target wasn't circles on paper, wasn't a rabid raccoon. The twelve-foot killing machine didn't look to have much in the way of weak spots, save the naked head she couldn't quite see over the massive metal shoulders. She aimed for a space between the plates on his back, exhaled, and squeezed the trigger.

Yardley slapped his back and stumbled. She ejected the round and shoved in another as the lights went out.

* * *

Matt tore the cables off of the wall with the crowbar, plunging the room into darkness, yanked a few more feet free, and turned.

Emergency lights kicked on, bathing the room in yellow sodium vapor.

Yardley had stumbled, one massive claw reaching behind to clutch at his back, the other catching him before he pitched on his face.

Matt stepped forward with the ground wire protruding a foot from where he'd tucked it in his armpit, the hot cable in his other—his only—hand. He contacted either side of the elbow of the arm supporting Yardley.

Sparks flew. Metal blackened. The air filled with the nauseating, appetizing smell of cooking flesh.

Yardley swiped Matt away with his free arm, but Matt anticipated the blow and rolled with it. The impact slammed him into a trunk twenty feet away, shattering it and spilling MREs all over the floor, but he leapt to his feet without serious injury.

Yardley stood and turned, sneering at Monica as she took aim for another shot. "Always need a woman's help, don't you, Rowley?"

Yardley flinched to the side as Monica fired and the shot pinged off his armor. Then he charged her, good arm raised, and Matt ran after him.

Monica ejected the round, grabbed another, and ran out of time. She bolted for the small entrance where Jason huddled with her son. Yardley hit the doorway the moment after she dove through it, shaking the earth and pulverizing stone.

Matt leapt and brought the crowbar down as hard as he could, but Yardley twisted and it deflected off of his shoulder. As the giant spun, Matt kept behind his cooked arm, charred and smoking and locked at the elbow. He jammed the bar under a panel on the frozen elbow and wrenched upward. It popped loose with the sound of shearing bolts.

Yardley lashed out with his foot. Matt danced back, but a talon hooked his calf and sent him crashing to the floor, the crowbar flying from his hand. Yardley turned and stomped, shaking the room again and again as Matt rolled out of the way.

A bullet pinged off Yardley's back, and another, but if he noticed he paid them no mind. Matt hit the wall and, with nowhere else to go, flipped up to his feet to jump out of the way.

A giant claw smashed Matt into the stone, crushing bone and jellying organs right through his body armor. Blood erupted from his mouth and his limbs went numb.

Monica screamed and ran for him. He tried to tell her to get back, tried to tell her to run. Instead he closed his eyes.

* * *

Through a haze of glory born of hatred and revenge and the thrill of carnage, Murdock Yardley heard his mother call him, her voice faint under a gale of wind.

"Murdy, it's time to come home."

He shook his head, confused. "Mama?"

"It's time to come home, Murdy. Your mama needs you."

His mother never needed anything. This voice belonged to someone else, pretending. He shook off the thought with a snarl.

* * *

As Yardley hesitated, Monica swept up the crowbar and jammed it into Yardley's exposed elbow. Hooking a hydraulic line, she yanked and twisted until hot orange fluid erupted from the mechanical artery.

The arm sagged as she stumbled back, and Matt slid down the wall to a sitting position, head lolled to the side, eyes closed. Monica waited, out of arms' reach, crowbar hefted like a baseball bat that wouldn't do her a damned bit of good. As the hydraulics failed Yardley sagged, then slumped, then fell over, the weight of the machine far too much for the former Aug's atrophied limbs.

She ran to Matt, lifted his head, kissed his bloody lips. "C'mon baby, don't you dare die on me. You got a baby to raise and a wife to love and so goddamned much to live for."

His eyes fluttered. One opened, the white orb red with broken blood vessels.

"I'm here." He mouthed it, but she understood.

Yardley's voice boomed behind her. "I told those men to rape you."

She stood, and turned, one hand on the pistol still in her holster.

"I told them to rape you to death in front of your son, and leave your body for your husband to find. And do you know what I say to that? Close enough."

Yardley's arm wiggled, his fingers straining for a red switch under a safety interlock.

"I'm getting real sick of your shit." She choked up the pistol as Yardley flipped up the switch guard.

"MONICA! NO!" Jason ran for her, arm outstretched.

She pulled the trigger.

* * *

Janet screamed as the power of her spell tore through her, a black flood that ripped her from reality and threw her into a sea of screaming, desperate hunger. Hunger for warmth, for life, for light, a never-ending maelstrom of souls begging for the peace of oblivion.

She held onto the pulsing thread that tied her to life, and dove for the abyss. Gray claws dripping with the remains of souls scraped at her, desperate for even the slightest hint of human warmth no matter what it cost the living. The pentagram held, and the abjurations borne of blood and pain. She dove farther.

"Brother." She had no voice, but her thoughts rang everywhere and nowhere, swept up in the gale of souls and scattered to the winds. Yet each tattered shred grew, bound with the power she had called, reeking of blood and purpose. "Brother, come to me."

A cherub broke off from the maelstrom and flitted over to stare at her with wide, black eyes. It smiled, revealing rows of serrated teeth, and between its legs it grew hard in a mockery of human love. Black drool spilling from its mouth, it lunged, and hit a wall of nothing inches from her breast. Shrieking in frustration it wheeled away, behind her and out of sight.

"Brother. Come to me."

Other creatures came. Skeletal bats, skinned angels, dragons, and dark mist with cunning eyes, every fear, every cruelty, every evil thought given form. They lunged, bit, scratched, but always turned away at the last moment. They broke off.

Unending beauty came to her next, gorgeous men and beautiful women and almost-human creatures of both sexes and none, in every combination, their heady musk reeking of unimaginable pleasure if only she would let go.

She ignored them all.

Her brother approached, hale and strong, and reached out his hand. She looked past the too-perfect form and it burst into a cloud of angry hornets, each with her brother's face twisted in never-ending rage. They swirled around her, an angry droning cloud, and disappeared.

"Brother. Come to me."

A pale shadow drifted to her, almost shy, a tattered, ephemeral thing, pathetic and desperate and so, so hungry, and she knew him, and smiled. "Take my hand. It's time to come home."

* * *

Monica watched the blood leaking from the hole in Yardley's temple, then looked up to Jason. "You can't tell me he didn't deserve it."

A great black maw opened in her mind, and she fell. A single silver thread connected her to herself, but as she grasped for it, it whipped out of reach.

* * *

Monica woke on a plain of hypodermic needles, a barren wasteland stretching to infinity under the blazing sun. Her body ached, and she had no idea how long since she'd last had a hit. Too long, too long. She knelt and dug through the broken glass, looking for any leftovers, a brown resin or white crystal, something, anything to take the edge off.

Metal pricked her fingers, glass shredded her hands, and she cried out but didn't stop her search. In all this there had to be something, anything, a taste or a touch, something to take the edge off. She needed it, more than life or love or oxygen.

Glass cut her knees, a sharp nothing compared to the craving. She crawled for unending days, searching. Sometimes a small part of her thought it strange that she'd be naked in a place like this, but then she'd see a sparkle, and dive, clutching in blind panic for the tiny rock. In her clumsiness it would scatter and fall from sight. She'd grovel forward, sweeping through the shards with bare arms, smearing the ground with ever more of her endless blood.

Tears blurred her vision as she scrambled through the glass, each desperate grasp another cut, another stab, another wail of frustration. *I just need something . . . something to take the edge off.* Days stretched to months, and months to years.

And one day, starving, bleeding, desperate, she stopped, froze in place, confused.

This isn't me. I don't belong here.

She looked up at the sun that wasn't a sun, a blazing maelstrom of endless night that cast the world in black light, a billion billion nightmares silently screaming for the void.

I know this place.

She'd dreamed of it—not the plain of glass and needles but the maelstrom—dreamed of it in the rectory, where she'd almost had a miscarriage, before Adam's birth.

Adam.

She looked down at the needles, at the cuts and track marks marring every inch of her body, and shuddered.

I don't want this. I don't need this. I need him. I need my son and my husband and life and warmth and love.

"Do you want to go home?"

She turned to find the most majestic woman she'd ever seen, a dark beauty with jade eyes, radiant in her power, great emerald wings of shimmering jade spread out behind her, refracting and intensifying and blotting out the sun that wasn't a sun. Her crown glinted in the black light, a simple circlet of wrought black iron.

"I asked you a question, child."

Yes, I want to go home.

"There is a price."

What is the price?

"You have to die."

She bowed her head. *Won't death bring me back here?*

The angel lifted her chin with a finger. "Don't be silly, child. This isn't your fate, it belongs to another."

What . . . what is my fate?

"None can say, yet. You've not been judged." She smiled, and the radiance dazzled Monica, made her head swim, her whole body weak with awe. The angel spread her arms. "Now come, child, come into my arms, and I will take you home."

Monica hesitated. *You do not love me. Why would you help?*

"Because the other whose fate this is deserves it." Her jade eyes blazed with wrath. "He belongs here, and I want him back."

So to get what you want I have to die.

"I cannot reverse the spell without power. All power requires sacrifice. Even mine."

Monica stepped into her embrace—

* * *

—and opened her eyes, and lowered the pistol. Blood spurted from Yardley's forehead, and his fingers sagged away from the switch.

She dropped the gun and ran for Adam, who'd wandered into the room after Jason had let him go. She cradled his head and turned him around, away from his broken father, away from the ruined body of Murdock Yardley.

Over his head she watched her husband. Matt's fingers flexed, his legs twitched. He blinked, first one eye, then two.

Jason approached, cautious. "What just happened?" His voice carried a note of gravity, heaviness, of more than the question asked.

Behind Monica's eyes a plain of shattered needles stretched forever. "He was reaching for a self-destruct or something, so I shot him. It was self-defense."

Jason frowned. "No, I mean what happened after you shot him?"

Adam put his head on her shoulder, and the plane of glass retreated to lurk in a dark corner of her mind, where it gibbered and gnawed at her sanity.

She closed her eyes and pushed it deeper. "I went somewhere, somewhere very bad, and I came back."

"Adam brought you back."

She shook her head. "No, not Adam. The place wasn't meant for me. Someone else belonged there, so I came back."

He watched her with his gray confessor's eyes, then turned to approach her shattered husband.

After a few minutes, Matt took some water, and twenty minutes after that ate six MREs, one after another, licking the containers clean, going so far as to suck down the hot sauce in the tiny bottles.

An hour later they returned to Jason's beat-up Camry.

* * *

Matt sagged into the car, reached forward and plucked Jason's phone out of the cup holder. He dialed Janet's private cell. She picked up on the third ring.

"Janet LaLonde."

"Janet. Matt."

"Holy crap what happened? They found a whole squad of marines just torn to pieces, and no sign of either of you."

"Yardley's dead. Hone in on the GPS of this phone and then go a half mile north-west straight through the woods. Send a recovery team, but make sure they're men we can trust."

"I'll call the FBI—"

"No! Keene betrayed us. Used Yardley to distract me while he took Sakura."

"Took Sakura."

"Yeah. She's gone. They have her."

"I'm on it. Be careful out there."

"Thanks, Janet."

* * *

Sitting naked in a pool of congealing blood, Janet looked from the ruined body of Anita Yardley to the split-open German Shepherd to the black char where her pentagram used to be, and burst into tears.

"I'm sorry, D. I'm so sorry."

Chapter 19

Libby Kamen held her head high as the bailiff led her toward the courtroom. In the white marble hallway, she tried not to smile at the FBI man she'd bribed to take her from that god-awful house near the turkey farm. He'd kept his word, but with nowhere for her to run he'd also kept her in custody.

She rounded the corner into a sea of reporters. No stranger to flashing bulbs, she wondered how her unkempt hair and orange prison jumpsuit would play on the tabloid covers. She cursed the garish whitehead on her right cheek, and the lack of foundation to cover it up.

Well, the fashion police had to talk about something, and jail gave her street cred.

The judge droned on about charges, stupid crap like resisting arrest and conspiracy to commit murder. She zoned out through the boring litany, perking up when her fat lawyer nudged her arm.

She raised her chin and spoke in a loud, clear voice, as coached. "Not guilty, your honor."

Lardo nodded his approval, chins jiggling.

The sexy dude in the cheap suit spoke next. "Your honor, the prosecution requests that the defendant be remanded to a maximum-security prison without bail. She is a flight risk with the means to go anywhere in the world, and has a history of volatile behavior."

With great effort Libby managed to not roll her eyes, and instead glared at Fatty McFatso.

He cleared his throat and held up a wad of papers. "Your honor, my client is a fifteen-year-old girl with no history of violence. Yes, she has some minor infractions on her record, but has never risen to the level of needing to be placed in jail, much less remanded without bail. Her accounts have been frozen, so she has no means. She got involved with some bad actors much older than she, and it is they who perpetuated these atrocities, not she. Miss Kamen is keen to face these baseless accusations against her character, and will appear before the court on the appointed day."

Her stomach knotted and she schooled her face to calm. Big K had been her mentor, her world. He'd taught her everything that mattered, the value of loyalty and dedication, to take no shit, no prisoners, and whatever you wanted. He'd committed himself to his friend Murdock even to the point of death. He'd taught her everything she knew about cause, about justice, about righteousness, about how to live. Hot rage flushed her face. How dare this blob of lard call him a "bad actor?"

The judge nodded to both lawyers. "After taking into consideration both concerns, Miss Kamen will be remanded to house arrest upon the remission of one hundred million dollars bond, or two hundred fifty million dollars cash."

He banged the gavel, and Libby whirled on her lawyer. "Pay it."

* * *

Matt stalked through One Center Plaza, a growing flurry of discombobulated functionaries and at least one security guard in his wake. He ignored their entreaties and took the stairs four at a time, leaving everyone in the dust, to Suite 600.

He crashed through the fire door at a steady walk, and

everyone turned in his direction, a bevy of white shirts and ties not quite tight and coffee cups and paperwork.

"Where's Keene?"

A brunette in her late forties, smartly dressed in a gray pants-suit that didn't quite cover her middle-aged pudge, approached him. "Do you have information on Agent Keene's whereabouts?"

Matt frowned. "I was hoping he was here."

She didn't react except to say, "When was the last time you saw Agent Keene?"

"Thursday."

"Five days ago Thursday?"

"Yes."

She exchanged looks with almost everyone. A young man ducked into an office and picked up a phone. "Mister . . ."

"Rowley."

"Mister Rowley, what is the nature of your relationship with Agent Keene?"

"He sold me out and kidnapped my partner."

The stairwell door burst open and two security guards huffed through, faces red, hands on their holsters. The woman in charge held up a hand but didn't dismiss them.

"Let's talk in my office."

Without waiting for his reply or agreement she walked into a glass-walled room, "Agent in Charge Cheryl Battisti" engraved in brass on the door. She allowed him through, closed it behind him, and walked around to sit at her oversized desk, cluttered with two computers and several stacks of files.

"Agent Keene hasn't reported to work in almost two weeks. The Bureau filed a missing persons report on his behalf eleven days ago. A search of his home found no signs of struggle, and aside from his keys and wallet missing there were no signs that he'd left town. Where did you see him Thursday?"

"Centralia, Pennsylvania." He explained the situation, leaving out Yardley's name and the giant sci-fi exo-suit, but deliberately brought up the dead squad of marines.

"The news called that a training accident."

Matt shook his head. "That's a cover up. We sent in a recovery team but they never made the site. The Shop had already taken over under guise of an environmental disaster relating to the mine fire and some minor earthquakes, but FEMA crews don't need military hardware for a toxic gas leak."

As he spoke, her expression went from dispassionate curiosity to bland distaste. She plucked a card from behind her keyboard and slid it across the desk. "If you have any other information, don't hesitate to call me."

She glanced up, out of the room, and stood, her palms on the desk.

Before the security guards could get there, Matt produced his own card and held it out. "You think I'm crazy, but I'm not."

She took it. "Special Threats, huh? That's the Bureau the President created after ICAP disintegrated." She waved down the guards. "And Special Threats was working with Agent Keene. Why didn't I know of this?"

He held up his hands in a plaintive gesture. "We have extensive communique records that show you did, including authorizing joint FBI-Penn PD ventures and a cooperating statement with USMC Recon."

She sat back down. "Never happened."

"Gathered that. Only it did." He slid a folder across her desk. "You going to help me find Keene or what?"

* * *

Janet LaLonde walked from the government sedan, up the marble steps, to the front door of Humans for Humanity's world headquarters. The cold snap had even reached Martonville, Texas, making it a brisk sixty-five degrees, but she'd chosen a low-cut cream-colored skirt suit that came almost halfway down her thighs and had cost her six thousand dollars. Given the leer from the security guard, it would do its job just fine.

She smiled and chomped on a piece of gum. "Hi there."

The giant black man in an expensive black suit kept his eyes glued to hers, and she could almost see him sweating with the effort. "Afternoon, ma'am. Do you have an appointment?"

"Nope. But I'm here to see Mr. Kellett about a donation. It's . . ." She leaned in, too close. ". . . urgent."

He cleared his throat. "Let me see if he's available."

Holding the door like a proper gentleman, he let her in out of the cold, then stepped back outside to talk on his radio. A schoolmarmish lady in a floral print dress sized her up, shook her head with a disapproving cluck, and went back to her paperwork behind a reception counter.

Two minutes later, Mr. Kellett appeared in the inner doorway. A frail old man with frail old manners, he extended an arm to help her navigate the ridiculous purple carpet in her four-inch heels. She took it, and ran a fingertip across his dry, wrinkled skin.

She entered his office, ten times more preposterous than the ornate hallway, and pretended to admire the giant painting, a Kellett hale and hearty, less taken by entropy if not much younger. They sat in a pair of plush chairs, facing one another, and his eyes flicked down between her legs as she sat and crossed them.

Yeah, old man. Scarlet lace. See it and want it. She strangled a twinge of remorse in its crib. Of the seven deadly sins, she'd mastered only one.

"So what is this about, Miss . . . ?"

She leaned forward and put out her hand, giving him just a glimpse down the front of her dress. He took her hand, kissed it with dry lips.

"Janet LaLonde. Call me Janet."

He pulled back. "What can I do for you, Janet?"

She removed a folded piece of paper from her thousand-dollar calfskin purse and slid it across the coffee table, the public and secondary reason she'd come.

He picked it up, unfolded it, and frowned. "You can't be serious."

She shrugged. "Couldn't trust a process server with that, sorry. Given the evidence we already have you'll probably go to jail, but meantime we'll be suing you for every penny you've ever had. We froze your US assets this morning, and scheduled the press release for two o'clock."

She stood and he leapt to his feet, hands balled into fists. *Wrath might work, if lust didn't.* She turned around, giving him a coy look over her shoulder as her hands reached up to the zipper under her hair and pulled it down.

"What is this? Get out of my office." He flushed, anger and, she hoped, something more.

Janet pulled the rest of the way, exposing the massive Jade Cross on her back, and whirled around. She tugged and her dress fell. His eyes widened—she wore no bra—and with a sigh he dropped to his knees, eyes transfixed by the gem between her breasts.

She plucked it from its chain and held it out, the ancient lapis lazuli orb bluer than the Texas sky. "Lust isn't just a sin, Mr. Kellett. It's a deadly sin, a mortal sin, one of seven, and to succumb to it is to forfeit your soul."

She approached, her dress falling to the floor, and his eyes followed the stone. Her high heels clacked across the marble tile as she stalked up to him. She looked down at him in her terrible glory, black wisps of power coalescing around her.

A tear appeared in his eye. "Why?"

"Because I may have need of you before all this is done, and if you're not already damned, close enough."

She stepped over him, putting her sex in his face, and pulled the red lace to the side. His tears fell freely now, and as he buried his mouth in her, his eyes never left the gem.

Ten minutes later, Janet shook Ronald Kellett's hand and left the building, his soul around her neck.

* * *

Matt picked up the phone. "Go ahead."

"Kellett gave me a little something," Janet said. "But I don't think it will pan out. I'll run with it, let you know what turns up."

"Okay." Salomon had been a dead end, too. "Battisti at FBI Boston is working a manhunt on the down-low. They suspect CIA or military, what with the quality of Yardley's hardware. It's way beyond anything DARPA's even dreamed of, so we'll have to dig deep. It'll get dangerous."

"Screw the danger. We'll find her."

"You're damned right we'll find her. Thanks again."

He hung up, and looked across the kitchen table. "We can't trust her."

Jason Rees sighed. "I know."

"How do you know?"

Jason shook his head. "The same way I knew how to get down into that cave, and that Monica had to be there. I did and she did, or you'd be dead and so would your son."

Matt looked at Adam, playing with a toy fire truck in front of the living room fireplace. "He's just a boy, Jason. There's nothing odd about him."

"So you feel nothing when you pick him up? Hold his hand?"

"Sure I do. But nothing more than any dad would feel, I guess."

"Peace? A disinclination toward violence?"

Matt ran his tongue over his teeth. "I'm always disinclined toward violence."

Rees sighed again. "I'm serious, man."

"So am I. I hurt and kill when I have to, but never for fun, never because I want to or like it." He looked out the window to where Monica worked on all fours, tearing out the last of the autumn weeds in the flower garden. "I kill to protect my family, my town, my country. I kill bad people when they need killing."

"It's that simple, is it?"

He shrugged. "I considered pacifism once, way back. Lasted about a week."

"Why'd you change your mind?"

"I saw the Jensen twins getting fresh on Cindy Baglio. Remember her?"

"Remember Fun-bags-lio? I dreamed about her my entire

adolescent life. How could I forget?"

"This was maybe eighth grade, so she was what, tenth? I come around the corner and those two shitwits had her backed against a wall, eyes closed, slapping at their hands as they groped her."

"Shit. Those kids were twice your size. What did you do?"

"Cracked their heads into the wall at a dead run, kneed them in the balls, and kicked them a couple times while they were down." He looked out the window at his wife and chuckled. Monica waved, and he smiled back. "Then Baglio kissed me—my first French kiss—and it took every ounce of willpower I had not to start in right where the Jensens had left off." He smirked around a cup of coffee. "Never amounted to anything. She was grateful, not attracted to a little pipsqueak like me. Still . . . ."

"And you never told anyone?"

He shrugged. "Monica, years later. My recruiter. The shrinks at ICAP—I had to tell them *everything*. Cindy asked me not to, you know?"

"So why tell me now?"

He shrugged again. "I don't know. It came up. How about you? You ever think about hurting anyone, Mr. Catholic Priest-man?"

Rees sat back. "I fantasized about your death for years. It wasn't a malicious thing, not in the true sense, but envy consumed me. I couldn't think about you without a white rage overcoming me. And then you showed up at my church with the girl of my dreams, asking for my help. And I had to help her."

"You betrayed me."

"I did."

"Men died because you betrayed me. Good men, doing their job to keep the world safe."

"I know, and I live with the shame of it every day. I won't ask you to forgive me, or ever trust me. I can only say that I've learned what guilt truly is."

Matt blinked. The world kept turning without the slightest inclination to forgive, but at the same time he didn't hate Jason. "I appreciate your help back there. But you ever even try to touch my wife I'll pull your arms off and beat you to death with them, and that's not an exaggeration."

"I know it." He turned to look at Adam. "It wouldn't be right for so many reasons."

Matt sighed, put his hands on the table, and stood. "Well, I've got to get to work, then spend some quality time with the girl of your dreams. So why don't you get the hell out of my house, and I'll see you next time?"

Jason stood, shook his hand, and headed for the door. "Bye, Matt. Thank you, and sorry."

Matt nodded.

He left, stopping on the deck to rub Ted's belly. The dog rolled onto his back without opening his eyes, and his delighted groans carried through the glass. Jason waved goodbye to Monica—she reached for her headphones but left them in when he didn't stop to chat—got in his car, and pulled out onto Turkey Vulture Lane.

Matt walked over to his son and picked him up, spinning him in the air before zerberting his exposed belly. They both laughed, and he booped Adam's nose.

"There something you're not telling me, little man?"

"Dada."

"Yup. That's what I thought."

He squirmed, pointing. "Doggie!"

Matt smiled. "That's a new one. Let's go say 'Hi' to the doggie."

Once on the floor the little man hobbled toward the deck on enthusiastic but uncoordinated legs. *They grow up so fast.*

He walked out onto the porch and sat next to Ted, who shifted as Adam plopped down and petted him with clumsy hands, leaning in to put his head against the dog's chest. Matt breathed in the brisk mountain air, dead leaves, pine, and clear, crisp water, and savored the moment.

His thoughts drifted to Sakura and the dead ends that led them no closer to finding her.

Monica pulled off her headphones. "What you thinking about, baby?"

He smiled, allowing the small joy to overwhelm the big worry. "I got to go to Washington for a couple days, to testify in front of some top-secret oversight committees about this Yardley mess. You want to come along? We'll make a vacation of it."

Her dazzling smile gave him his answer. He hopped off the steps, bounded to her, and swept her off her feet. She giggled as he kissed her and nibbled her shoulder, and responded with a bite.

"Ow!"

"Oh, I've seen you take worse, you big baby."

He kissed her again. "Pack up and we'll leave tonight. I hope Ted does okay on the helicopter."

Chapter 20

"You're kidding me." Libby Kamen glared down at the man she'd paid ten thousand dollars to come to her house, no questions asked, just so he could sit her on the couch and tell her "no."

"I'm sorry." Already kneeling on the floor in front of her, he tapped the ankle bracelet. "These things are state-of-the-art technology, with all kinds of redundant backups. A fiber-optic prevents you from taking it off or even loosening it too much, and you'd have to move faster than light to foil that. You can't mask the GPS or remove the battery without setting off the alarm. It's like a dead-man's switch, you know?"

"No, I don't fucking know," she snarled. "How am I supposed to take the fucking thing off, then?"

He laughed. "You're not. That's the point."

"Are you laughing at me?"

He choked it down. "No, I'm not laughing at you. Sorry."

"Sorry for what? Not laughing?"

He held up his hands. "Look, I didn't mean anything by it. You're just stuck with it is all. They're literally foolproof."

She smiled and scooched forward, letting her legs fall open just a little. "If you could do it, I could make it worth your while."

His eyes wandered up her thighs and he licked his lips. "Uh, I can't. I mean, we could remove it, but they'd know instantly."

"What about a fake signal? Could you jack the GPS and send a false location?"

He sighed. "They'd still get the real one. Without hacking their system—and no, that's not going to happen without months of work, and probably not even then—they'd get two signals and it'd tip them off anyway."

She dropped off the couch and shoved her tits in his face. "If you help me cut it off, I'd be really grateful."

"They'll know."

She bit his bottom lip, pulling it out with her teeth while rubbing her tongue along it. "It's the fucking cops. I'll be long gone before they get here."

"It's not smart."

She grabbed his belt and yanked it free. "Nobody's ever accused me of being smart."

* * *

Matt texted Monica on the way out of the Capitol Building. His four-hour deposition consisted of a million times saying, "I don't know" and an uncomfortable moment when he'd questioned them about Sakura's disappearance and looked for reactions. Unfortunately, he'd always depended on her to read the liars, and he'd learned nothing.

Monica met him under the Washington Monument amidst a heavy lunchtime crowd, the Indian Summer having drawn the residents and workers out of their homes and offices to bask in the near-seventy-degree sunshine. She had Ted leashed to the stroller and looking none the worse for wear after the most traumatic helicopter ride in the history of dogs or helicopters. He kissed her, then leaned down to scratch Ted behind the ears. "Must be nice to be too dumb to remember, huh?"

Monica slapped his ass. "That for me or the dog?"

He stood and kissed her again, then pulled back and grinned. "Why not both?"

She patted his cheek. "You watch it, mister. I've killed men twice your size."

He looked for guile or pain or anything in her eyes, and found her as inscrutable as ever. He brushed his knuckles down her cheek.

"You okay with that?"

She shrugged and looked out toward the Lincoln Memorial. "Had to happen. I ain't going to feel bad about self-defense."

"And that's that?"

She smooched him. "No. But yes. It's got to be."

She turned and pushed the stroller down the sidewalk then stopped to look at a plaque on the trees by the FDR Memorial. "That's ironic."

He raised an eyebrow.

She read the plaque. "In nineteen-twelve on this spot, three thousand and twenty Sakura cherry blossom trees were planted in a spirit of friendship between the cities of Washington, D.C. and Tokyo, Japan. Under the guidance of First Lady Helen Herron Taft and fulfilling the dream of Mrs. Eliza Ruhamah Scidmore, these first trees led to mass plantings throughout the Tidal Basin for several decades."

The plaque continued for several more paragraphs, but she didn't read it aloud. They stood in silence, until Ted broke it with a loud fart.

"Really, Ted?" Matt said. Ted wagged his tail at his name, and looked back and forth between the two of them, assessing his best options for treats or loving.

"I hope she's okay."

He hugged Monica with one arm and led her away from the spot. "She's the toughest woman—the toughest person—I've ever met."

They approached the water, and Monica pulled Adam out of the stroller. He rubbed sleep from his eyes but didn't fuss—at this point Adam never fussed—and suffered the baby leash with aplomb as Monica prevented him from chasing the few remaining Canadian Geese lingering around the reflecting pool.

Monica wandered down the side of the pool, and Matt watched her take in the sights. A young woman jogged by in a heavy jacket and running shoes, large sunglasses covering most of her face. As she passed, a half-folded paper fell from her pocket.

Matt picked it up. In streaks of black marker it read,

* * *

You took my happiness. I'm taking yours.

* * *

Matt bolted for his wife. "MONICA!"

Monica looked up as the jogger passed her and raised a pistol, her happy wave turning into a downcast look of sorrow and resignation. The jogger removed her sunglasses and smiled at Matt.

Someone screamed, and the world slowed down. Ten steps away. Nine. Eight. The whispers cackled in elated glee.

Libby Kamen pulled the trigger. Seven steps.

Monica's eyes closed. Her head listed to the side. And then it erupted, a spray of blood and brains out across the water.

Six steps. The geese scattered at the sudden noise.

Monica collapsed on the bank next to their son, who stared around with wide eyes. The world shrieked back to normal time.

Matt brought his hands to his head and stumbled to his knees, sliding across the sidewalk, a wail of complete anguish erupting from his throat.

Libby's eyes blazed green, a look of sheer terror wracking her face as she put the gun to her own temple and fired. A red puff and she collapsed, the weapon clattering to the concrete. Ted barked, turning in confused circles, tail between his legs.

People ran, most away, some toward the bodies. Cell phones streamed video, cameras flashed, and through it all Matt screamed, raw and unending, a maelstrom of whispered hell given victim and voice.

Adam looked down at his dead mother and shook his head. Over and around and through the cacophony he said, "No, Mama." He dropped to his knees and wrapped his arms around her neck. Matt crawled toward them, unable to stand, unable to reason.

A silver light enveloped Adam, a million tiny particles glowing with internal flame. It shifted, took in the light from the reflecting pool, stole the light from the midday sun. Shimmering motes became feathers of silver and ice and light, and his wings unfolded to blanket the sky. He cradled Monica's head and stroked her hair, and the silver light slithered into her.

The bleeding stopped, the exit wound collapsed in on itself, and new flesh covered the red ruin. Adam beat his wings and they both rose from the ground, limned in silver. Monica's eyes fluttered open, she lifted her head. As her feet touched the ground the light died, and Adam fell into her waiting arms as his wings disintegrated in the rising wind.

Matt stood, stumbled to her, wrapped her in his arms, then sobbed. He closed his eyes and kissed her hair, kissed his son, held them and cried, hot tears streaming down his face from under his eyelids.

"Look, Dada."

He opened his eyes at Adam's touch. Through blurred vision he saw them, hundreds of people on their knees, eyes raised in rapture at his family, some of those present with cellphones raised, red lights staring like baleful eyes.

Ted licked his ankle, tail wagging. In the distance, sirens blared.

THE END

Patrick Freivald is an author, teacher (physics, robotics, and American Sign Language), and beekeeper. He lives in Western New York with his beautiful wife, two birds, three dogs, too many cats, and several million stinging insects. A member of the Horror Writers' Association and International Thriller Writers, he's always had a soft spot for slavering monsters of all kinds. When he's not writing, he's reading, keeping bees, building robots with his FIRST Robotics team, proofreading college application essays, and teaching kids the wonders of science and technology. *Black Tide* is his fifth novel. There will be more.

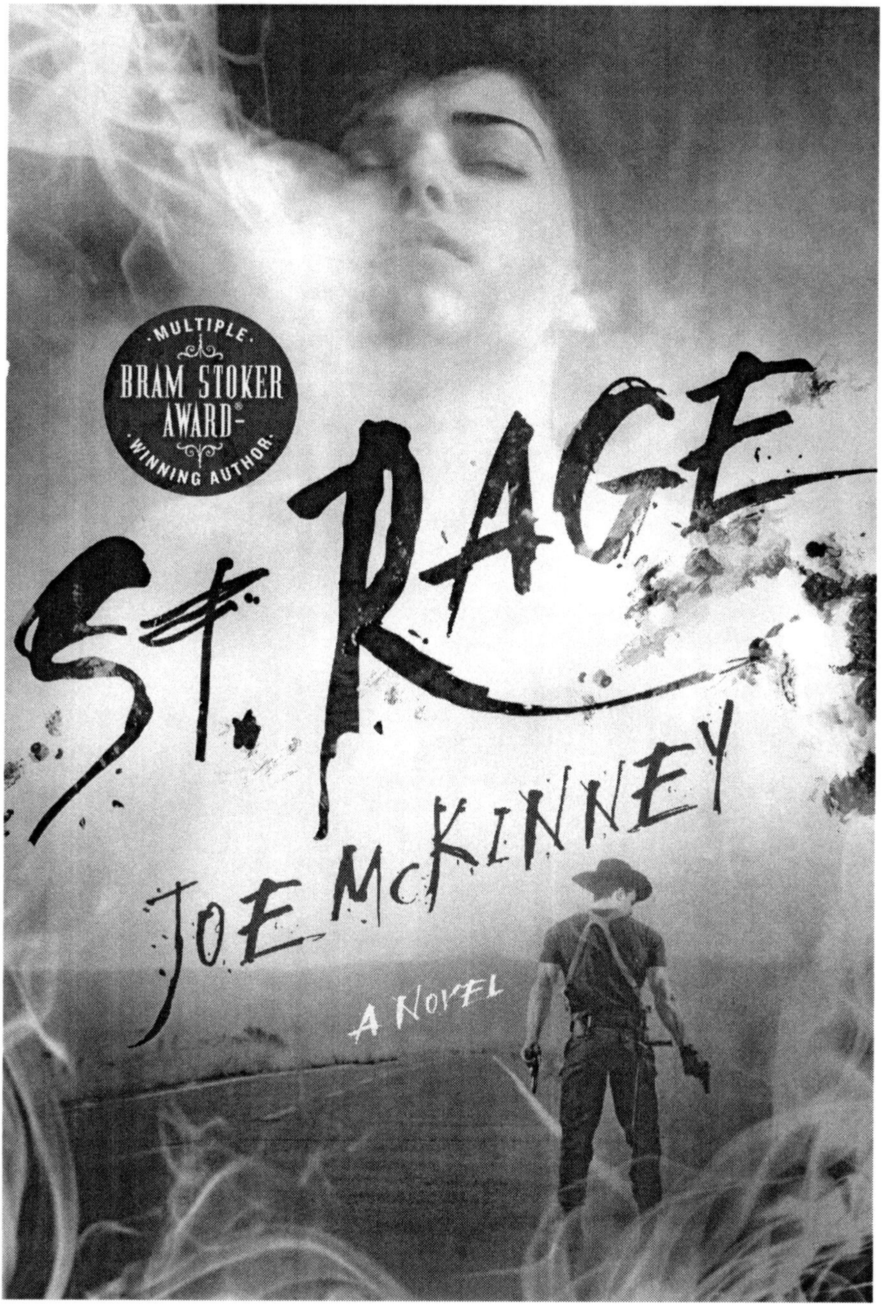
MULTIPLE
BRAM STOKER
AWARD®
WINNING AUTHOR
ST. RAGE
JOE MCKINNEY
A NOVEL

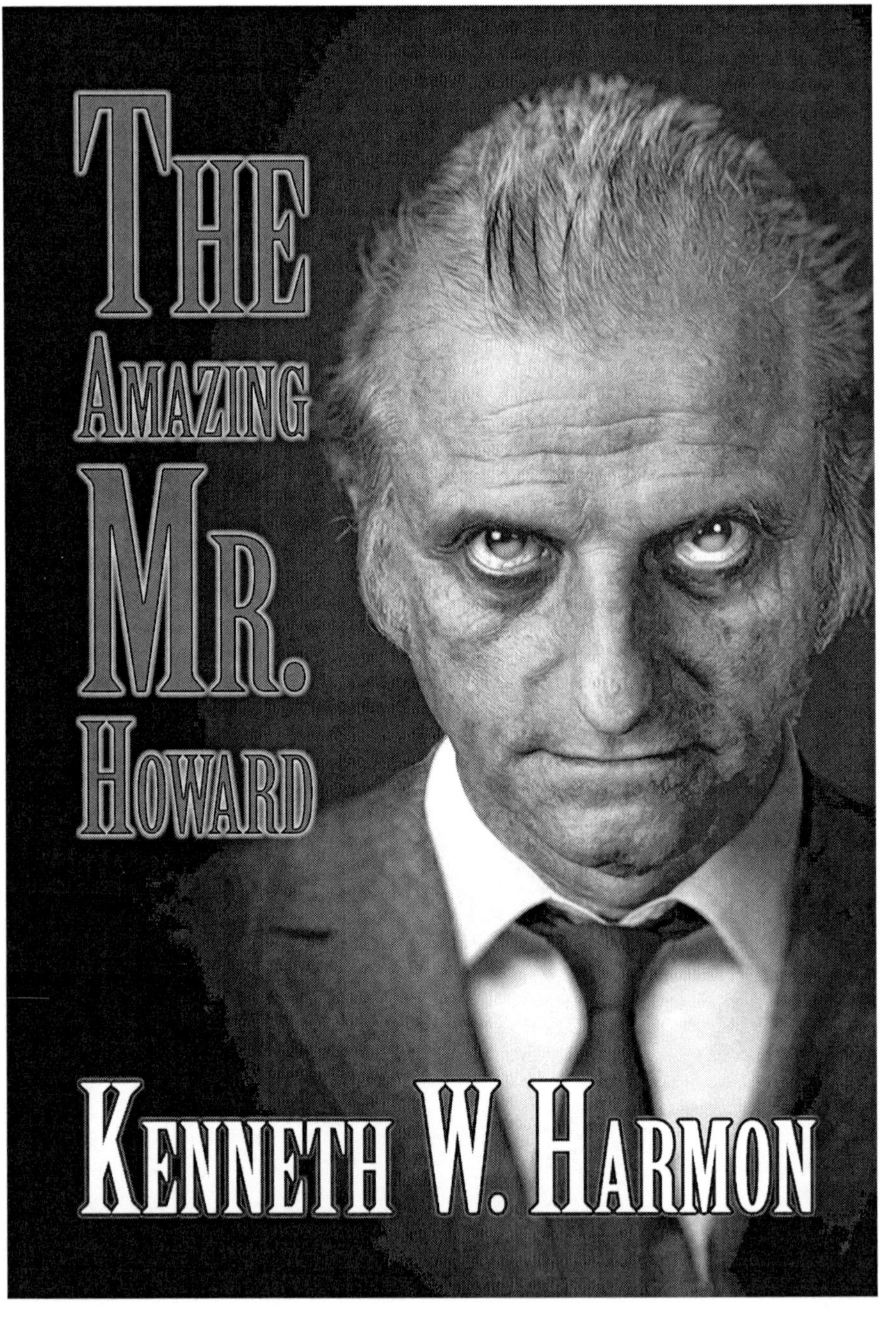
THE
AMAZING
MR.
HOWARD
KENNETH W. HARMON

JADE
SKY
PATRICK FREIVALD
• A MATT ROWLEY NOVEL •

DIVINE
SCREAM
A NOVEL
BENJAMIN KANE ETHRIDGE
BRAM STOKER AWARD® WINNING AUTHOR

CPSIA information can be obtained at www.ICGtesting.com
Printed in the USA
BVOW02s1611020415

394483BV00001B/1/P

9 781942 712008